## Praise for Nicole Locke

"*Secrets of a Highland Warrior* is romantic, engaging and has a wonderful depth that kept me invested in both the characters and story!"
—*Rae Reads* on *Secrets of a Highland Warrior*

"An engaging...and wonderfully romantic love story that has got so much of the author's heart in it. Ms. Locke's passion for this era and this story is evident on every page. I cannot wait to see what comes next."
—*Chicks, Rogues and Scandals* on *Reclaimed by the Knight*

"This story was so much more than just a romance. I honestly had a hard time putting it down. With fascinating secondary characters, drama, humor and of course a fabulous romance this has everything you could want in a book."
—*Rose is Reading* on *The Knight's Broken Promise*

## Author Note

I'm certain a heroine archer slash assassin may come as a surprise for all you #LoversandLegends readers, but Cressida has been in many of the stories all along, always as this mysterious Archer who shoots an arrow from the darkest of corners.

I never meant to keep her in the dark, and since she saved Mairead Buchanan's life in *Her Enemy Highlander*, I knew she'd have her own story. But what kind of hero could stand with such a heroine?

That was easy. It was always going to be Eldric from *Her Christmas Knight*. A man who sought vengeance against the Archer for killing his friends, who found an arrow on his pillow and who danced with a mysterious masked woman...

# NICOLE LOCKE

---

## Captured by Her Enemy Knight

# HARLEQUIN®
## HISTORICAL™

Recycling programs
for this product may
not exist in your area.

ISBN-13: 978-1-335-50555-2

Captured by Her Enemy Knight

Copyright © 2020 by Nicole Locke

This edition published by arrangement with Harlequin Books S.A.

For questions and comments about the quality of this book,
please contact us at CustomerService@Harlequin.com.

Harlequin Enterprises ULC
22 Adelaide St. West, 40th Floor
Toronto, Ontario M5H 4E3, Canada
www.Harlequin.com

**Printed in U.S.A.**

**Nicole Locke** discovered her first romance novels in her grandmother's closet, where they were secretly hidden. Convinced that books that were hidden must be better than those that weren't, Nicole greedily read them. It was only natural for her to start writing them—but now not so secretly.

### Books by Nicole Locke

### Harlequin Historical

### *The Lochmore Legacy*
*Secrets of a Highland Warrior*

### *Lovers and Legends*

*The Knight's Broken Promise*
*Her Enemy Highlander*
*The Highland Laird's Bride*
*In Debt to the Enemy Lord*
*The Knight's Scarred Maiden*
*Her Christmas Knight*
*Reclaimed by the Knight*
*Her Dark Knight's Redemption*
*Captured by Her Enemy Knight*

Visit the Author Profile page
at Harlequin.com.

There are strangers, acquaintances and friends in your life. If we're lucky, once in a while someone comes along who is that extra bit more, and it's difficult to explain how treasured they are.

Virginia Heath, friend till we're all crinkly with age and fellow writing adventurist... I'm ever so glad you came along.

# *Chapter One*

Spring 1297—England

It was the stink of the port that she hated the most. A cross between a hacked cadaver whose entrails had been exposed too long to a blistering sun, the vigorously repeated discharge of urine and the crisp, salted sea air that carried a promise of a better life somewhere else.

Those promises were a lie. Cressida Howe knew there was nothing better. Which served her well most days. Today wasn't that day.

Today she needed fortune or fate to give her some grain of luck. She knew they wouldn't, however, and not because she'd stopped praying, but because six months ago she'd prevented an obsessive mercenary from completing his intended murder.

A person whom he ordered *she* kill, but she hadn't. Not that she had failed. She never failed. She'd simply... disobeyed orders. And now that exacting mercenary wanted her punished.

Evading his wrath wasn't an option because he was hired by the Warstones, the most bloodthirsty of families; thus, he had unlimited resources and unlimited hate. He was also her father. Her only family.

Weaving her way through the throng of commerce and vagrants, she balanced between the uneven planks of the walkway, all the while keeping her hood sufficiently tucked to hide any chance of recognition.

Her being a woman wasn't why she feared discovery. If any dared attack they'd realise their fatal mistake soon enough. No, what she had to hide above all else was *who* she was.

The Archer. The sole weapon and creation of her father, Sir Richard Howe... The Englishman. Years of training with every weapon save a sword. But she didn't need that iron when she held her bow and a quiver of arrows, especially the ones she had carved herself in the hours spent alone. Which were more frequent as she went from being a child to a woman and her father's commitment to hiding her intensified. Until her face wasn't seen by anyone unless he chose it.

Everything was as he chose it. She was raised to be a weapon without thought, without questioning the rights and wrongs of what he ordered. She obeyed him at all costs.

Thus, it was shocking to both of them when she'd disobeyed him, shooting the arrow that stopped him killing his target. The look on his face... Her utter wretchedness could not have been worse than when God banished the angels from heaven.

And banished she was, for he left her behind. He was everything to her: life, death, survival. Her only contact with him now was through messages. He gave her tasks to do. It had been that way for months. Her loyalty to him in question, she obeyed his every command now.

Except…except the last message, the last task, came with a terrible rumour—that her father had kidnapped a child to raise. It had to be a lie, one she meant to discover the truth of for herself, so, between tasks, she'd followed her father's trail here to the docks. To find him, to confront him and demand to be taken back.

Until then, she needed to find a sufficient hiding place for the day. One from which she could freely observe, but not be seen. Fortunately, she knew just where to observe the ships and the people. It was the same place she went yesterday and the day before that and the day before that because for a sennight she'd been climbing one of the port's last remaining copse of trees.

She didn't know why the trees survived the copious amounts of building around the docks. Perhaps it was for shade, perhaps for a landmark, but for now she would take advantage of it.

First circling her tree to test the crowd and determine if she was being followed, she waited one heartbeat more to be satisfied no one watched before climbing quickly to a secure branch, one where she could wait in relative comfort. It was half-hidden with foliage, low enough to jump from and not break her legs, but high enough to see passengers boarding and disembarking from the merchant ships to France. Dover was a Cinque Port, one which was required to provide ships and crew to the King should he need it. When she had arrived, she'd spent much time scanning each of the faces around her. But it had been like this for days and now she was exhausted.

So very tired of the games, of the travel. Of hiding and, when she couldn't hide, she was tired of fighting. Her father was punishing her. First with exile, then with mercenaries who attacked and whom she couldn't kill. She knew this to be the truth for the messages the mercenaries carried told her so.

But the mercenaries were also the ones who had told her the terrible rumour.

Cressida settled on the branch, leaned her back against the truck and closed her eyes. She was so tired. As no ships were leaving, there was no urgency yet. Over the years, she'd learned to rest when she could. Soon enough there would be a battle. She expected more mercenaries to find her, to fight, spar and to disperse once again.

As for death? She didn't worry about her own life, for that had been forfeit upon her very birth, but she did worry about her father no longer loving her. It was something she must remedy. If she didn't have him, she would be a weapon alone.

Her fear was that he'd already crossed the water to France before she could get here. It couldn't be. She was younger and the better rider. She merely had to wait and watch some more.

She closed her eyes again. There were no ships sailing right now, no entourage that looked to be her father's, she'd rest only a moment…

The lethal clamp of a calloused hand on her ankle broke her rest. Asleep? Cressida kicked to free herself and reached for a weapon. Her bow and quiver hanging from a branch above were useless. Her daggers were caught under her cloak and unreachable. The manacled fingers only gripped tighter.

A man's hand, a warrior's. Her eyes snapped to her captor.

'All this time, I never thought you'd make a mistake. I never thought I'd catch you.'

Achingly familiar thick, long brown hair, and the bluest of eyes gleaming with victory. A jawline cut from the side of cliffs covered in lush stubble. Broad shoulders, thick, pronounced arms, all his features entirely too close because Eldric of Hawksmoor was a giant among men.

No matter how near or far, she always knew who he was.

'You,' she croaked.

A very unfamiliar sardonic twist to his lips as he answered, 'Me.'

Cressida gripped the branch over her head, anchored her body and slammed her free foot to the side of his head.

A grunt, a grip loosened and she scrambled to a higher branch. He dived for her other foot and she jerked it out of his way, only to lose her grip. Lurching too far to the left, he leapt to get under her.

Clenching her right fist with her left palm, she jammed her elbow into his neck, he staggered back, but her balance was off. Grasping for her bow, then quiver, she fell to the hard-packed earth.

No breath. One moment, two, she curled in a ball and rolled as the warrior vaulted down from the tree.

With his fingertips brushing her cloak, she bounded to her feet. He leaned forward to snatch her and she gripped his outstretched wrist. Without letting go, she kicked him in the ribs two times. Relishing his lost breath, she spun into the crowd.

Trapped by people. Darting left, she hesitated and it cost her. Eldric grasped her cloak and yanked.

She dropped on her back, her breath lost again upon impact. No moment to recover as she rolled to avoid the slam of his fist. He hit the dirt, but she felt the scrape of his knuckles.

Too close. His hand caught in her cloak and ripped the hood away. He pulled back for another punch and jerked, his fist spasming before her nose.

'A *woman*,' he rasped.

Wide blue eyes, parted lips. His shock was as visceral to her as much as to him. No one saw her like this. A female. A weapon; utterly exposed and vulnerable.

Cressida slammed her head into his nose.

'God's bones!' He reared back.

She pulled her own fist back to hit him again, he caught it and jammed it down to the side of her head. She struck with her left and he pinned his legs on either side of her thighs to restrain that limb above her head as well.

His eyes watering, nose bleeding, hair tangled and plastered to his brow, Eldric of Hawksmoor, the only man who could, the only man who shouldn't, had caught and trapped her.

Eldric's ringing ears, his pounding bruised ribs and his throbbing throat were marked cues this wasn't a dream or nightmare. The pain was substantial enough to know with certainty he was awake.

Awake and staring down at the palest of wide blue eyes and the lushest of white-gold hair in multiple plaits that didn't tame the loose curls framing the rest of her dramatic features.

Her skin wasn't as pale as her other colouring, but instead spoke of time spent in the sun, though spring had barely begun. Her cheeks were rounded, her lips a full, soft-rose colour.

The rest of her… Everything about her woman's form lying flush on her back, his hands wrapped around her wrists, was stunning. She was small, her bones fine, but strong, the curve of breasts, the indent of hips, all wrapped in warrior's garb. Inside her dark clothing were sewn multiple straps holding several daggers that dug into his legs. Her boot blade was lying in the dirt beside them. Spilled around them was a quiver and bow that had fallen along with her from the branch above.

A woman, but also a merciless killer. It was a marked clue he wasn't dreaming because he could never have imagined this. The woman pinned beneath him was the very enemy he'd been pursuing for months. *She* was the warrior, the Archer, who had killed his comrades.

She also seemed…familiar to him, though that had to be because of his shock. He'd only ever seen her from a distance fully garbed, covered and hidden in tree foliage. She could not be familiar; else he would have known her gender…he would have—Eldric shook his head.

The Archer struggled beneath him; her wide eyes

remaining on his, as if she was as stunned for being caught as he was for realising her identity. The ringing in his ears grew louder. The murmurings of the crowd slapped against the words repeating inside his head.

*The Archer was a woman. The Archer who killed his friends was a stunningly beautiful woman.*

The words became almost a chant until she bucked to free herself and he jammed his weight against her. The rush of breath and her sudden stillness centred his conflicting thoughts.

For years, he'd fought for King Edward's causes and earned his distinction to become a knight, then a spy. In the battles since the King's campaign against Scotland began, he'd fought valiantly and for what was right. Then, in a battle, an arrow had slashed across his right arm and struck the friend who watched his back. More fighting, another arrow slash and Michael was felled. Among the men fighting and fallen he had tried to find the one who dared shoot an arrow among those clashing with swords, but he saw no one and called for a retreat.

Another battle, another slash to the same arm. The scenario was all too acutely familiar. He swung his gaze until he saw a figure in a tree. Sword out to anyone who dared approach, but the cry of pain and Philip falling held him back.

Blinded by wrath, bound by duty, determined to pursue a cowardly murderer and frantic to share words with a dying friend, Eldric knelt while Philip died in his arms. By the time he looked to the trees again, the Archer was gone. After that day, Eldric was no longer merely King Edward's knight. He was a man with a vow, a quest: to seize this killer and deliver justice for his friends.

The Archer was his prey and now his captive. He had her in his very grip. Vengeance for him; justice met when the King executed her at the Tower. He seethed with the very need to fulfil his vow.

'You're hurting me,' she gasped.

Her eyes widened more; her lips parted. Yes, this was right. She would beg for his mercy and he would give none. She deserved no man's pity. 'Say it again. Tell me.'

A pinched crease in the middle of her brow. 'I can't breathe.'

The Archer was...a *woman*. He was a warrior knight, trained to protect. He eased his weight and released his hands. God's toes, what had he become? What—?

A fist flew into his crunched nose. He saw nothing but blackness and stars, felt her twist out from under him. Through debilitating pain, he opened a clenched eye and snatched her fleeing leg. Her arms full of her dropped weaponry, she smacked hard to the ground.

A grunt, a rush of breath. She didn't move. Partially dragging himself until she was trapped in his arms again, he flipped her over.

She was limp; her eyes closed. Dead? He put a hand on her chest. She breathed, but she wouldn't wake.

The murmurings of the crowd, of people staring and walking by, intruded into his world. He scooped up the woman, held her to his chest and faced them all. For a moment, a declaration began in his chest, a thumping of something primal, a *claiming*, before he clutched her closer and shoved his way through the crowd.

## Chapter Two

The Archer woke as Eldric tied her other wrist to the bed. She jerked to free herself, but it was too late. Her ankles were bound together and each of her wrists were secured to the headboard behind her. Around her mouth was a cloth so she could make no sound until he determined she would.

Completely defenceless, her eyes blazed frustration and indignation. Eldric felt a small thrill at her defiance and, perplexing most of all, relieved. Because she was well enough to want to fight him. Their...altercation... had not harmed her.

Brutish body, brutish hands. His parents had often teased he was left on their doorstep by a mighty oak. Always larger than anyone else, he was acutely aware of his size and the damage he could cause. Other kids would jump from one side of the stream bed to the other, whereas he merely took a step. If there was a rope to swing out over water and dive, it was never for his use and enjoyment. Merely climbing a tree caused sturdy branches to break.

Unless he was unleashed in battle where his entire body was free, he was constantly contained. Indoors was difficult. Low ceilings, small entryways, narrow hallways. Garderobes were the worst. Dining in a hall required him to sit at the end of a table—even then, he took the place of three others.

Only in battle could he be free…and in his imagination. He had spent months relishing the imagery of fighting the Archer, of exacting significant harm. He knew his enemy was small and slight, but that meant nothing. Everyone was small and slight compared to him. He had no intention of containing any of his strength and, before he knew the Archer was a woman, that was exactly what he'd done. Then her hood tore free and revealed…beauty.

The Archer being a female was unfathomable. His fighting a female was equally unheard of. His nose, throbbing and swelling from her strike, altered his thinking. Still, when he trapped her leg, he had only meant to halt her pursuit as she twisted out from under him. But when she thumped to the ground at his merest touch, echoes of his past taunted him.

All the time he carried her through the crowds, she didn't wake. He concentrated on the fluttering of her breath, the flickering of her closed eyelids and… worried.

Over the Archer, who had killed his friends and, no doubt, other Englishmen. His rage at this enemy only increased because he was *caring*. All for naught. The Archer was awake and even now furtively trying to slacken her bindings.

'Stop trying to loosen the gag with your tongue,' he

said. 'You'll only cause yourself thirst and I have no intention to quench it.'

She swallowed and stilled her jaw.

'That's better, isn't it?' he said with a smirk.

She kicked her bound legs, pushing the coverlet to the floor.

'Even if you could loosen those ropes, do you think I'd let you out of the room? No, you're here for as long as I want you here.'

It was the only place they could be. When he'd approached that copse of trees, he had no thought other than capturing the Archer. Numerous times over the last few months he'd got close. Discovered he entered one door of a building while his enemy exited by another.

He learned that hesitating, waiting at all, cost him. No more. Trapped in a tree, unaware he'd approached from behind, was an opportunity he wouldn't waste.

If the Archer had been a man, it would come down to a fight he would win, then dragging his enemy's body through the port until guards stopped him. There would be a swift explanation, then he would proceed on to buying a cart, rope, etc. All to tie the Archer down and trap him on the way to London. Eldric didn't care about the Archer's comfort. If he pissed over himself on the way to his formal execution, it mattered not. He only cared to finally secure an enemy who had alluded him for far too long.

And he had captured the Archer, but she was an unconscious woman because of his brutal hands, brutal strength. The buying of a cart and mere explanation were no longer feasible and he'd not readied a location to take her where they wouldn't be seen.

Unfortunately, he could hardly be hidden and his deeds... He'd fought a woman! If she hadn't been swift enough, the fist blow he'd aimed for her face would have... He couldn't think of it.

Others were thinking it, the crowd for one, and he couldn't blame them. Some of the children who had watched them fight were scampering behind them. Their excited chatter and scuffling feet abraded him at every step. He wanted to roar for them to leave. As a knight, his actions were unconscionable. As a spy for King Edward, they were grievous.

Children thinking him a monster. What could he say to change their opinion? That it was the tiny frail woman in his arms who was the true evil? She looked anything but. Her colour, her vibrancy... Her beauty alone muddled his thoughts. The way she could fight muddled his reasoning.

And it was a bitter reminder of who she truly was. The Archer at all costs must be contained. Urgency overtook him to find somewhere to confront her.

In the end, coin was on his side, as was the sword against his hip. He entered the nearest inn and ordered the best room, which was on the ground floor. Large enough to sleep many, but sparsely filled, which provided space inside for his heavy frame. The only bed seemed adequate to support him.

Out of every scenario he had ever envisaged when he finally captured the Archer, her being a woman tied to his bed was never one of them. Every accusation he expected to fling, every slam of his fists, every broken finger and absolute punishment thwarted.

He had the Archer and no way to release his wrath. The world for him was only good and evil. Right and wrong. When there was evil, there was justice. The Archer was a woman? God's bones, toes and any other body part, now he had questions.

Using his left hand, and staring down at her diminutive form, he yanked the gag away. 'Explain yourself.'

Licking her lips, Cressida stared at Eldric. *Her* Eldric. Only once had she dared be this close to him. It was at a Christmas dance in Swaffham where she thought to observe this warrior from afar, but he'd requested a dance. To hide her identity, she'd darkened her hair and worn a mask, but every moment her heart had pounded in her chest much like it was doing now.

'Explain myself? For what? You snatched me from a tree and have tied me—' She opened her eyes and feigned shock. 'I've my maidenhead. Please don't hurt me. My family will pay whatever silver you want.'

'Don't,' he growled.

'Don't what?' she pleaded with all the innocence she'd never felt. She must keep Eldric distracted until she escaped. 'I have done nothing! I—'

'Nothing!' Eyes burning with retribution, his vibrating body loomed over her. Bound tight, she pulled her head away and caved her stomach to avoid what blows she could.

A rough sound escaped his throat as he stepped back. She had truly hurt him when they'd fought. His nose and one of his eyes were swelling. There was a mark at the side of his neck where she had elbowed him. Tomorrow that would be purple, as would the rest of his face. She'd given him all of her fiercest of blows and none of them had been enough to take him down.

'Don't,' he enunciated very carefully, 'do that either.'

This time she didn't know what she'd done. Her confusion real.

His brows drew in. 'Did you think I would strike you?'

Never, her action was only instinct and training. Unless in battle, Eldric was all too careful with his body. When she dared watch him with women—before she couldn't watch any more—he was painfully formal, his arms unnaturally at his sides. The women always appeared inadequate for him. It didn't seem to matter for him, they often… Cressida squashed the familiar burning of jealousy in her chest.

'How would I know what you would do?' She tried to put disdain into her words. Knew they were weak because of past hurts she had no right to feel. 'I don't know you!'

'Thank you for your lies. A dear reminder of who you are.' He unsheathed a dagger at his waist, aimed the blade towards her throat. 'No flinching?' he mocked. 'Don't presume I wouldn't hurt you. For months now, that is all I have thought of.'

'You wouldn't hurt a woman,' she answered, knowing the truth. Unbeknown to him, she'd watched him for years.

He pressed it to her throat. 'You don't know me, though, remember?'

How many times would she forget her ruse? She

felt the cool metal press her skin, but it did not bite. 'Knights don't hurt women.'

He eased the blade up, but his eyes flared. 'Chivalry has long been gone from knighthood. It has no place during war. And we both know you're no mere woman.'

Every ounce of Eldric was steeped in chivalry, though he hid it well when he did Edward's nefarious deeds. As for the insult…that she deserved. Even now she could feel the sting on her forehead from when she'd tried to break his nose. Her foot throbbed where she'd kicked him and, after falling and losing her breath several times until she fainted, she still couldn't catch her breath. A woman would normally only have these issues because she'd fainted from tightened undergarments. A true woman wouldn't be bruised in the ribs after plunging from a tree to escape an enemy.

A *true* woman wouldn't know what an injury was, let alone be able to inflict them on a giant of a man. No, she wasn't a mere woman. If it wasn't for that dance they had shared last winter, where she'd dressed and for one night pretended, she'd wonder if she was a woman at all.

'I'm not anything,' she said, covering her lies in partial truths. She was born and raised to be only what her father wished. 'If it's coin you want—'

'Coin! I want your head and you well know it.'

It was a fact she wished wasn't true. 'Please, if you'd only listen to me—' she didn't need to hide the pain in her voice '—I can give you coin. I have family. If you let me go, I can get it for you.'

Eldric snorted. 'You play a dangerous game, taunting me. Pretending I don't know who you are or what you have done. I've caught you; I've bound you. You must know your life is mine to forfeit.'

Her forfeited life was something which was never in doubt.

Her father had raised her from infancy, kept her cloistered in different abbeys until she turned ten. On that birth date, he altered her role with him. No longer was she trained in private and kept hidden within the highest of walls; instead, as long as she wore her hood, she could travel with him. To learn to spy, to observe from afar and sometimes to thieve.

At first, he didn't risk her life on enemy camps, but on fellow English ones. And that was when, a year or two later, she had first seen Eldric. It wasn't his size that caught her attention. By then she'd travelled and seen enough of men that she only noted their weaknesses in case they should become targets.

No, it was Eldric's actions that had arrested her. He *whistled*. She had never heard music until then. Prior to that, there had been no festival or celebratory events for her. The constantly rotating abbeys she was kept in secluded her in private chambers and the inhabitants never spoke to her.

At first it had been shocking to be around camps and noise, but Eldric was something other than mere noise. The songs he made were hauntingly beautiful.

Thus, she'd watched him most of all; she was grateful for his size, for it made it easy to see him as he went about his day with ease and laughter. And all the while from one tent to another, from one task to another— even in training. Constantly whistling.

Perhaps because of his size, strength and skill, he

felt safe enough in the world for such exotic behaviour. If she had such a noticeable habit, her father would have carved out her tongue.

It also made it easy to find him again as the years went by and he kept his strange custom. And as time passed her fascination with him changed from that of a child to that of a woman. Until one day, when her father had given her another mission. Eldric had accepted King Edward's position to spy. So, her father had ordered what he always did with Edward's spies: for her to kill him.

'What do you intend to do with me, or rather, with the person you believe I am?' she whispered, coming back to the present with the awareness that his expression had changed to malice once more.

'Think! I have pursued you for seasons now. Do I act like a man who is not certain? I know exactly what I will do with you. You are bound for the Tower of London for execution.' His smile did not reach his eyes. 'Ah, finally a reaction.'

'Of course I'd react. I don't know who you think I am. You snatched me from sleep, bound me to rape me and now tell me you want my head. Sir, please, you have the wrong—'

The pounding on the door made them jump. Aware of her vulnerability, she wrenched on the bindings until the bed creaked.

'Stay still and quiet,' he hissed. 'It is only the supplies I ordered.'

As her father's weapon, the Archer, she'd stay quiet, but as a female unlawfully abducted, her best bet would be to call out for help. She breathed in to call out—

'Do you think to cry out?' he sneered. 'How would that favour you?'

He was right. She couldn't trust the being on the other side to believe she was innocent. But she had to keep her ruse as a frightened female.

'Let me go!' She struggled.

'You're not going anywhere.' With a harsh laugh, Eldric cracked open the door and stepped out. A moment or two more and he carried in a large tray with a small water basin and several linens and set it down on a chest. Another moment outside and he brought inside a smaller tray, laden with food and drink, and set it on the one available table.

The aromas of food and ale filled the room. Despite her training to go without, her mouth watered. He eyed her eyeing the food and smirked.

'I didn't think it would be so easy to break you,' he said.

'I'm already broken—what man ties a woman—?'

'One that knows better when it comes to you, despite your gender. Despite your—' His eyes skittered from her bound wrists down the curves of her body to her wrapped feet. Fear, and something else, brushed just under her skin as his gaze darkened and became almost calculating before his frown grew fierce and he jerked his head away.

She suddenly wished she hadn't kicked off the linen that covered her. It was a weak protection, but at least in this moment it would prevent him from seeing her so clearly. The fact anyone could see her was a vulnerability. But for Eldric to do so was—

No, Eldric wasn't looking at her as a woman. He

was taking note of her size and seeing if the bindings held. Fully revealed to him, he could see the odd colours of her hair and eyes. When sunlight came, he'd see her freckles across her nose, the numerous scars. He'd compare her to his other women.

She'd only imagined his eyes lingered on her bound hands, at her body stretched against the bed. Imagined he saw her as a woman. Eldric would never see her as anyone other than the person who had killed his friends.

Her only option was to lie until she could escape. 'You only think you know who I am. I'm trying to tell you, if there's someone you're trying to…capture, I'm not they. You've got me here, but the person you want could be escaping even now.'

'Of course, you would continue to lie since every weapon you have is gone. Please, tell me more. Entertain me. I have all the time in the world to find the truth.' He scoffed as if he was amused with her words, but a muscle ticked in his jaw as if her falsehood got under his skin. He gestured to the food. 'I can eat while you starve. I can leave for the garderobe while you soil yourself. I can and will do what is necessary because we both know you're anything but broken. But I will get you there.'

As if to prove his point, he leisurely unfastened his outer vest, throwing it towards a chair, though it slid to the floor. At the tray with the basin of water, he soaked the linen and wrung it. He did this slowly, methodically, as if his every thought were on those water droplets.

After all the accusations, the room seethed with a

taut wariness punctuated by the sounds of splashing water and the wringing of cloth. She was used to her father and his games. Used to being ignored until he focused everything on her. And that focus was always violent. Words. Deeds.

Eldric wasn't her father, but she was woefully without any other comparison. She might have watched others from afar, but she herself had never interacted with anyone. She didn't know what to expect. Would he launch the dagger he threatened her with? Force her mouth and nose into the sodden linen until she suffocated?

Abruptly, he looked over his shoulder and caught her eye. She didn't turn her gaze—it was all she had, to watch him as if he was just any other man to her. She concentrated on easing her heart rate, slowing her breath. Faked a bored mien though she could do nothing about the heated restlessness that coursed under her skin which she knew had everything to do with the proximity of this man. Another matter she could do nothing about. She'd been fascinated by him for far too long not to react when he was this near.

With a huff, he reached behind, yanked off his tunic and threw it towards the same chair. It also slid and billowed to the floor. Keeping that eerie silence between them, he lifted the cloth to his face, held it there. Dipped it back into the basin to soak.

All these years, she'd watched him from afar as he went about his daily routine. Never close enough, never fully, truly seeing him. Not like now.

His clothing couldn't hide the structure of his body, but she could never have been prepared for what was underneath. The width of his shoulders defined by the mounds and striations of muscles from his arms to his neck. His spinal cord providing a straight boundary for the arrow-like cording that arched outwards.

The entirety of his back tapered fast and hard to his waist where his breeches hugged. The fabric was thickly woven and his back was to her, but now that his tunic was gone, there was nothing that hid his gender from her. His breeches outlined every honed muscle.

She swallowed.

How did she dare fight or think she could escape him? He was nothing but formidable strength and magnificent male. If she assessed him as simply an enemy, there would be no stopping him, his arms providing an easy reach should he snatch her and too long for her to get up close with a dagger. That was before he applied any strength. No, only with an arrow could he be killed.

The thought was unbearably desolate. The fact that there could be a way to fell him, that anything or anyone could harm him at all.

A grunt from him brought her eyes back up. He held the cloth to his face. She watched him minutely move his arms as if he was adjusting his nose. It was swelling, but she didn't think she'd broken it.

She wanted, needed, to know. As far as he was concerned, she was an enemy, but for her…she didn't want him hurt. 'Is it broken?'

Another huff of breath and he dropped the linen. 'If it was, would you add it to your trophies?'

Trophies were for those who wanted to boast of their winnings. Trophies, like mementos of sentimentality, were kept around a house to fondly remember past days. She had neither friends to regale, nor a home to hold such things…even if she owned anything. Even if the trophy was a mere ring, she couldn't keep it. Anything that wasn't essential to her survival was forbidden. In truth, she didn't expect to keep her own life to fondly remember any past.

If fondly was a way to describe her past, which she doubted.

No, his talk of trophies made little sense to her, but the bite behind Eldric's words did. She knew why he raged and wished her dead. She'd known it the moment his friend fell because her arrow pierced him. Though she hadn't meant to harm his friend at the time, she had.

She'd been ordered to kill Eldric, but of course she couldn't. Unbeknown to her father, she'd already been immersed in the warrior's music and laughter. But she had to appease her father…and something in her wanted to help her warrior as well. She'd notched the arrow, meaning only to skim his arm so he'd swerve away from her reach. Her intention was to tell her father that the target was too far away.

Cressida tried to stop the next memory of that day. Tried to cease the piercing ache of guilt from creeping into her thoughts. But she couldn't stop either, just as she couldn't stop the past. She'd timed the arrow and the warning shot with absolute precision…and then the English warrior flanking Eldric's side had dodged another opponent and unerringly went into the trajectory of her arrow. She watched as the man fell, as Eldric roared and searched the field so he could make amends.

The absolute anguish on his face, the whispering of

vows made. She knew then that the dead man wasn't merely a fellow warrior. She'd killed Eldric's friend without meaning to, but that mattered little. Death was final and intentions meant nothing.

Ever since, Eldric had searched for her…the weapon, the murderer. All so he could tear her down and exact his vengeance. He had a right to his wrath, but it pained her all the same.

Eldric turned and she realised she hadn't answered his question. His gaze skimmed her features and seemed disappointed, before he raised the linen to his face again. The water couldn't be cold enough to stop the swelling.

'You need peppermint,' she whispered through a throat closed with remorse. She had hurt him…again.

Throwing the linen in the basin, splashing the water out of the bowl, he said, 'Poison. That's not your way.'

She was a weapon and possessed many lethal skills. In fact, she was quite adept at poison; still, he was right that she preferred the more direct route. One that separated her from her enemy. More and more she found she used the arrow as her means to kill. She feared it had nothing to do with her proficiency in it, but rather that she was beginning to feel something for her victims.

'I—I don't know what you mean,' she purposely stammered as if she feared him and his accusations. 'Being a healer, I understand about poisoning, but I… would never poison someone. That goes against everything I am. I'm only suggesting something that could help you.'

'This is the lie you come up with to entertain me? I will tell you this, it doesn't. Attempt something else.'

She shook her head, knowing there was no answer for that. His presence was enough to make it difficult to keep the ruse that she was merely a woman visiting at the docks. She knew enough not to feign that she was the woman who threw up her skirts for coin and food, but she could be a traveller, one who was merely resting out in the open until her ship left.

But being around Eldric when he was so familiar made fissures in her ruse. The fact he refused to believe her even more. But he couldn't know who she was, not really. He didn't appear to recognise her from that night they had danced, when his hands had touched hers and her skirts had swirled between his legs.

Nor could he know for certain she was the Archer for her father. She'd maintained her distance from this man, from all men. No one saw her.

So maintaining she was somehow innocent was her only available option. It was a cover that couldn't be maintained long term, but if there was the smallest chance she could cause doubt, convince him he had captured the wrong person, she would. Otherwise…

Otherwise, she'd have to be what her father made her. But even she knew she could never be a true weapon around Eldric. Didn't even want to test the assumption. So she was left with falsehood or the truth. It was safer for Eldric if she lied.

'Peppermint isn't poison,' she continued as if he'd answered her. 'When crushed until its oil is released, it cools.'

He retrieved the linen and brushed it across his shoulders and arms, along his torso, as if he was bathing in his chamber alone. As if she didn't exist. She watched the small linen as it was shoved brutally across his skin, sloughing off the embedded dirt from their altercation and from whatever journey he'd made to reach her.

How could she not know he was following her? In pursuing her father, she'd made herself vulnerable. Allowing her entire focus to be consumed with a rumour. Foolish mistake. No one had surprised her ever before. Eldric, a giant of a man who whistled, truly shouldn't be capable of stealth.

Not that Eldric was her enemy, though she knew she was his. Or...at least, he thought her an enemy. And for his safety, it would remain that way until she was dead.

Another brush of the linen up his neck and around to his chest. He rubbed roughly there. She could imagine what it felt like, the water cool after the heat of the morning and their fight. She'd hit him hard and wished he'd turn completely so she could see the extent of the damage...if he needed peppermint or wrapping. After all, if she was bound and he injured, they would be at a disadvantage if they were attacked.

That was the reason she cared, not because of bruising, swelling or pain. If those existed, peppermint would help. Rubbed along his tender side, swirled to reach... Trying in vain to stop her errant thoughts of applying the oil herself, she kept up with her useless babble while that strange restlessness increased and she shifted her body to ease it. 'I was a healer in my other village before I'd decided to take a ship to—'

Throwing the linen with such force the wooden bowl rattled against the table, he strode to the refreshments. Swiping the flagon in one hand, he didn't bother with the goblet and drank straight from the curved jug. His profile to her, she watched his throat take in the liquid in one, two, three gulps before he slammed the vessel on the table. It toppled over, empty.

He didn't bother to straighten it. She glanced to his strewn clothes, the washing area slopped over with his mud-and-blood-splattered linen. That was when his gaze acutely returned to her.

She swallowed. 'I could make some for you. It won't heal instantly. But it will feel better. You must be in pain.'

He rolled his shoulders and a harsh breath flared his nostrils. Pivoting, he took the two steps to his satchel on the floor and yanked out a tunic that he shoved over his head.

'Perhaps comfrey,' she continued as if they were carrying on a conversation. 'That may help with the colouring of it all, though I suppose you're not bothered with aesthetics. And it should be used sparingly. But it'll aid with—'

He scraped a chair over to the bed, turned it around backwards and straddled it to face her. It brought the hulk of him perilously close. Enough to smell the fragrant ale and the saltwater he'd washed in. Enough to smell *him*…a scent like frost on evergreen.

Keeping his silence, he laid his hands against the back of the chair and leaned his chin on them. Like this, he looked…boyish. Draped on the chair, his body in repose, he could have been any mother's son.

But the look in his blue eyes was a man's. And the lethal glare told her he sat this way not to be congenial, but to barricade himself.

Since she was already bound, the shield wasn't from her, it was to block his own action, his own reach. And some twisted thing inside her cherished his trying to protect her...even if it was she who aggravated him. No one had ever tried to protect her before.

Yet, for both their sakes, she must still provoke him. She must escape. 'I don't know what you want with me, what...you intend to do with me, but I feel we must have got off on the wrong foot. I'm a traveller, like you.'

He tilted his head, his blue eyes, already swallowed by the dilating of his pupils, darkened even further. His chin remained rested on the back of the chair, but now his hands clenched the seatback, the tips of his fingers turning white.

'I'm travelling to France, to meet my family.' It was as much of the truth as she could muster. 'I didn't mean to hurt you, you simply took me by surprise... I was defending myself. Surely you can realise that, you grabbed me and—'

'Are you done?' His deep voice resonated around the room like a sentence. It wasn't a question; it was an order. 'Because I'm done.'

'I don't know what—'

He made a sound of frustrated anguish and soared out of his chair so fast the heavy oak slipped and slammed on the bed. The carved back of it didn't hit her, but she felt the heavy weight of it against the over-stuffed mattress.

It was the man towering above her who was the true danger. His hands clenching and unclenching at his sides, his chest heavy. He seemed to want to get hold of himself and couldn't.

If he picked up the chair, he could easily slam it against her. Bash her head in and there would be nothing she could do about it. This wasn't even something she could arch her body to avoid. Nothing. But she did keep her eyes open, her mouth shut.

'You lie,' he growled. 'You lie so terribly, that even if I didn't know it was a falsehood, I'd know you weren't telling the truth. And you *know* this. God's bones, do you know this. You are tied to that bed and I could starve you to death. Slowly scrape my blade across every inch of your skin until you bled out. Or I could pick up a blanket and smother you in an instant. And still you defy me.' He looked wildly about before his gaze swung back to hers.

'You waste time,' he said, 'but remember it's your time you waste, not mine. Perhaps I should demonstrate the dynamics between us. I am free. You are not. A day? Perhaps two? A sennight, a fortnight. Trapped in here, tied to this bed, how long do you expect to live?'

Without a backward glance, he stormed out of the room, the lock crashing into place behind him.

## *Chapter Three*

He'd...left her.

She waited one, two heartbeats, but not even the stamp of feet could be heard from the hallway. Immediately, she worked to loosen her bindings, her fingers on her left hand just long enough to reach the wrapping around her wrist to worry the fabric enough to slacken it.

All the while, the room echoed Eldric's wrath. Reverberated with the words he'd targeted her with. He wanted her dead and she believed him. She'd frustrated him with her lies and, knowing him as she did, she hadn't left him with much else to do but to harm her. Starvation was a brilliant decision on his part.

She could have answered him because she knew how long she could last before she became delirious with dehydration. It was a lesson her father had taught her long ago. And if she went longer than that, she would die.

But she couldn't. Not because she had a sense of self-preservation. A weapon didn't care if it lived or died. Her father had long ago stripped that weakness from her. It also wasn't because she felt an injustice of being kept against her will. A weapon did not reflect on rights and wrongs; it merely did what it was told to do.

That's why she'd always remained faithful to him. The rumour of the other daughter must be a lie. For years, her father's sole focus had been to secure something the Warstone family desperately wanted: the Jewel of Kings. A legendary jewel which had influence much like Excalibur in King Arthur's realm. Except Excalibur was merely a story; the Jewel of Kings was truth.

Since England now fought with Scotland such a legend could sway many. Such power was enviable and the Warstones coveted it. Her father had lost it when, six months ago, she disobeyed and didn't kill Mairead of Clan Buchanan. When, for a mere moment, she thought him wrong to harm a brave woman. So she'd released her arrow and shot him in the shoulder instead. Mairead and Caird of Clan Colquhoun had escaped while Cressida was exiled from the only person she knew.

Her father was angry with her, testing her, but he'd never abandoned her. He gave her messages still. Further, he continued his training by sending warriors for her to fight. He must care for her still. She needed to be free from here. She couldn't die with the doubt her father no longer wanted her.

She arched her whole body, stretched until the bed creaked and her muscles ached, then she relaxed as much as she could. She hoped she stretched the bindings, but her legs were still bound too tight, her right hand unmovable. The left-wrist binding was reachable with her fingers, but she couldn't get the right angle. She needed to wedge a finger under, but couldn't.

She eyed the heavy oak chair he'd abandoned against her bed, but it was out of reach to be used as any kind of leverage. Arching again, she curled her limbs in with all her strength. When she flopped against the bed again, she expected the chair to slide to the floor, but it was a heavy oak thing and refused to budge. As did her bindings.

It was her turn to huff. To simply rest against the bed, which was one of the most comfortable ones she'd ever lain on. Certainly, the ones in the abbey had never been well filled or secured with thick linens so that none of the straw was felt beneath her back.

The entire room was opulent, if sparse. Not that she could see that much under the chaos he had left, leaving the contents of the room as they were. The askew chair, the basin and flagon. Had he been this messy before? She wondered if it was a sign of his frustration, or a shortcoming in her observations of him. That night in Swaffham last winter, when she laid her arrow on his pillow…the bed had been unmade, the quilt crumpled on the floor.

She saw Eldric's sloppiness as a weakness. One of her keys to self-preservation was to leave behind no trace she'd occupied a space. If a chair had been shoved under a table at an odd angle, she made sure to leave it so. If a mattress was so soft that the indent of her body could be noted, she slept on the floor.

Eldric left a wake of wreckage and he'd only been in the room mere moments. Water splashed against stone would be impossible to cover up. For a moment, she entertained the conversation she'd have with him on the subject, simply to offer survival help, and imagined how it would proceed. Poorly, no doubt.

A man secure enough to whistle wouldn't care who found him. She couldn't fathom being so cavalier, but then an arrow didn't imagine itself a table. If she stretched her imagination, she could see herself as a sword, but that was only another weapon. To be a warrior and welcome an enemy instead of hide from one was too strange a difference to comprehend. Eldric lived and behaved so differently from her.

Unfortunately, wondering on their differences without knowing all of them wasn't enough to fill in the time before he returned. Another deep breath as she waited…and waited again. When he didn't storm back in, she started to count the objects in the room and to count the time she tapped her toes in her boots.

Whatever she could do to not fall asleep. It spelled her doom if she slept. But she hadn't slept properly in weeks; her rest in the tree had been too brief and the exhaustion in her limbs from straining against her bindings had drained her. However, as angry as he was, surely he'd return. He'd left food here. Surely he'd want to eat. Surely…

Eldric stood over the sleeping form of the Archer. Hours had passed since he completely lost his temper. He didn't even know he had one. In battle, he had unnatural strength and, certainly since he'd targeted the Archer, his rage had weathered and tightened to splintered wood within him.

But a temper where the rage burst from his being with no target to aim it towards? Never before. Only this time. With this enemy. With this *woman* who lied.

He expected those he captured to lie and, over the years, he'd learned what to do about it. Now, he could do nothing. Nothing. Threats wouldn't stop her; she was too resilient for that.

And being in the room with her ever-watchful eyes? Even if he could get over their colour, the *way* she looked at him… It was as if she was waiting for something. Or knew something of him.

So he'd left, knowing that, no matter how strong she was, she couldn't break her bindings. Remembering, too, to never underestimate her, he'd paid two boys to watch the room so he could walk the docks and come to terms with what was revealed to him.

To what he knew. On the battlefield, he'd held his friend as he died and made a vow to avenge his death. He vowed again to God now and burned a candle in church. He'd made another vow when he'd accepted a hunting horn from King Edward of England. Some would argue that vow could be the most important one of all. One that couldn't be forgiven or altered as could be done with a deity or the dead.

With certainty, that meeting with Edward might prove the most fateful. For there in the monarch's chambers he'd agreed to obtain the Archer for the King.

Eldric knew he'd made a deal with the devil and agreed to pay the price. And why not? The King's wants and his own were the same. They both desired the Archer's head. But it went further than that. Because by pledging this vow and loyalty to the King, he could also conceal the disloyal act he'd done.

Christmas past, Edward had ordered him to Swaffham to locate the traitor who had sent private messages to the Scots. A specific traitor who possessed a half-thistle seal.

The traitor was Hugh of Shoebury, a childhood friend, and one whom he'd trained with at Edward's court. It was revealed that Hugh had a viable reason to convey certain information to the Scots...because Hugh was protecting Robert of Dent, Black Robert.

Robert, who was reported dead, was in fact hiding from the King. He did it so he could have his life with his Scottish wife, Gaira, and their adopted children. The private information was sent to Robert and his wife, Gaira of Clan Colquhoun, to specifically protect them.

And Robert... Robert was also his friend who needed any information that could be passed to him. For the last several months, he and the Colquhoun Clan had been searching frantically for the daughter who was stolen from them.

Of course, he'd immediately given his loyalty to his friends.

Eldric realised then that loyalty had many sides. Thus, he was left with only one choice. He'd lied to King Edward to protect them. Robert had faked his own death and, so, Hugh with the woman he loved faked theirs. Leaving him, a spy, to report that the half-thistle-seal traitor was dead.

Thus, three people Edward had concerns over no longer existed. It would risk too much to contact them again. Ah…but loyalty. Eldric knew he needed to make right with the world again. To make clear the lines of good and evil, right and wrong. Two lies to the King meant he'd doubly bound himself to the Sovereign.

So he vowed to bring the Archer to Edward and accepted the royal hunting horn, the coin, the royal papers to flaunt and terrorise with when needed. Because he knew last Christmas that if there was a price to pay, he'd make the Archer pay it. He'd do it not only for vengeance for his friends who were dead, but also to protect those beings who were alive and wished to remain hidden.

Edward must never know he was disloyal or the lies would unwind like pegs in a well-worn instrument. Hugh, Robert and their families must stay safe.

Except the Archer was a woman. Now, it wasn't a simple matter of transporting an enemy to the Tower of London to be done with disloyalty and treason. Because now there were more falsehoods. He needed to make a decision: to hide or reveal them?

He could see now he should have been cautious last winter. Walking the docks, allowing the putrid air and the chaos to thump against him, he had examined the meeting with the King in a different light. He'd been so concerned and focused on his own words and deeds in that room, he hadn't properly analysed the ruler's.

The King had informed him he knew that Eldric had been pursuing the Archer because of his friends' deaths. The King had been spying on his spy. It was a possibility the King knew the Archer was a woman. It was very likely he also knew what she was about, her deeds…and purpose.

The Archer being a woman changed everything.

Not because she was a female and wasn't capable of murder. Knowing his own mother, he knew the strength of women. He didn't argue the Archer's skills either…he'd seen that first-hand.

No, it was the methodical way the Archer did such deeds that called them into question. So he made another vow, this one to himself. To keep her here until she confessed. To reflect on the ramifications and different angles of the pieces. To be more cautious. Something he should have done when he was summoned to King Edward's private chambers when there wasn't anyone else in attendance.

He couldn't execute her without knowing who she was and why she did what she did. Would he have waited if she was a man? Would he have cared for reasons then? No. If the Archer had been a man, he wouldn't have questioned anything. He'd have merely tied and slammed his enemy in the back of a cart to roll around for days until they reached London. Instead, he did wonder why and how a female was his enemy. Why it was different, he couldn't say.

No. He did know. She was a surprise. An unknown. His world had always been simple. The fact she was not was unacceptable. Unwanted.

And whatever actions he needed to take to gain those answers would be acceptable. His monstrous strength did not pertain to this situation. If harsh words and harsh deeds were needed until she broke, he would do them. To keep his vows to his friends both here and gone, he'd have to break a lifetime of habit. With a determined heart, prepared to confront her, he entered the room…only to find her asleep.

His first thought was to wake her by pressing a blade against her heart so that each steady breath she took would prick until she awoke to the danger. Instead, he grabbed the bowl with filthy water and prepared to fling it on her.

She was…restless. Her stunning eyes closed, he could see more clearly the dark circles under them, hear her uneven breaths. Dreaming, or a nightmare?

Clenching the bowl in both his hands, he warred with himself as he had done all day while she was bound in this room. While he'd walked, returned to the inn, eaten, watched the day turning into twilight, he'd wondered how she fared alone in the room.

He had intended to wait even longer, but that plan failed. She'd escaped him too long for him to be sure she was truly trapped.

Now he stood over her, and wondered about her dreams? He hated this woman; shouldn't care if she was awake or asleep. Shouldn't wonder if she merely dreamed or if she was plagued with something darker. He needed these lies over with. The longer they went on, the more involved they became, the more likely they would unravel.

But he couldn't bring her harm. She looked… She looked exhausted. The kind of bone weariness that only the hunted carried with them.

Beauty, that was still there. There wasn't another woman like her and the sleep softened her exotic features to something almost unearthly. But he could see the sunken hollows of her cheeks from lack of food.

Could recognise the tell-tale signs of exhaustion in her body as her limbs twitched because they were unused to rest, because she had to keep alert to nearby danger.

And she *was* in danger. He was her captor. She was bound, in an unknown location. The fact she slept when this vulnerable was a testament to her true depletion.

She gave the softest of sounds. A whimper. One that held a fragment of pain and he was brought back to reality. This woman was not music and no matter how great her beauty was, she was no angel. If she was, she was part of the fallen and very deadly. Lethal and ethereal.

He stood over her ruminating, but he could easily be the true enemy with a knife in his hand. He was death to her and she slept. Exhausted beyond her strength.

If she was as poorly rundown as this, how had she fought him? His face was throbbing; each breath he took pricked with the kicks she'd landed against his ribs. She was fierce. He'd returned as many blows to her. The fact they didn't land wasn't a saving grace. He didn't cause her the same harm because he'd held back. She wasn't as harmed as him because she had fought, blocked and fallen from a tree!

He'd heard and felt the impact when she hit the ground. How much more could she take? Could there be another way to gain his answers? Could he…pretend to befriend her? Or, at least, give her a false sense of safety? She could rest and gain the sleep she so obviously needed. He could feed her until the pallor of her skin disappeared. Maybe kindness could be a way to—

But the mere thought of his friend Thomas's last breaths choked that idea. Knowing that Robert had a family laid rest to any kindness. He couldn't do it. It was also clear the longer he stood over her, he wouldn't be tossing the cold dirty water and interrogating her until she broke.

He'd trained to be a spy, knew the methods needed. Enemies didn't confess or capitulate when they were strong, they only did so when they were weakened. He needed her sleep deprived, hungry, her position vulnerable. He needed to break her. Her brows drew in and she let out a keening whimper.

He felt his own brows furrow at such a helpless sound. A nightmare, then. What did a killer dream of? This woman was a weapon he must find the owner of before throwing her in the fire to be melted, far from anyone's grasp.

God's bones! With a frustrating reluctance, he lifted the chair off her bed and slammed it on the ground.

## Chapter Four

Cressida thrashed awake. The clench of the ropes around her ankles panicked her, the ropes on her wrist cut deep. Her gaze locked on the man looming over her. Heart thundering, she felt the blood slam through her body, readying her to run, to fight. With instinct to survive battering her, she screamed.

Somewhere wood hit stone and water splashed. All she knew was the punishing grip of the man's hands on her shoulders.

'Enough!' he roared.

Where was she? Not in an abbey, not in a tree. A room she didn't recognise. A darkness enveloping it that jarred against her attempts to understand. It shouldn't be dark.

'Leave me!' she cried, flinging her body up to break free, but the grip tightened, a weight pressing her deep into the mattress.

To suffocate her! She gasped deep, gathering as much air before it became too late. She fought harder.

The man loomed until his face was a breath from hers. 'Stop this!'

Cressida blinked. Could that be Eldric?

She was dying, going into her dreams before sleeping for ever. She must be. Eldric wasn't here, not this close, not touching her.

She wrenched on the cords binding her, welcomed the jagged bite as they drew blood. If she broke her wrist, if she lacerated the skin, the blood and loss of skin would loosen knots. Pulling, pulling!

The grip shook her body before it seized around her wrists, stopping her bid for freedom. 'Nooo!' she keened.

'Wake, Archer! What are you doing?'

The voice…she recognised. Eldric. So close his hair waved down to brush across her cheek. To see the blue of his eyes altered by the darkness of his pupils. There was something there: concern.

Eldric in a room where he'd bound her. But she fought it, still, because it couldn't be truth. She remembered when he'd stormed from the room. There could never be concern or caring when it came to him. 'It's dark. It was morning when you left. *Morning.*'

He released his grip, but her eyes had adjusted to the dim light; she could see all of him now. 'It is turning to night.'

'I slept all day?'

He canted his head and straightened, but did not move away from the bed. She could smell the sea on him and something else. Bread from his hands where he brushed her shoulders. He'd eaten. Time had passed.

'You slept,' he repeated.

'You let me?'

His spine snapped straight, the concern she'd fleet-ingly witnessed gone. She'd said something wrong. 'I was gone because as my enemy you were bound se-curely in this room. All day here to contemplate the uselessness of your lying to me.'

'But I slept.' She couldn't get past that point. When was the last time she'd slept? And never when survival was tantamount.

'And I woke you. You'll feel it. The need to relieve yourself, your hunger, thirst? All of it must be begin-ning.'

She was too confused to feel anything else. Eldric touched her. It was rough, but the purpose of it didn't feel as though it was to hurt her. He demanded she wake, he stopped her from harming her wrists. 'Why did you try to wake me?'

He frowned. 'So you could suffer.'

But she was suffering already when locked in a nightmare. It'd happened to her before when her father trained her too hard. There were moments when the truth of her torture clashed with what had happened to her weeks before, and weeks before that. And on and on until she didn't know where or who she was. She'd only become a weapon who survived to be wielded again.

Which only made the truth more acute. She needed to be free, find her father, to become his weapon again because without that, without her father, she didn't know who she was.

Just this little time in the presence of someone else, talking with someone else, was confusing. Like now. This Eldric was different than the one who'd stormed from the room. He'd behaved differently when he shook her awake as if he was desperate to wake her, to make her stop.

However, in the time she'd slept, he'd done things—maybe he had had second thoughts. Maybe he was the Eldric who whistled and laughed. Maybe this was the kind Eldric.

Her eyes swept to her wrist. 'I've suffered. I'm hurting now.'

He glanced to her bindings, which were secure, but oddly hadn't pained until she wrenched them in her panic.

'Good,' he said before his expression became absolutely resolute. 'The entirety of this is your own doing.'

Not if she wasn't who he thought she was. Not if she kept her ruse. 'Where am I?'

'It matters not where you are,' he said.

'I can smell the port, we can't be far,' she said.

He arched a brow. 'And that would be significant because?'

Because her father could be in the port. He could be alone or with another daughter. In the worst case, they would be on a merchant ship already bound for France where it would be near impossible to find him.

When her whole existence in life was in jeopardy, she needed her freedom most. But to say anything would harm her relationship with her father. To reveal anything to Eldric would be fatal for him.

Even though it might irreparably harm her own life, she would tell Eldric nothing. She would, as she had always done, protect the man who hated her.

She jerked her chin and flexed her fingers, which tightened the rope around her wrists.

'Because I need to be on the port.'

His eyes gleamed. 'Why?'

To give him a reason he'd believe? 'To meet my family.'

'Tell me.' His eyes never left hers.

Too much. Too close to the truth. There was still a chance to find her father. To repair whatever harm she had done. How had she fallen asleep? To be so vulnerable again! This time, she knew an enemy was there, knew Eldric was far worse to her than some faceless mercenary she could easily fight. Eldric had loyalties, he had vows and vengeance he wanted to exact.

'None of this makes sense to me. You have to know none of it does.' She spoke a lie, but it felt like a truth. 'Let me free.'

'No,' he rasped. His chest heaved, his shoulder bunched.

'Then tell me. Tell me what you intend to do with me.'

He took one more breath and stilled. Something changed in his eyes, as his gaze swept across her body to the tangled linens between her legs, up again to her bound hands. Stayed there and turned...calculating.

It wasn't something she could readily comprehend, but it felt familiar, none the less. Oh, yes, he'd looked that way at her once before—when he'd held out his hand to dance with her. And, like then, her body tracked faster than her thoughts. His pupils dilating, a flush to his cheeks. On that day, he'd looked so deep into her eyes she thought she'd be discovered.

Now, he looked everywhere but and it didn't matter. Her body felt her reaction to him all the same. Except now, she didn't have the protection of the mask and layers of clothing. Now, she was bound, exposed. And she felt something in her wanting to blurt out her words, to tell him—

He ripped his eyes away and cursed under his breath. 'What game is it you think you play?'

Nothing, yet to have him look at her… Just a glimpse of something other than hatred. She'd give *anything*, yet she had to be wrong. He didn't look at her with anything but loathing. It was her own longing, her own stupidity for not understanding people as well as she should.

His eyes narrowed. 'Tell me who you are.'

She swallowed her emotions, the way her body felt. She'd get through this. 'I told you. I'm a healer.'

Eldric was glad for his walk, for his sustenance before he'd returned to confront this enemy. But the nightmare she'd been gripped in… The fact she couldn't wake from it unsettled him.

What to do with her, bound by his hand, helpless, vulnerable? Yet she still defied him with lies, with some sort of fragility he couldn't navigate himself around. When she looked at him with those eyes…

He couldn't shake that she was familiar to him. That he knew her. He couldn't seem to forget that she was a woman bound on his bed. Unfailingly stunning with something else that lured him closer to her, to desire her, which was a sick madness he couldn't seem to reason against. It made no sense.

She. Had. Killed. His. Friends.

'Enough of this! We will get nowhere if you continue with lies. Why do you pretend? I know who you are, little Archer.'

She flinched, just a little, just enough for him to see, and he relished it, but that was all she gave him. 'Archer? I'm a woman. Archers are men who battle from parapets against Scotland.'

'So aware of warriors you know their position in battle?' he said. 'And have you forgot you were in a tree with a bow and quiver hanging at the ready? It fell to the ground along with you. Spilled at my feet, defeated as surely as you were at that moment. And, like you, it's trapped in this room.'

Her eyes narrowed, but they stayed on him. He both admired and detested her will. He knew she wanted to survey the room, to determine its position so, when she did free herself, she'd have the weapon at the ready. It was that very reason he'd hid it under her bed.

'You may think you know me, sir,' she said, 'but I can assure you, I do not know you.'

'You lie so easily. How can I believe you? You have been too difficult to capture not to be aware of me.' He welcomed the malicious impulse that bolted through him then. 'Maybe you need a reminder.'

He whipped off his tunic, turned to reveal his right arm to her and traced the top two scars. 'Do you remember these?'

Her eyes never betrayed her. Her body remained perfectly still and he felt his anger press once again to the surface.

She should display nerves; she should *be* nervous.

Instead, he was unnerved. He didn't know what to do, what he would do, from one moment to another. Trained as a warrior and a spy, he only had one type of enemy these many years: ones he defeated with force.

He had fought every one of them with determination and a will to live, to defeat. They were enemies who needed to be captured or conquered, that was all.

But the Archer... This woman was the worst of them all because it felt...personal when she had killed his friends. He couldn't explain it, but her marking him as precisely as she did; her ability to murder his closest companions wasn't dispassionate.

And when it came to her, he didn't burn with a righteous determination to conquer her. His hatred for her was personal. Many others had been killed by his hand, but he hadn't bargained with the King pursuing with singularity any of them. On the battlefield, he meted out his vengeance and those who survived and escaped, he simply fought again on another field.

Not so the Archer. No, she'd marked him. Marked him and shown him what she was capable of and his need for retribution against her felt as though he'd marked her as well. Marked her as the one enemy he would defeat.

So sure of this belief that they were personal enemies, that the fact the Archer was a desirable woman— the fact she lied about her role in his life—only made his frustration blaze brighter. Why was she lying to him? He would get answers!

'You should be aware, I didn't actually feel the first cut you gave me,' he said. 'I was too intent on fighting the enemy in front of me. But Thomas's sudden drop from his position, his sword arm flinging within my line of sight, alerted me. I was so…so aware of Thomas's death. A friend since we were young. I felt that bolt he received in his chest.

'Felt it, but could do nothing about it. I was still surrounded. You can imagine how I fought after that. What am I saying? You don't have to imagine it; you watched it, didn't you? My God, why haven't I thought of this before? Of course you watched me. You marked me. Did my pain amuse you?

'It must have amused you greatly because during that same battle you did it again. That one burned across my arm. Already consumed with Thomas's death, I had to face Michael's. You know what I did then, don't you: called for retreat. With that arrow lodged in his throat, I called for retreat!'

Her breathing stayed the same, no finger twitched. As a warrior, everything in him demanded instant retribution. As a spy who needed information, he had to get more…creative.

Over the years, he'd promised pain to his enemies. Held a knife to throats; placed perfect cuts along the most tenderest of skin. He'd seen other spies, other warriors, mete out their own justice. Since Thomas's death, the rage had carried him forward. The Archer deserved the harshest of punishments.

And here she was, captured, bound. He could do anything to her. Anything. Yet he found himself frustratingly bound by custom, by some moral code instilled in him.

He couldn't raise a blade to her, couldn't harm her. Could do nothing but rage words at her and they fell uselessly in front of him. She simply laid there, keeping her eyes on him, her breath even. With her wrists bleeding from nightmares, she looked at him as if *he* was the madman.

If he was mad, she was the one who brought him there. 'This one—' Eldric pointed to the wound directly underneath the other two '—I earned from you as well. It, too, preceded the killing of a man who was watching my left flank. I knew, immediately, it was you. What did you feel when I spotted you in that tree?'

She shook her head, refusing him or acknowledging his anger and pain?

This was personal. He was sure of it. He felt it in his soul.

'Tell me this, when I found you that day. *Why* did you mark me? I knew it was you. You know I knew it was you. There was no need to kill Philip.'

## Chapter Five

Every word a blade sliced across her chest and she felt the cut of each one. All to tell him the truth. Her father asked her to kill him, but she couldn't. So she'd warned him away. It didn't matter, it didn't matter that her arrow accidentally killed his friend the first time.

It didn't matter that it was her father who killed Philip...or Michael. Those men, the anguish on Eldric's face, haunted her, but now she knew their names. Names!

To tell him the truth and prove her disloyalty to her father? To tell him, so he'd pursue her father with certainty and get himself killed? Never.

If she could have, she, too, would have roared and left the room as Eldric had done. But she couldn't, she couldn't. All she had left was, 'I need to relieve myself.'

His head jerked as if she'd slapped him. One thundering step until he leaned over her. Took in every one of her flaws. She knew he did as his eyes flicked from one cheek to the other, her eyes, her lips, where his eyes stayed for one moment, two before they wrenched to her bound hands.

He growled. 'This is what you say to me. This!'

She knew what he wanted. But it was truth, at least after a day bound. Raising her chin, she answered, 'You're the one who captured me and imprisoned me here. What did you plan to do when it came to this?'

She knew what her father would do. He'd leave her. She knew what Eldric wanted to do, his anger was so great. If possible, he grew colder, more formidable.

But that was his expression. Everything else… He didn't put on his tunic. His body remained partially bared. Forgotten in his anger? She couldn't forget. The scars she gave him were stark. Jagged. Accusing, if such a word could be used for wounds purposefully inflicted.

On a harsh breath, he wrenched on the ties around her ankles to release them, then abruptly stepped back. 'Thinking to kick me?' he said.

His scars. *Her* scars distracted her from keeping up her ruse of protesting, begging him to release her. Instead, to ease the ache, she curled her legs into herself. 'They hurt. I was—' She shook her head. What would he believe?

'Lay them flat. *Now.*'

Protest? No. This wasn't a situation she knew. Slowly, she lowered them until she felt his gaze. She adjusted her back, her shoulders, if only to relieve whatever tension this was.

'You mean to release me?' she said.

He wrenched on another tie and her left arm was

free. When his eyes snapped to her hand, she lowered it as well.

'No release. And I'll be watching your moves, Archer, as I've no intention of falling for that again.' He pointed to his nose. He'd said it was not broken, but the swelling was spreading along both cheekbones.

'Comfrey...' she said.

'Turn on your stomach,' he bit out.

Blood drained from her face and, despite her trying to keep as still as possible, because she truly did have to relieve herself, her limbs twitched.

'Are you ill?'

She didn't want to turn on her stomach, there would be no way to protect herself. And her father had her do this when... No, she didn't want to recall that at all.

'Why do this? Why not have me use a pot?' she said.

'I don't welcome trouble by bringing in a servant. And I don't desire to clean a pot, Archer. Especially yours.'

The blush spread up from her chest to the roots of her hair. She hated that she had that disadvantage. Her father had used it against her many times and he'd varied the punishments, thinking she could unlearn it. She'd tried to please him. She'd tried so that no one would know—

Eldric noticed it now. The blue of his gaze changing again. She wished she could understand what such a reaction meant, but she had no reference for it. No one looked at her the way he did. And if Eldric looked this way at another, she never saw it.

His stare was riveting, as if she was prey, and he was calculating her weaknesses. No, it was different.

How? The longer she stared the more he stared right back. The pupils of his eyes darkened until his gaze felt intense and *warm*.

Her blush deepened. Horrified, she flipped on to her stomach.

For the longest of moments, nothing happened. Turning her head to the side, she captured a bit of how still he stood before a harsh breath left him.

Curious, she tilted her head to catch more of him; winced as it pulled something that much tighter in her bound hand. Bewilderment, as he roughly untied her other hand.

'Turn on to your back again.' His voice roughened.

She could move freely, her tunic and leggings loose. Unfortunately, with the way she'd been tied, then with her flipping to her back, the extra fabric was now a hindrance.

'I can't.'

'You'll do it now.'

His voice brooked no compromise and she didn't want to argue. She truly needed to get to the garderobe. 'I'm trapped. My clothing twisted. I'll need to lift up from the bed to—'

'Don't move.' Cursing, he gripped the back of her leg. She felt the practical way he lifted it, his efficient tug of the fabric before he released her leg and did the same to the other. Except it didn't feel practical or efficient. The backs of her legs were sensitive.

When he grabbed the second one, she couldn't stop her body's reaction to his touch.

'Don't fight me.' He tugged again, his fingers digging when the fabric of her leggings didn't release, and suddenly she wanted much, much more of his fingers, of his hands. Her blush deepened.

Too many weaknesses! Sleeping, hunger, blushing, being caught. She didn't need any more when it came to him! 'Let go of my leg.'

He didn't. She wouldn't tolerate it. With a huff, she flipped on her back so she could face her enemy. Fight him the way her father would want. Escape if possible, the way she should. She was free.

Unlike Eldric, who seemed locked over her, his hand still clutching her leg. All of it simple. But Eldric was tall, his grip kept her leg up and out towards him.

Only a few candles were lit, but even in the dim flickering light that kept the corners of the room in shadows, she could see her actions surprised him.

He gave off a choked sound, not like hers at all. No. Nothing light and surprised and useless like hiding a laugh. It was almost a shocked helplessness to it. But deeper, rough…possessive.

His hold slackened enough so that she could have eased her leg back on to the bed. Except for the way he was looking at her. If she moved, if she blinked, she didn't know what he would do.

Would he react as if she was fighting him? She didn't want to fight him.

'I'll stay still,' she assured him.

His gaze, which had been riveted on her leg in his hand, broke away, travelled to the juncture in between. To her very exposed belly which brought her acutely aware of how he held her, with his bare hands, arms. His bare chest. The bottom of her foot pressed lightly to his lower rib. To the marks and lines, and scars that made him everything he was: a warrior, a spy. A man.

Did she think she had weaknesses with her back to him? This...this was far more dangerous. She'd watched this man since she was a child. She knew what she felt for him. The longer he held her, the longer they stayed like this, the more chance she'd do something and reveal what she shouldn't.

'I won't fight you,' she said, her voice sounding as irregular as his. 'Tie my hands in the front, I can—'

He shook his head hard, once, twice. The softness of his lips from before pressed hard as he ground his teeth. He flung her leg to the bed. 'What do you play at?' he said.

'Play?'

'Flipping on the bed, tightening your clothes...is this how you free yourself when men capture you?'

He used words, but she couldn't put them in context. He was angry, but she'd only followed his instructions. And he might have let go of her leg, but his eyes roved and touched every bit of her as if compelled to do so.

'I've never been captured.' At the gleam in his eyes, she added, 'Why would anyone capture a healer waiting for her family to arrive?'

'Lies and games. What do you think to do? Use *this*—' he waved over her '—as a distraction?'

A distraction. She couldn't think around him. Kept imagining something else in his eyes when it was she who felt, she who wanted. The longer she stayed around him, the more confusing it became. Constantly she wanted to blurt the truth, her feelings, everything. Reveal every embarrassing vulnerability. And he thought her a distraction?

She might not understand fully what made him bewildered, but she understood she didn't want to be here. Eldric might believe he was entitled to his vengeance against her, but she had her own desires. She'd be damned if he had his before she discovered the truth of the rumours. She was lying there, but she wasn't defenceless.

'I play no games and only followed your exact instructions, though I am under no obligation to do so. You've untied me, Sir Knight. How easy would it be for me to roll off this bed and slice the back of your legs with the dagger attached to your waist.'

'Such *healing* words. And you remind me again why I loathe you. Let's not forget it's for your comfort we do this.' He lifted the ropes in his hand. 'What shall it be?'

She might have made her point, but Eldric's long reach meant there was no certainty of escape. The only certainty was losing whatever this tiny bit of trust was. Next time, she wouldn't be allowed the garderobe. For now, she needed trust when they were on the road to the Tower. That was her best chance to escape.

She would get free. He might know how to swing a sword and tie some knots, but she'd been trained to elude and vanish. Watching his eyes for any change to his decision, she clasped her palms together and raised her hands.

If anything, his frown grew darker. Displeased she was cooperating with him tying her wrists? He cinched the last of it, snatched his tunic and yanked it on. All the while his eyes never went to hers.

'Get up,' he ordered.

The rope bit into the cuts she'd made earlier in panic. Knowing he meant to hurt her this time, she didn't give him the pleasure of making a sound. If she had her wits about her from now on, she wouldn't give another reaction or say another word. She'd shown him enough of how best to hurt her.

The Archer lied horribly, but Eldric found no comfort in that fact. Nor did he find comfort in the straw mattress, the five thick wool blankets, nor the four down pillows he'd demanded from the innkeepers once the Archer was through with the garderobe and tied up again to the bed.

He'd also ordered fresh food and drink. He ate every crumb of the bread and cheese from earlier along with the steaming bowl of stew. No wine, but a weakened ale that he drank fully of, and after a bit gave her some as well.

Through it all, she stayed quiet, which suited him fine. The rest…he was too open with her, as if someone had scoured his skin on the inside and then felt it wasn't enough. The heartache he had of losing his comrades, his pursuit of the Archer, then being thwarted again and again burned inside him.

To capture her only to be trapped in a room. Too close. No chance for her to escape, but none for him as well. He didn't want to risk her escaping… Risk her rolling off the bed and slicing the dagger across the back of his knees.

A healer! No healer would have such a clever and

resourceful way of felling an enemy. To loathe and admire her was unfathomable.

To desire her? Unconscionable! And yet…she was stunning—he'd acknowledged that when her hood fell back and all her glory was presented. He'd never seen hair or eyes her colour. The golden hue to her skin, the painted bud of her lips.

And her form, her strength, the way her body curved beneath him as he felt her foot against his side and he looked down at her splayed on the bed. Her body…how she could wield it like a weapon. How effectively she used it against him! She had trained and someone had taught her. Who? How?

Those were the matters he should be thinking of and discovering more about. There were surprises other than her gender. Far too many to simply turn her over to the King.

No. He might have been too hasty in taking the hunting horn from his King and entering a pact. From now on, he'd find his own answers.

One answer he must face. He more than desired the Archer. All those moments his body jolted with awareness, with possessiveness, with *need*: carrying her through the crowd to the inn, tying her to the bed, holding, and being unable to release her ankle…all because she lay under him.

Did this ferocity stem because she was the enemy? Perhaps, having pursued her, his body equated his vengeance with his desire and pursuit of women. If so, he could reason his way out. Pursue another female. His enemy was tied to a bed, he could find one now.

No. Even the thought didn't hold merit. Her lure

for him was something else. Some familiarity that shouldn't be there. Her! He desired her, was tempted by her. A mix of vulnerability and strength. Of innocence and deadly intent.

He could never act on it. Never. The sooner he discovered her secrets, the sooner he could rid himself of her. Forget this moment in time. No victory. No satisfaction. Just finish it. Until then…

He welcomed her silence. He was incapable of words, of conversations, of pressing for answers.

No words could be said as his body locked on to quelling a heated response when his hand clamped to her wrist, when her body fell into step with his. Arm against arm, against hip, against leg. Sharing one side of his body with hers as he took her down the hall and back again.

He argued with himself it was necessary. Outward restraints might be noticed and bring questions or, worse, some fool to her rescue. Holding her any further away and, given her talents, she'd try to escape.

So he kept her that close. She should have been too tiny for him, his hatred of her too strong, but the touch of her body, the scent of her skin, all he felt was some unfathomable rightness.

Only one other time had it felt like that for him. Once at a dance in Swaffham last winter where he met a masked woman…one that he hadn't been able to forget. He dreamed of her late at night, saw her in every woman that even slightly resembled her, dark hair, eyes that met his. Their encounter was brief, he only touched her hand, but she haunted him. As the weeks turned into months, she became everything he wished for, if he could only find her again.

Maybe if he hadn't lost her that night, he'd realise she was nothing special. But they shared one dance and then she disappeared. He'd tried to find her afterwards, but no one knew who she was. He had no time to linger. His pursuit of his enemy was all consuming. His pursuit of *this* woman. The masked woman had to remain a dream.

All the while, he listened to his enemy breathe, watched the fluttering of her pulse in her neck. Noticed her blushes as he tied her once again to the bed. The swallows she took of the weakened ale. Her eyes open to his, his palm cradling her head. The feel of her hair wrapping around his fingers. Mistrust until he took a drink from the same cup as her. Then defiance as she drank from that same side. From placing her lips where his had been.

He couldn't arrange his bedding for the night quickly enough. All against the door. An almost insurmountable trap, while he could sleep in comfort.

And he needed to sleep. He couldn't remember the last time he'd done so, knowing the Archer was close, and he refused, *refused* to allow her to escape him.

But now she was secured and he could succumb to his exhaustion. She might have slept, but there were dark circles under her eyes, she needed more.

The fact he understood she needed sleep, that he was giving it to her, grated. But nothing else needed to be done for the night. To sleep. To rest, and tomorrow to start again. This from a place of knowing who she was and what she was capable of. To not underestimate her or the way he felt with her.

Tomorrow would be different. He had the power now and he'd use it. Moments passed. The inn's patrons retiring for the night left larger gaps of silence. Leaving just them in the room. Awake.

She didn't move. She didn't speak. But he knew all the same, she was as awake as he. Every bone in his body demanded he rest, but she was within reach.

Maybe here, now, would be different. Maybe now he could coax a secret. The need pounded in him to end this. He felt…he knew…too much time in her presence would only confuse what must be done. He had made a pact with the King, one he must fulfil or else jeopardise his friends. Whatever he felt when he was close to her must mean nothing. She could only ever be the Archer for him.

Still, there wouldn't be any harm if he asked questions. If she gave him lies, he'd end for the night and sleep.

'I will take you to the Tower whether you tell me the truth or not,' he said and waited. 'Why bother to hide who you truly are?' he continued even though she stayed quiet. 'Don't you take pride in your work? Those shots across my arm were beautifully executed. A friend of mine thought I had them done for art's sake. Surely you have to know your skill is unparalleled. Why don't you tell me of it?'

She remained unerringly still, staring up at that ceiling, and he hated that he remained by the door where he could not see her expression.

Sleep waited, but now that he asked these questions,

he wanted to continue doing so. Even if she didn't answer them, even if she didn't…

'No answer? How about your ability to kick? You are a slight thing, yet you've bruised my ribs and my nose swells. You recommended something to heal them. What was it?'

Somehow her chest rose and fell enough for him to discern it under the quilt. A sigh, or was she weakening?

'No words on how to heal me. No words at all. It will be a very long journey to the Tower. To your execution. Many men like to talk. To reminisce. To beg at these points. Men think it'll soften me to their plight, or perhaps they want to be remembered. But you're not a man, are you? Clever to disguise yourself as one. Or is it a disguise? You couldn't kick me in a gown. Maybe you dress this way for all those trees you climb.'

Still nothing. There were others in the past who'd kept their secrets until by some application of torture or threat, they broke. But words weren't working here.

What did he know of women? That they had strength, compassion. He couldn't imagine her, a killer, to have any, but…nothing else was working. If she had compassion, if he had to make himself bleed to get answers from her he would. If this is what it took to bring her to confession—to torture himself—he would.

Maybe it was sleep deprivation, maybe merely desperation. But he'd tell her all, tell her what he had lost. Tell her to call to some humanity within her. He killed when it became a matter of his life. She killed from a distance, when there was no possibility of coming to harm, and he didn't know why. She wasn't the enemy. Her accent was English.

'The three men who were protecting me? I met Thomas when we were only five. He loved jests. Terrible ones. They didn't make any sense, but he'd make them up while his mouth was half-full of stew and he'd almost choke himself to death laughing at his own humour.'

He rolled his shoulders, feeling grief begin its painful grip. Each sentence, each memory opened wounds that cut far deeper than the ones she had given him.

'Michael was far too quiet until he drank ale and we were always making sure he drank too much. Philip? I don't know where he got his coin, but he had plenty and he spent it on the most ridiculous things that he had no use for.'

The Archer stared at the ceiling, her chest rising and falling, but when he told of Michael, it caught, stuttered. He took a malicious pride in that reaction. Talking of his friends burned away whatever spell she cast with her looks, the softness of her hair in his palm.

'What of your friends, have you lost them as well?' he said. Another stutter to her chest, this time with a sound. Quick, brutal. Victory. 'Tell me, little Archer, have you lost friends as well?'

'I can't—' She jerked. 'I'm not who you think I am.'

A reaction or a lie? To see her expression! Though if he lit a candle, if he rose from the barricade he'd made by the door, he knew she'd say nothing more.

'You can't…what?' he coaxed, keeping his voice even, almost soothing. Maybe this killer needed the dark to whisper her heinous confession.

'Nothing.'

'I know you're not who you pretend to be, but that's the point of this conversation. I've told you of me. What of you?'

Silence only.

'I have been pursuing you for many seasons. I've studied you as much as you'd let me. I've come to conclusions which can only lead to your death. Don't you wish to enlighten me to save your life?'

She turned her head. He could almost see her now and was certain, with the shadows by the door, she couldn't see him.

'I said what I meant to say,' she said. 'You are mistaken. I am not the person you seek.'

He'd kick the covers off him if it didn't give his frustration away. Twice now. Twice she'd brought him to the edge. All this time, he'd imagined when he captured the Archer he'd feel only victory. He'd imagined that the vow inside him would be put to rest and he'd find some peace within him. Find whatever contentment and happiness she'd stolen from him.

But, no, she'd keep to her horrible lies and obfuscation, her deceit. Taunting him with her mesmerising hair and unfathomable eyes. With a body that was honed as fine as her bow skills. And all of it sliced through his grief.

He'd stormed away from her once and everything in him wanted to do it again. And she just lay there, her words meticulously controlled.

'Not the person I seek?' The words burned in his throat, in his heart. 'You are hell to me. *Hell.*'

## Chapter Six

It wasn't a sound that woke Cressida. She could hardly hear anything above Eldric's steady breath which hadn't changed since he fell asleep atop the hill of blankets he'd insisted the inn provide him. The floor was well-worn wood, softened over the years and built with nary a gap between the planks. No draughts, a roof over her head, she would have contentedly fallen asleep without alerting others to her presence.

But Eldric insisted on the thickest of blankets and a spare mattress from another room. Which all meant that even if he moved away from the door—a barrier to her escape—the weight of the rest of his comforts would preclude her from breaking past him.

Every moment stuck was another agonising moment of imagining her father on a ship. A full day trapped and now her imagination had him with another child, with another weapon who would take her place.

It wasn't like her to agonise over rumours and thoughts. She was never idle, always running to the next camp to spy and gather information. Sometimes to be that weapon her father needed. Two days of being bound. Of someone else gathering food and taking care of her needs. All she had were these thoughts keeping her up all night.

Though Eldric, in his tower of comfort, clearly had no difficulty sleeping. Even after he told her of the friends he lost because of her. Told and almost broke her. How weak she was with him! How much she wanted to comfort him for his loss when she was the one who had caused it!

Not that he'd accept her offered comfort. Not ever. And even if she wasn't who she was, why would he want her? She was…physically flawed, covered with her failings.

After sleeping all day, she had no chance to sleep this night. In truth, she needed little sleep and Eldric… was Eldric, permeating all her thoughts awake and sleeping. Every move he made under the covers. Every turn and brush of his limbs against wool, every thump of his hand against the wooded door, or a dull bump of a foot against the floor plank, she heard and felt.

To her everything he did was noisy, though he was probably no louder than any other. Everyone was noisier than her. But her focus on Eldric made anything else around them difficult to perceive, and that could easily result in her death…in his death if she wasn't as well trained as she was.

So her sudden alertness could only mean one thing. Danger. Stilling her breath and body, she ached to hear the now-familiar tromping of feet and muffled voices of the other inn residents she had been able to sift through over the last day. There were the feet of those travellers who came for the day and left quickly afterward. Then there was the innkeeper and his wife, the two girl servants and the three young men who carried buckets and food. There was one other regular set of footsteps. One she had assumed was a traveller staying for a few days in a fine inn, but now she knew differently, because she'd heard that distinct step before, that particular gait along the plankboards outside their door. It was here, again.

This was no mere traveller rushing to the garderobe at the end of the hall. Her eyes went to Eldric, but he slept on.

A shadow swept past the shutters just outside the room. The window was high in the wall and the light provided wasn't moonlight, but flickering torches. Men at the door, others by the window. They were surrounded and she was bound. If she alerted Eldric, if she shouted out, it would only notify the men surrounding them.

Another shadow. A moment of sound like a cough contained. They were too close now and she was truly helpless for the first time in her life. She looked to Eldric, only to see he wasn't asleep. He lay in the same position, his back to the door, his body curled, facing her, but his eyes were open and pinned on her. With the softest of movements, he placed his finger against his lips for her to keep quiet.

She moved her wrist, begging him to release her. His only response was to show his hand around the pommel of his sword, as he slowly stood up and moved to the right of the door.

Leaving her completely trussed up like an offer-

ing to the mercenaries behind the windows and the
door. Her heart hammered, but not for her safety. She
knew what these men meant. Her father had been sending them to her since her disloyalty. They came, they
fought and she received another mission. Right now,
their surrounding them was merely another test she
needed to pass.

They wouldn't permanently harm her; they wouldn't
dare. Even if they tried, she was usually prepared to
quickly disable them and retrieve the next message
from her father. It was the message, not the men, that
was important.

But this time was different. Now she was bound
and Eldric gripped his sword. Eldric, who didn't know
this was one of her father's games, who would take the
threat in earnest; most likely fight to the death because
that was how he was trained.

What would happen then? Would the mercenaries
forget the game as well? Would fatal blood be spilled?
Worse, a mercenary could escape and report she was
trapped, that Eldric was here. He would be in more
danger than he already was.

She shook her head and mouthed one word: *No!*

He raised one brow as the door slammed open.
The first mercenary tripped on the bedding and Eldric swung his sword.

'Don't kill him!'

With a twist of his wrist, the flat of the sword hit
the mercenary in the chest. She heard an arm break
as the man fell. Two others forced their way in. Eldric
gave a downward swing which caught the first one in

the back of the head, but the other ducked and rolled over the overstuffed mattress.

A bang on the window shutters warned of others. Eldric cursed as he fought the mercenary who had the advantage because Eldric's back was to the opened door. Another bang outside, of feet scrambling to find purchase on wood.

'Don't leave me like this!'

'You're mine! They can't have you.' Eldric ducked the mercenary's sword and dived towards the bed.

'They don't want me.' That wasn't exactly true, but how to tell him partial truths? She wasn't used to talking at all, only holding secrets. Of hiding. 'They—'

'You told me not to kill!' Eldric swung again, forcing the man to retreat further into the room. Closer to her and Eldric's back was still vulnerable to the opened door. 'You know them; tell me who they are.'

'They're here to harm me.'

A crash of splintered wood. The shutters giving way beneath hands and iron.

'They can wait their turn.' Eldric rushed the man before him and bashed his fist against his temple. The man crumpled. Sprinting towards the bed, he cut her bound hands.

Two more men poured through the door.

This wasn't right. There were too many. Many more than her father had ever dispatched before. And in this enclosed space she was unable to use her bow and arrow, her deadliest asset.

Swords crashed on swords now. A grunt, the heavy shuffling of feet as Eldric fought two. So much noise and no one came to their rescue. That also didn't bode well. Her hands were unsteady as she untied the knots around her ankles. Too many knots!

She freed her feet just as the first man tumbled though the window. Lunging, she locked her arms around his neck until he passed out. She dragged his body into the room and grabbed his dagger as another man popped his head up. She dived under the window until he, too, hoisted himself over the sill, and she slammed the hilt on to the back of his head. He slumped and she dragged him into the room as well, then waited. Silence outside, while the movements of the men inside grew more reckless. She wouldn't be distracted; she felt another person outside still.

A crash into the wall as a body was slammed. Eldric? She looked; his sword was at an odd angle. His body was momentarily pinned to the wall, his chest and heart utterly exposed.

He needed help! A scraping of a boot against wood outside. She couldn't leave her position.

Eldric dropped as a sword hacked into the wall right where he had been. Cressida cursed. The mercenaries were ordered not to kill her, but that didn't extend to witnesses.

To stay here endangered Eldric, to not fight the man outside was fatal as well. The moment her back was turned, the mercenary would have the element of surprise.

No choice for it, she'd risk her life. Jumping, she pulled herself up to the sill and looked down. By the unfettered malevolence of his expression, if the climbing mercenary could have yanked her over the sill and down below, he would have. Without a word, he dropped back to the ground and into the night. Most likely to gain entrance another way.

She whirled around. Eldric now fought only one of them. Neither man had their swords, but his opponent had his dagger, twirling it as if deciding to throw or slice.

With a yell, she charged. Eldric cried out as she leapt against the mercenary's back, locking her arms around his throat to block his air. He grabbed her arms and flipped her over his body.

She slammed into the floor, every bruise she'd already suffered roaring to life; she lost her bearings, couldn't dodge the mercenary's fist aiming for her chest.

Not a fist! She tilted her body. The blade scored across her back and pricked the floor. His weight flung off her as Eldric tossed him towards the bed. His head, then his arm hit the post with a snap, he flopped to the ground and the dagger slid towards her.

Skidding through the door, the man from under the window rushed in. His focus intent on Eldric, she threw the dagger. It lodged in his chest, knocked him back, his eyes locked with hers before he fell face forward. The thud echoed in the room.

Silence for one, two heartbeats.

'You killed him,' Eldric said.

Men lay at Eldric's feet, a few of them already stirring. Her eyes sweeping for targets, she leapt across the floor, slamming the back of heads, knocking them out.

Utterly aware of Eldric standing and watching everything, she dragged the two bodies under the window together, swiped the bindings he'd used on her and tied them to each other. There wasn't enough binding for their feet, but if she tied their hands, used the furniture, it would hold them until she escaped.

'What are you doing?'

'I have to—' She clenched the tunic of another mercenary and dragged him until he was closer to another. Every movement stung as the wound in her back pulled and fresh blood poured. No hope for it. She needed to be done quickly and leave before the mercenaries woke or the game would begin once more. Injured, she would be too weak to fight again.

'You killed him. You told me not to kill—why did I not kill them?' He shook his head.

She had killed a mercenary. She had killed one of her father's men. She hadn't been thinking. Instinct. The heat of the moment? No, she did it because Eldric was risked. Because…she was protecting him.

'It was an accident,' she said.

His eyes, which had blazed with retribution, censored at once. 'You never have accidents. Not a murderer like you.'

She couldn't say anything to that. On both accounts, it was the truth. It was no accident; she'd kill again to save Eldric. As for her being a murderer…it was and would always be how he saw her. No choice now. No ruse or fakery. She'd shown her true self when she fought the mercenaries.

Now she needed to do what needed to be done. Then…then she'd find a way to apologise to her father. She simply needed more time. Lifting the bindings in one hand, she said, 'I need to leave. Help me before they waken.'

'*We* need to leave,' he corrected. 'You're my captive and this location is compromised.'

'I am no captive,' she said.

She could run right now, but she needed to search for the missive attached to one of the men. Which pouch? How to search when Eldric's entire focus was her?

'Something is wrong.' Eldric looked out in the corridor. 'Dead of night, but we made sound. Where are the innkeepers?'

'They would have been paid.'

His head swung to hers, she ignored his glare and knotted the rope around another pair of wrists.

'Even the patrons?' At her shrug, he continued, 'You've done this before. You knew they were coming.'

There was no pretending she was some healer, or an innocent maiden he'd mistakenly kidnapped. She could barely maintain the ruse before her father's men attacked. 'If I was alone, they would have only harmed me. *If* they could have got to me. They mostly never do, but here in this room there was no choice. Being bound made this far more dangerous. They never would have intended—'

'Harmed you? Intended! He thrust a blade at your heart!' Eldric pointed to the man slumped against the wall. 'That one tried to gut me.'

'It's not true,' she said, scrambling to her feet, not wanting to think on that or the ramifications of the man she'd killed. She hid her grimace as she felt her back wound tear that much more. The pain froze her for a moment, two before she could take the next few steps to Eldric's packed tunic to tear it into strips. 'It can't be true. We…misinterpreted what they were doing. We need more bindings to gag them.'

'Bones!' Eldric yanked the clothing from her to rip himself. 'Tell me who those men were. Why did you not want me to kill them?'

If she meant to protect Eldric, she could tell him nothing. Yet, she knew he would keep questioning her. He'd let nothing go since she released that first arrow and marked his arm. Something bound them that day. Something…inevitable.

Like heartache. Loss. As much as she cared for him, he would always hate her.

Her back throbbed and dizziness hit her. She needed to find the missive from her father telling her what he expected next. His orders centred her, gave her purpose. Reminded her of what was right and true. Then she could find a shelter and hide until she was safe to travel again.

Too much time with Eldric. With their words exchanged and his deeds. Saying he wanted only her death, but giving her food, shelter, ensuring the bindings would not cut. Too many words, his unfailingly all-too-close presence. All of it confusing. Her life wasn't meant to share with another. Her father and his missions were all she was, all she should be.

There! She spotted the red pouch attached to one of the men by the window and flipped it open. Inside was the almost comforting sealed parchment. Her father was still with her. He was here even among this chaos and Eldric's questions. Ripping it open, she read words on the page. Ones that couldn't be—

A moan from one of the captives as Eldric yanked

him up. He rammed part of his tunic into the man's
open mouth and cinched the ropes around the last two
mercenaries' wrists. Their limbs whitened around each
rope knot.

He caught her eye. 'Do not think I do your bidding
now. These men tried to kill me no matter what you
believe. They deserve every bit of pain I mete out to
them before we go to— What are you reading?'

Nothing. She felt the paper in her hand; forced her
chin to lower. Begged her eyes to decipher a different
set of sentences. The same. Letters swirling before her.
Triple-checked the handwriting, and the seal. It was
her father's. Everything in her knew it was her father's,
but it couldn't be.

'Nothing.' She crushed it. 'I'd hoped that it would
be some—'

Eldric snatched the message, stepped back, read it.
Glanced at her as if he didn't know who she was. She
didn't blame him. She didn't know herself.

Hours of him demanding answers. She needed a
few of her own. She shook the bound mercenary who
had the pouch. His eyes fluttered, but his head stayed
lulled.

'Stop it,' Eldric ordered. 'Do you mean to undo our
deeds?'

Cursing, she shook the next mercenary, felt the skin
in her back tear until white stars threatened her vision.
Somewhere she heard a groan, but her captive didn't
wake. Impatient, she slapped his face. His eyes shot
open and she stared straight into them.

'Do you know who I am?'

He moaned.

Shaking him again, she demanded, 'Do you?'

He swallowed. 'You're his first daughter.'

She should be his only daughter. 'What was your mission?'

He sneered. 'To kill you.'

She locked her suddenly weakened spine. 'Tell me.'

'You're expendable. He has another.' His grin widened. 'There will be others. There will be others and they'll come for you as well. Finally, you'll get what's coming to you. Replaced by a half-Scottish child no less. Stolen and half-filth and still he wants her more than you. You're not his favourite any more and you know what that means. You know—'

He jerked; blood poured from his lips. Cressida dropped him, finally recognised the dagger in his chest. She turned.

'You can't tell me not to kill that one,' Eldric said. 'Should I do the rest?'

There was no answer to that. She didn't make the decisions on whether someone lived or died. That was her father's choice. Except for Eldric and his music, the rest of the world didn't exist for her, yet she suddenly seemed to be in the middle of it.

It was too much. Too much and all too soon. She felt oddly weak from it all.

Eldric's eyes narrowed on her. 'Are you fainting?'

She didn't think so, but what did she know of fainting? She'd been knocked unconscious before and this felt like that, but her eyes were open. All she knew with certainty was the world wasn't as steady as it once was.

'Tell me who you are.' His fingers flexed as if wanting his sword. To gut her? To die by Eldric's hands was all too believable an end for her.

'Who do you think I am?'

He growled low, without mercy, 'What you have always been to me: my enemy, the Archer.'

She closed her eyes on that truth. She was only death and it was all she deserved as well. 'I am...what my father made me.'

# *Chapter Seven*

Eldric didn't know anything. Oh, he was certain this was the woman who had killed his friends—the same Archer he was required to bring to King Edward for beheading, for torture—and she'd proven who she was when she fought him and the trained men. No woman fought like that without years of gaining these deadly skills.

She was a killer and, after months of hatred, hatred he still harboured, he'd captured her. But everything else... He kept her here trying to gain answers, but at this moment, facing her, his blood ramming through his veins, he no longer knew the correct questions.

That message. When she declared it was nothing and crushed it in her fist, he had to have it. He clenched it still and felt the crisp prick of the parchment weaken. But he continued to reel from the punch the words threw him. 'This missive. Is this some sort of code? Does it have another meaning?'

She parted her lips, but didn't make any more effort to answer his question. He had patience. The heat of battle hadn't left his limbs. He jammed wool into the warrior's mouths to gag their cries and secured knots around wrists and chairs. Now, with no ready task before him, his body felt unsteady. A few breaths caught and all would be easier.

For once, the Archer didn't look much better than he felt. White-blonde hair snarled across her shoulders, her pallor almost sickly. He could determine nothing of her emotions. Her eyes were fixed on the floor before her bent knees.

She had fought like a warrior, dispatched the men with grace and skill. Even after being knocked breathless, when the mercenary thrust his blade towards her chest, there was no hesitation in her movements. Now... she wasn't resting or waiting like him to ease the fight from her body. Instead, everything about her was subdued. Beaten.

What he needed to determine from her he must do somewhere else, not amid these prone bodies who posed a threat. The innkeepers and patrons must have been paid off, but they would return. He and the Archer needed to be far away from Dover, but right now neither of them moved.

'If this isn't a code...' he swallowed '...what does it mean?' He didn't need to read it again. 'What does it mean when it says, *"If you are reading this, then I have failed to end your life. If so, it will only be the first attempt. There will be another and another until the deed is done. Accept it or do the deed yourself."*?'

She flinched at his words as if he was punching her with every one of them. She couldn't seem to answer any question. Still, he continued them. 'This is a message for you, isn't it? You saw that red pouch; you knew what you were looking for. Said these men were sent before, but the red pouch you were expecting as well.'

She swayed a bit, but didn't raise her eyes. 'Many times before. Many times, but not always. It wasn't supposed to be for always. These men, the fight, my acquiring the pouch and the mission…the message. This isn't the first time.'

Her voice was unstable. Weak, but he noticed her slip of the tongue. A mission. She was given missions. But not this time. 'Look at me.'

Her chest rose and fell a bit faster, but she kept her eyes to the floor. Truth flared within him. 'This isn't a code. This person wants you dead.'

'It can't be—' Her bent legs shuffled under her as if trying to escape. 'We need to go. I need to find… I have to know.'

None of the mercenaries were awake or stirred, and no one came crashing down the hall. She'd told him the witnesses were paid off, but how could a whole town be paid off? How much wealth was spent for tonight's entertainment? His patience with this game was gone. If innkeepers or patrons interrupted them, another blade would fly into a chest.

Seasons of pursuing this enemy of his, hours of interrogating her, attempting to torture her with truths he knew. He felt further from understanding her than ever before.

'How much do you know? How much are you not telling me?'

She raised her eyes at that, but didn't look at him. It was as if she was seeing something far in the future, or far in the past. 'I know so much and can't tell you any of it, Eldric.'

A splinter of fear woke his hot body. Hours together and they hadn't exchanged names. He still didn't know hers. He was no fool. He knew she must know something of who he was. The way she looked at him, the words she almost said.

But her saying his name wasn't what caused him to leap across the floor and skid to her side. It was the way she said it. It was the way her eyes were unfocused as she looked at him now. Battling the hesitation, he laid his hands on her shoulders. She felt like ice. Shock? After reading the missive and hearing that mercenary's words, she'd paled, but now he wondered if it was something else. 'Are you injured?'

Her eyes fluttered, but kept firm on him, as if fascinated by his features. He thought he'd seen such an expression once or twice since he bound her, but she always shuttered her expression too quickly to be certain. Now she stared with openness as if she had nothing to hide or was incapable of it.

'Are you hurt?' he repeated. When her eyes shut and she slumped into his hands, he clutched her to him. She moaned, but didn't wake. There weren't enough curse words in the world as he felt what he should have known before. The heated liquid of blood against her back. The dagger! He'd watched her evade the point, but she hadn't been quick enough. The bastard had carved her.

He had nothing on him for such a wound. A healer! But he didn't know this port town. He didn't know... He knew ships. Trying to staunch the flow of blood, he swept her in his arms and pelted out the door, his heavy footsteps thundering down the empty hall and out into the night where a few workers still lingered on the docks. The ships blazed with patrols and activity.

Scanning a few of them for possibilities, he chose the most maintained. When his feet echoed on the gangplank, her eyes opened. 'Where are you…?'

'Stay awake,' he said.

'This isn't your ship.'

Of course she would know that. She'd been successfully hiding the truth from him, but he knew full well why information so easily flowed from her now. Shock, injury. He was a bastard, but he would take advantage of it. 'Tell me how you know me.'

Her hand on his shoulder slipped, caressed the area above his elbow. Stunned, he felt the purposeful tracing through his tunic before ice rushed down his spine and his skin prickled. She caressed the scars she'd given him. Three strikes from arrow points across his arm as she killed his friends.

'Because I've watched over you.'

Her eyes remained partially unfocused; he could feel the blood now dripping through his fingers. She rambled words that made no sense. Was she dying?

'Hold on!' he demanded even though it was better if she remained unconscious for what he had to do.

Crossing the plank to the deck, he called out and a man with a short sword drawn stepped out of the rooms below.

Dover as a Cinque Port meant that at any time the King could commission a ship docked here and he just happened to have royal papers that would allow him to do the same. Releasing the pouch at his waist, he tossed it to the man. 'Do you have a healer?'

The man was dishevelled, but his clothes spoke of wealth. No doubt the Commander. Sheathing his sword, he opened the pouch, unrolled the message and his eyes widened. When he began to bend at the knee, Eldric lost the last of his patience.

'Don't bow. Get me a healer and privacy.'

The Commander waved away the patrols that had appeared since he called out. The men didn't hesitate. Either well trained or something of his own glower warned them off.

'There's none on board. I'll fetch one, for a price. As for privacy, this way.' The Commander indicated with his chin.

Eldric followed the man, then realised the impossibility of it. Ships' stairs were small, the hull's ceilings low, he'd have to fold himself into a crouch to get through the doorway. He refused to release the Archer. 'Bring him to me here.'

The man opened his mouth to protest. Save him from fools and small places. 'Do it!'

While he waited, he knelt and laid her by the doorway so those searching the docks couldn't easily spot them.

'Never seen you shout at people before,' she said, her eyes almost guileless.

He steadied his breath, which caught too many times when he didn't brace himself for the beauty of her eyes. Hours in her presence and he still couldn't grasp that such opacity existed. But it wasn't their colour and clarity that riveted him this time, it was the look within them. Only in sleep had he seen any softness to her. But now was different. Now she was awake and her wide blue eyes held a fragility that was at odds with everything he believed she was.

'Do you hurt?'

She shook her head. Grimaced as something in her tugged. 'No.'

'Don't move,' he said. How long did it take to find a healer?

She settled in his embrace and the cold wooden deck rocked and creaked underneath them. Overhead dawn came and with it the sound of seagulls and some carts lumbering against uneven cobblestones.

She didn't look away from him and he couldn't look anywhere else. Her hair had lost the plaits during the fighting. The white curls tangled, slanted across her cheeks as if still locked in a mêlée. There was an unnatural paleness to her skin, which only accentuated the unusual colour of her lips.

Beautiful. Deadly. A liar. She hurt terribly or else she'd never let him see her or talk to him like this. He was a bastard, but this wasn't the time for chivalry. He had to press his advantage.

The message burned in his mind, but he'd get to it soon enough. Someone wanted her dead and had sent mercenaries to kill her. But mercenaries and missives weren't what he truly needed to know.

Because her words implied something he couldn't allow. Secrets he held, but not only his own. If she had followed him, if she knew more about him than just his vengeance against her for his fellow comrades…

'Did I give myself away these past months? When you

murdered Philip and I followed you, did you see me at some point? Did you watch for me because I meant to kill you? Were you in those trees waiting for me?'

Her brow creased, her hand waving a bit before it flopped down. 'Been watching you for years and years and years. I was meant to kill *you*.'

Eldric's entire world locked on to her words. 'What—?'

Pounding footsteps on the deck. Eldric coiled his body over the Archer and slashed out with a dagger.

Shuffling footsteps. 'This is unpardon—'

'Excuse me, sir,' the Commander's voice interrupted and registered. Barely.

The healed scars in Eldric's arms burned. The Archer's words, her actions. Everything in him demanded retribution. The wondering guilelessness in her eyes clashing with her intent to murder…him. He *required* answers.

Just keeping back his snarl, he turned. 'What do you want?'

The Commander nodded. 'This is the healer, found two ships down.'

Eldric looked at the older, portly man with pouches upon pouches around his waist. His eyes looked warily from him to the dagger in his hand. 'Does she live?'

His gaze swung to the Archer, who was half-slumped against him. Her eyes were now closed. Injured, terribly, and he'd cost her with his questions. But he felt her breath and, if he paid attention, he could feel the pounding of her heart as well.

'Unconscious.'

The healer walked in front, though he kept some

distance. Enough to make Eldric realise he hadn't truly kept back that growl when they came upon him. He eased back.

'It's her back. She's bleeding through and needs stitches.'

The doctor turned to the Commander. 'I can't work out here like this with a woman. She'll have to be undressed.'

He hadn't thought to undress her to get to the wounds. He hadn't thought anything at all, except her words...that missive. Now all he could do was think of their predicament. Even if he could comfortably carry her below, they'd be trapped.

'I won't go below. The Commander leaves and you will do it here.'

'Save me from overprotective husbands,' the healer said, as the Commander marched across the deck.

Husband. Eldric let his presumption drop since there was no alternative. As for the Commander, where he went, Eldric didn't care. As long as there was privacy and as long as no one else saw her... Possessiveness. The irony was not lost on him. Apparently, husbands and hunters all had their claims.

Easing her over to her stomach, he cradled her head into his lap. Without his hands holding her tunic together, the wound was more clearly seen, but not enough.

'What happened?' The healer set down a bag and got out a pair of shears.

Eldric didn't trust them, or the healer's question. 'Let me.' He unsheathed the smallest dagger and nicked the already torn fabric. It fell easily away to reveal a clean diagonal slice from almost the base of her back to the curve of her waist. Around the edges looked torn. Since she stilled, only a little blood pooled across the dried blood on her back.

''Tis deep,' the healer said. 'It may need to be cauterised.'

To burn her skin would be quick and they could escape if needed. He baulked at the scar it would leave, but shook that instinct away. This wasn't a mere woman; she was the Archer.

Eldric nodded his head. 'Do it.'

The healer stood, and Eldric swiped his cloak down her back to remove the excess blood—and revealed all her skin.

The healer gave a rough exhale.

It took far too long for Eldric to understand what he was seeing. When he did, he bit out a curse, then another as everything inflamed inside him. Possession. Claiming. Rage. None of them made sense.

But the spy and warrior in him was aware of the healer staring, gathering information that would be harmful to them all. 'You'll tell no one of this or you won't live.'

The healer stayed quiet and Eldric looked over his shoulder.

The healer gestured behind him. 'I need to retrieve the tools to seal the wound.'

'No fire. Stitch it and make them the finest you've ever done. I won't… She won't scar again.'

At the healer's hesitation, Eldric bit out, 'Now.'

The healer knelt. Eldric adjusted his body to give the man access to her, but he didn't let her go. Aware always of his surroundings, aware, too, of just how careful the healer was with her. How fierce his frown.

It most certainly reflected his own. He could murder the one who had done this to her. Irrational when only a few hours before he'd wanted to harm her as well.

She'd been whipped. Several times, over different days and long ago. As a child, perhaps. The thin scars were nothing but white shimmering wisps across her back, but so many. And none of them looked as if they tore into the other. She'd been whipped once, then allowed to heal before she was whipped again.

Dissecting all these thin lines were blunter ones. Some shallow and broad. Blade cuts, scrapes. Like the one the healer was mending now.

He had chased the Archer, knew the strength of him…her. Her cleverness. Knew at one point she had had to climb up on to a thatch roof to escape him. An impossible feat. She must have been injured along the way. He'd relished that she was injured while he pursued her. A drop of blood spilt for all the blood she had spilled.

But seeing the effects of what she did, perhaps what he had forced her to do when she fled from him… And those men. She seemed…familiar with them and they wanted her dead. As did he.

'I didn't—' Eldric stopped.

The healer's brow was sheened with sweat and he didn't glance up at Eldric's stumbled words. What was he to say? That he didn't know about her wounds; therefore was not her husband. That he didn't harm her? The guilty would proclaim innocence. Eldric kept his counsel. 'There's coin for you.'

The healer simply hummed. His attention on the thread, on her back. The slice wasn't any longer than his hand, but deep enough to bleed, to hurt.

The Archer remained unconscious, but her body twitched with almost every stab of the needle. He swore he could feel every one of them himself.

He'd been trained at Edward's court. The punishments for mistakes were fierce, but never permanent. Never disfiguring. Who she was, what she was, he had no idea. Tonight, she'd saved his life. She'd killed to do so and looked dismayed right after. She'd confessed to watching over him. Why?

All this time, he thought only of the horror she had meted out. He never thought, not once, of the horror she came from. *'I am what my father made me.'* Could it be…was it possible her father had done this to her? If so, what else…?

Knotting the last stitch, the healer placed his hands on his knees and leaned back to drag his pouch over. Putting away his supplies, Eldric saw that his hands remained steady, though his expression returned to the wariness of before.

'You did well,' Eldric said and meant it. The stitches were as fine as he'd ever seen. No blood seeped. If she did scar, it would be thin…like the rest of them on her back.

'Keep her rested and give her liquid often. A bone broth would be best. She's thin.'

'Your coin,' Eldric said, lifting the pouch at his waist.

The healer stopped wiping his hands. 'I don't need that much coin, warrior.'

'Your service was needed and you came.'

'My service requires only one of those coins and even that is generous, as well you know. But my children have children, so I'll take two none the less.'

Eldric pinched two coins and left the rest in his pouch. His instincts should be clamouring to threaten this healer, to bribe with more coin. Something to secure his safety. It was all too easy.

'Why?' he said instead.

The healer took the coins and smiled. 'Ah. Why do I not call the guards or pretend some umbrage because you are not her husband? Why don't I demand more coin than you have?'

Eldric couldn't answer any of those questions.

'It's simple. I know you didn't do this and why do I know that?' The healer gave a soft smile and turned to leave. 'You care too much for her.'

The Archer's weight was on his lap, her back exposed to the air, to him. He did not move, but watched the old healer say a few words to the Commander, who slowly approached.

'I have rooms below, sir.' The Commander shifted his feet. 'It seems you might need one.'

The man's clothes were English, but still dishevelled, and his crew were more pirate than soldier. 'You sail ships and are far from London. What care have you to protect us? I'm not so naive to think the seal I carry has more influence on you than it has already commanded.'

'I'm loyal to England, sir.'

'Your crew are loyal to you; I recognise the mark on their arms. Not all of them are loyal to England.'

The Commander shrugged. 'Your sword is fine.'

Ah. How much room did he have to bargain? None. No manoeuvre that did not expose him and the Archer in some way. Putting her on a cart and heading to the Tower when those men roamed free was also not a choice. It wasn't for her sake, but for his own plans.

'You want my sword?' he said. 'Why not kill me, my back has been presented enough.'

The Commander scoffed. 'My men are better at thieving than fighting. I'm not a fool, sir. That fine a blade with a well-worn pommel means you use it and use it well. Nothing wrong with…negotiating first.'

Negotiation with a pirate. Did he think he had power any more? The Archer slept in his arms now, but the wound was deep and she'd lost blood. Far worse, he had more questions. 'How long can we rest?'

'I must sail to France later this afternoon. A few passengers, mostly cargo to load, but when in France I will be conducting business. With your royal papers, I would ask that you stay in the room when we dock. For at least a day.'

Trapped and compromised by illegal dealings and he was in no position to go against such a request. It wasn't onerous and, by the look in the Commander's eye, it wasn't negotiable. 'Your men truly are better thieves than crew? This is a poorly protected ship and I see no routine maintenance as is being done on the others.'

'Much better thieves, *monsieur*.' The Commander raised one brow. 'Check your purse.'

He had his purse when he paid the healer. No one had been anywhere close since then. Still… 'Passable attempt at trickery.'

The Commander laughed. 'But your expression! You weren't certain at all. That is how good we are. As to the rest? My crew, when they see a desperate well-dressed man, they know better than to chase him away. It's better to lure the rabbit to the trap, you see.'

So he'd boarded the ship with their knowledge. Clever, and he could be bought. They could be protected here.

Another day. Surrounded on a boat where the mercenaries couldn't get to them. Another day in which to question her. Time for her to rest, too. To heal from her injuries. He shook his thoughts. He couldn't, shouldn't, soften when it came to her. She was still the Archer, despite her taking a dagger to her back, the fact she was whipped as a child, the fact she'd protected him. The fact he hunkered over her protectively. Damn God's bones!

'I have coin,' Eldric said. 'You will be amply awarded if you let no other well-dressed man or men on your ship.'

The Commander's eyes narrowed. 'How many more men and how well trained?'

'Well trained and more than I could fight alone.' This Commander looked like any other appointed Englishman, but he was no fool. 'But all the coin that could be yours is not on me.'

'Hidden silver.' The Commander flashed a grin. 'My favourite kind.'

Eldric wasn't fooled by the easy grin. This man could be trusted as long as he had coin. Which only meant others could give him more coin to betray them.

'You and your men didn't fight me because the odds

weren't in your favour,' he said. 'Know that if you betray my trust, it's not only me you have to fear.'

'Now you attempt to intimidate, so what do you have to tell me next?' The man crossed his arms. 'Let's see if it was worth allowing you on my ship.'

This Commander wasn't as trustworthy as Eldric liked, but he was intelligent and so he had to take the risk. There was, indeed, one more factor to negotiate and it all had to do with the mercenary's words.

The Archer had a father, who had kidnapped a child. The Archer who followed him for years, who possibly knew who his friends were.

And that familiarity that he couldn't shake, that he was somehow tied to her. He was beginning to believe there were no coincidences here. And if her father kidnapped a child who was half-Scottish and he knew of a Scottish family who had lost a child, then... Then even if it was all conjecture, it didn't matter. He had to tell the Colquhoun clan. Tell his friend Robert and his Scottish wife Gaira he might have found the trail to their adopted daughter Maisie. A child who had been kidnapped, who they still couldn't find.

And he was trusting all this to a man who took money for loyalty. And yet...the Commander was providing a safe haven instead of simply taking the coin. Eldric suspected there was more to the man than he let on.

'Do you have a name?' Eldric asked.

The man smirked. 'Do you?'

Eldric exhaled. 'There is more to negotiate and more coin to be had,' he said. 'In particular, I need one of your men, without fail, to deliver a message.'

The Commander canted his head. 'Terric. My name is Terric.'

'Your true name?' Eldric asked.

'Would it matter if that was my true name?'

If this man could be trusted, Eldric would prefer him to be on his side. 'See that message delivered, Commander, and I'll tell you my name.'

## *Chapter Eight*

Cressida woke with her back on fire, but the remainder of her rested on the plush comfort of perhaps two mattresses and at least six pillows. 'Eldric.'

'Here.'

She turned her head, took in the horizontal boards, no windows, the smell of ocean and the rocking. 'We're on that ship?'

'Yes.'

'Where are you taking me?'

'Easy. Don't get up.'

One sharp move had her understanding his order. The pain which burned in her back now flamed everywhere. It didn't matter, she'd toil through the pain. She always did. Pulling herself to the edge of the bed, she slithered to the ground.

Eldric launched from the seat in the corner and caught her halfway. Her hands on the floor, her body on the bed. She felt familiar pinpoint stings.

'You stitched me?'

'That's what you want to talk of?' he said, trying

to push her up. She dropped her head to make it more difficult, but she couldn't match his strength.

Seething, she settled back, but when he started to adjust the pillows around her like some babe, she'd had enough.

'Do you ever stop?' Eldric reached over the bed to grab her. 'How far do you think you'll get crawling out of the other side?'

'I have to go.'

'No one's getting on this ship.'

'I need to get *off*.'

'You won't get past me.'

His words were stern, but his voice… Something was different. She didn't know what it was. He should be in a rage because the mercenaries had attacked and would again. Not this careful…this caring of her.

'They'll return,' she said, settling in. She'd wait until he slept and escape then.

Keeping his eyes on her, he walked backwards to the chair and sat. 'I'm counting on it.'

She looked back at the ceiling. 'You mean to make us targets?'

'You already are a target. My presence makes no difference.'

She waved her hand, revelled in the movement even through the sting from her wound. 'Other than it's your death they'll achieve. Let me out and you won't have to worry about it.'

'It's you who would worry over me, isn't it? You saved me from that mercenary—why?'

She should have hidden her reaction, but she couldn't. She was remembering now. What she told

Eldric. Her confession about her father, about Eldric, that she watched and protected him like some lovesick fool! The heat of a blush only furthered her embarrassment. 'After the mercenaries came. After that blade struck, you…you asked me questions.'

'And you answered a few. But I have many more. Why did you save me? My death would have freed you, wouldn't it?'

She didn't blink. 'We were both being attacked. I acted on instinct.'

His frown deepened. 'No truth, even now? What about who you are?'

Never did she want to answer these questions. Never did she want the truth revealed. Embarrassed for what she had confessed; shamed because she had. She was a warrior as strong as any other! She could ignore the slash in her back. The agony of loss that slowly squeezed her heart. 'I was in pain, injured, and you took advantage of me.'

He held up his hand. 'Let's not travel down that path again and my questions will far outlast your avoiding them. Who is your father?'

Oh, that she had her bow and arrow to shoot the appendage down. 'Whatever ramblings I did in my delirium, you should ignore. Drunk people say ridiculous things. I'm sure I said nothing sane.'

'You weren't drunk and we both know you're far more resilient than you claim, injured or not.'

She knew what was different now in his voice and could not be more defeated. Blinking to keep the sting out of her eyes, she glared at the ceiling.

Wounded, stitches in her back. Eldric saw the result

of her failures, her ugliness. He'd never want her now. As if he ever would. Her father didn't.

The message. Eldric had read the message as well. How much further could she be humiliated? How much more pain could she bear? She'd been trained to withstand anything, but she had always…always had someone who loved her no matter how bad her deeds. No longer did agony squeeze. The pain in her chest was like a thousand thin piercing daggers.

'You need to talk,' he said. 'No more healer stories, no more lies. Who is the child that your father stole?'

She hurt so much. If she talked, she didn't know if she'd stop. What did she know of the child stolen? Far too little. It was as if now that Eldric knew of the other daughter, she was more of a truth. That a mercenary confirmed it only made it all the more believable that the daughter existed.

Her father had kidnapped a child to replace her.

Only once did she betray him and even then was it truly a betrayal? They had positioned themselves in a tiny Scottish village, the intent to obtain a dagger and gem for the Warstone family.

She was kept hidden while he made plans with his men on how to best go about it when the very object, the very woman and man who carried the objects, stumbled into the village.

But then…but then it became clear that her father wouldn't only wrest the object for his own, he also meant to harm the woman and her companion. He didn't need to harm that woman. Didn't need to cause her so much…pain. Her words, her grief over her brother, she was in so much pain, Cressida couldn't stand it.

So she released an arrow and stopped her father. Her father was resourceful, cunning, there would be other opportunities to get objects for his benefactors.

She'd stopped him. Merely stopped him, that was all, and right there he raised his gaze to her. Gave her position away with a gaze so full of wrath, she was sure God spoke through him.

She'd stayed hidden, watching the events unfold, shaking the entire time. Waiting, knowing she would be punished—instead, she was banished. Sent away like a biblical character from the garden. Her entire life devoted to him, her entire soul and existence bent on returning to him.

And her father wanted her dead.

Too much pain! Too many vulnerabilities. It was better to fight than show any more to Eldric. He had seen her disfigured back. And what of her other disfigurements and failures displayed all over her body? No, she wouldn't yield, wounded or not. She would see her duty to the end. Despite his strength, despite his whistling, whatever he wanted to achieve, it wouldn't come easy for him. 'So…' she cleared her throat '… I'm to change, but you're not?'

'Change? I'm asking questions that you won't answer and I have more. Why were you sent to kill me?'

'I'm to confess to whatever it is you think you need to know, but you'll still take me to the Tower? If I lie or don't, the result is the same.' She tilted her head to look at him. 'But if you let me go, then your death won't be at the end of it as well.'

He leaned forward, rested his elbows on his knees and clasped his hands before him. 'I heard that mercenary. Why are you so certain of my death, but not yours? See? I have more questions and I'll take an answer to any of them.'

That mercenary. The rumour of another daughter was true. Was she also to devote her life to the man she called father? A prick behind her eyes. Tears threatening. Tears! She would think about this in private. Not now, not while Eldric's eyes were peering at her too closely. 'I told you I expected them. It's a game we play.'

'You lie terribly, Archer. Why don't we make this simple? You say I won't change, but you do nothing to change my opinion.'

Why would he not leave her be! He needed to leave. 'What would it matter?'

He tapped his fingertips. 'Perhaps everything.'

Everything? Nothing! Nothing would change. She was nothing to her father. Nothing to Eldric. She'd killed his friend, Thomas. Didn't prevent the other two from their deaths. He'd never forgive her. 'So a mere scratch on my back overrides your hatred of me?'

'Admittance now?'

She clenched her teeth, refusing to answer him. Something was overcoming inside her. Defeating her from within. It...it hurt.

Eyes narrowing, but keeping the same relaxed posture, he said, 'I know you're a woman; I know you're the Archer who killed my friends and sliced my arms. I know you were truly waiting at the docks for family. I know you were whipped, almost ritualistically, as a child, perhaps by the father who created you. I know that there's a kidnapped child out there, and you don't want to talk of her. I know that that message was no game and they truly meant to harm you.'

He clasped his hands again. 'Will you deny any of it?'

She was a weapon without an owner. A daughter without a father. A woman who longed for a man who would hate her for ever. She wanted to deny everything he said. Not to thwart him, but to deny her past ever happened. Deny the whipping, the training, the missives, the duties. The day she'd first heard Eldric whistle.

She wanted to deny everything. The pain in her chest! Because if she didn't... She blinked back the overwhelming grief threatening. Threatening. Because—

She cried.

In all his days, the Archer's response wasn't anything Eldric could have prepared for. It was as though he had suddenly been stolen from the comforts of his home and hurled on to a battlefield surrounded by phantom adversaries.

Malicious foes who weren't there to taunt and torture and slash at him, but a defenceless other—this woman—and everything in him welled up to fight against them. To his shock, the fierce protectiveness wasn't because she was crying. The maddening possessiveness wasn't because she'd been injured.

It was because the Archer broke. Utterly broke and, before he could truly understand what he was doing or why, he sat beside her on the bed, gathered her in his arms and held her.

When she stiffened, he pulled her on to his lap and folded over her. She never, not once, stopped her tears and he didn't want her to. They streamed from her eyes like everything else she'd done since he'd known her: with fierceness and that elusive fragility that he couldn't comprehend when he caught her and now all too terribly might have a glimpse into understanding.

A moment of breath, another, and her hands laid against his chest, her nose pressed firmly in between as if she thought to bury and hide her response from him. As if he couldn't feel every jagged breath and hear each wrecked sound.

So aware of his size, he laid a hand on the back of her head, another on the small of her waist and gathered her against him. He could no longer see the tears, but he felt their scalding wetness soaking his tunic. Another sound, almost one of defeat on an inhale that shook her. Her capable hands now brushing the sides of her cheeks as the tears slowed.

What had she lost? He could guess. But all his guesses were unfathomable; he wanted to cease his thoughts, to gather her more tightly to him and rest his head upon her as she did him. Swollen cheeks, swollen eyes. Reddened, starkly contrasting with her eyes' unusual colour. Making her otherworldly. She *was* otherworldly.

Despite what occurred, despite what he guessed, most of him should be raging against her. Not…holding her and refusing to let go.

Why was it this way with her? Was it because she'd

saved his life? Or the fact that he'd read that message? Mere glimpses, but that was all it took for everything to change between them. Enough of a sliver underneath all his hatred and wrath. Buried somewhere between his questions and his wondering of why she killed his friends, why she marked him. *Why?*

They couldn't continue to fight as they had. Those men came. That message was read. His friends were killed, his vows were taken. He had some answers now and even more questions. She'd fought him up to now, but now was different.

Holding her, he felt different. What was it between them and how to proceed? He wasn't a spy here, or even a warrior. He suspected when it came to her, he was merely a man with his own vulnerabilities.

'We're not going back to how we were.' He said his words as gently as he could, but in the silence that followed her weeping, there was still a harsh brutality about them. A reminder of what was between them.

Stiffening, she pushed against his chest to extract herself, but he didn't let her. A few more pushes before she snatched her hands off his chest as though he was something that would harm her.

Brutal hands. Brutal body. He almost raised his hands from her, but her expression stopped him. She looked down as if she was embarrassed. No, it was… as if she was *shamed*.

He cupped her jaw. She allowed him to raise her gaze to his and he searched its depths. Underneath the little flutter of wary embarrassment in her eyes, just below the meaning of her tapping fingers against his chest, there was something…

She riveted him. Her white-gold hair tumbled like rolling waves of river over rock. The soft slant of her cheekbones, the coloured hue of her skin like sunlight at dawn. And then, the white-gold framing of lashes around eyes that shouldn't be real. Like crystals held to a summer sky.

He couldn't shake this feeling that he knew her. Something beyond his obsession of the Archer. Something else. Had he known she was there all this time? 'How long did you watch me?'

Her lips parted and his focus went to them. A darker colour, almost like a sun setting. Had he ever held a woman thus? When the dart of her tongue went to the seam, he bent his head. A quick intake of breath that drew him in.

He pulled her closer. In his arms, she felt familiar, as though he had held her before. He remembered being reluctant to let her go—how? He looked up and fell into her gaze.

Her eyes wide. That fragility about her again, and he…wanted her with something that went beyond her beauty. Closer, until their lips were there. Sharing breaths. Until everything in him that was male demanded he close that distance.

So he did.

Giant fierce warrior. Holding her face with tender touches along her cheeks. His lips pressing against hers. Asking. It was too much. Her fear and pain from her father had built inside her until they burst out of her in torrents. Until she was empty and aware of being held for the first time. His warmth, strength.

All-encompassing because of his size, his scent, because of who he was. Eldric.

Eldric, who canted his head, pressed more. She felt his fingers curve into her curls. Felt his tongue run along her lower lip.

Then...then she only felt. Her hands sweeping over broad shoulders, brushing across stubbled skin, to dig into the waves of his hair. To open her own lips, to answer whatever question this was. His tongue meeting hers.

She didn't know this could exist. Not ever. Him pressing her closer, to mould her body to his. Closer yet. The heat of this kiss, of him. Like kindling scraping, scraping to create fire.

A sound made. Of want, need...yearning. So much want boiling to the surface, like her emotions for her father. She was unused to touches, to kisses. She couldn't take it, couldn't bear to be ripped apart again. Not this much.

She jerked her chin away from his hands and Eldric immediately broke the kiss. He sat frozen, his harsh exhale buffeting against her chin, which still felt the abrasion of his jaw.

He straightened, an unevenness to his movements, pulling himself from her at the same time as making his large frame smaller, rounding his shoulders, his great arms tucked back.

He jerked his gaze to the side. A flush to his cheeks showed an uneasiness she'd seen before, but couldn't recall when or how. Not now when her body, her very soul, was attempting to understand what had happened.

'I...apologise,' he said. 'You cried.'

Everything in her reared up in horrifying clarity. It had been her first time being held by someone. Even as a child she was never held, comforted. Cared for. Her first kiss.

That fact that both were with Eldric, the man she had longed for, for years, the man she had hunted, and she'd responded. Worse, she had made sounds, dug her fingers into his hair, pressed her body to his.

And he...he'd done it because she cried. He was providing comfort and because she wanted, wanted, wanted—she'd made a fool of herself.

Blushing, she pulled her eyes away from his, bit out words that hid her emotions, pleased when the anger at herself could be heard with each enunciation. 'So I cried. You haven't?'

## Chapter Nine

He swung his gaze back to hers, the uneasiness gone. His blue eyes cold. 'You know I have.'

Ah, this. Yes, she did know he had cried. When she killed Thomas, when her father killed the others. Slapping a fist against his chest, she said, 'Let me free.'

He opened his palms and splayed his fingers, and she freed herself from him. Slowly, clumsily. His size, the fact she was plastered to him making it awkward. Her feet firmly back on the ground, she spun away.

'Your name,' he said.

Cressida didn't face him. The room was too small to avoid him. Her back to him was the only way to escape the horror of what she had done. She welcomed the pinch of pain in her back to distract her. She'd heard Eldric shift to stand and come closer?

'Cressida. My name is Cressida.'

The rustle of the mattress alerting her that he had eased back down again. 'Is your family… Greek? Italian?'

'I don't…' An unsettling thought occurred. 'I don't

know why they named me that.' And she wasn't all that clear why she told him the truth. She felt…lightheaded. The crying, the message. Her limbs shook.

'You need to rest.'

Vulnerabilities! She whirled around. 'I'm not weak!'

He huffed. 'I believe I, among all your acquaintances, understand that.'

His words hurt, yet how they were said…

'Do you…jest?'

'I do. Contradictory, I know, but then so are you. Maybe that is what we are to each other: contradictions.'

A quirk to his lips. Laughter, the strike of defiance in his blue eyes. His rich brown hair waved to his shoulder, the shadow of a beard accentuating the lips she had touched. A fierce beauty to him. A weapon he wielded with uncanny ability against her. She was weak when it came to him.

Ironic. She was trained to know her opponents' weaknesses and strengths; with Eldric, she could guess, but never seem to grasp what it was in his eyes or manners that did this to her. And nothing in her past helped her understand. She'd never been this close for this length of time with anyone. Her father certainly never gazed at her so profoundly.

When Eldric held her, kissed her, it felt as though he wanted her, which must be a mistake. It was her own wanting that confused everything between them.

'We're not *anything* to each other,' she said.

His brows drew in and he sighed. 'We need to talk of the missive. This isn't about me questioning you and you not answering. We need to discuss how to stay alive.'

The sting in her heart was worse than the pain in her back. 'It doesn't matter now.'

'Those men were trying to kill you.'

She shivered. She shivered and, because Eldric was watching her so carefully, he saw it. 'Why didn't you let me go? I'm a woman, you see that now. I can't be—'

'You know why I can't let you go!'

She did. He wouldn't be Eldric if he released his enemy. Loyal, kind, he'd never simply forget his friends' deaths. It didn't matter if she was the one who had killed them or not. She often thought she could have stopped her father, yet...

'The past cannot be changed even if you take me to the Tower.'

He rubbed his hand over his face. 'But even so, even so... More is occurring than what happened on those battlefields. The fact you're a woman, that missive, the stolen child. Wrongs must be set right and more wrongs need to be prevented.'

Everything was in disarray. She'd exposed too many emotions and he didn't understand. Wouldn't ever understand. 'So sure what is right and what is wrong? You know nothing, nothing!'

'You won't tell me what's transpiring presently. I know nothing about your past. I've seen your back, your scars. It was your father who did that to you, wasn't it, Cressida?'

Eldric saying her name. How many times had she imagined how it would sound from his lips? Her father rarely said her name. Maybe once, twice in her entire life. She'd assumed he never risked it in case they were overheard. She had never begrudged it because she dreamed of Eldric saying it and now he had. Except a question taunted her.

'Why did he name me that?' she said.

He stopped, and she knew she'd surprised him.

'I know the poem. We travelled. There were lessons and literature and… Cressida means someone who cheated. Why would my father name me that? All my life, I've never cheated, I've always followed the rules. Every time, except that once.'

'Once,' he said.

She shivered. 'Only once. Was that all it took to lose him?'

'How did you lose your father?'

Cressida acknowledged that Eldric stood mere feet in front of her, that he overheard her troubled thoughts. That he was inserting words into their conversation, but they weren't having a conversation.

She didn't want to talk with him. No, she wanted to rail and rage. She wanted her weaponry. To shoot her bow at a target until her fingers gave way and her arms trembled from exhaustion. Too many emotions, weaknesses, vulnerabilities when her father and his new daughter could be on another ship now. Could be in France and far away from her.

For the first time, she understood that though she'd been left alone most of her life, this time she was truly alone. Without a home or protection. Her father was always supposed to protect her. Wasn't that why she bore the brunt of his training?

'My father punished me,' she said. 'When I failed

as a child to retrieve a piece of information, I received one lash. He could do it with a perfect flick of his wrist to achieve the exact depth he wanted. My father is trying to—*will*—kill me. He's behind all of this. Behind me, the way I am, and I don't know how it all went so wrong.'

She startled when he grabbed her hand. He wasn't supposed to touch her, not after she threw herself at him. Ardently kissed him when she was supposed to do nothing but cry prettily, dabbing her eyes with a cloth that was at the ready.

The front of his tunic was still darkened from where her tears soaked through the linen. 'Let go of my hand.'

He squeezed her fingers. 'Tell me who he is.'

She wrenched her hand free. 'No.'

'You protect him?' He shook his head. 'There are matters… Your being brought to the King must occur, but if your father had a play in all that you do, perhaps there would be leniency.'

That sounded like a promise made by the ocean. In other words, it was a lie. All the worse for she could still feel his arms comforting her. 'There is no leniency for one like me.'

'But if—'

'No!' she bit out. 'You, who have so much, can't have everything. You aren't telling me all, are you? You and your questions. You said there's more here than your friends dying on the battlefields. What more is it? And don't pretend there's only more because of me or my father.'

A muscle ticked in his clenched jaw. 'If he's committing treason, then everything changes.'

'Nothing changes! Your friends are dead. If you wanted your vengeance, you'd simply kill me. Instead, you want to take me to King Edward. Why!' She pointed at him. 'Hah! You won't tell me everything either.'

'So what will you tell me?' His brows drew down. 'You killed my friends and I've been pursuing you to bring you to justice, and all this time you've known it. You've known it and evaded me, but you can't now. So tell me.'

She paced, looked around the small cabin. The fact they could take two steps between them meant their quarters were luxurious, but the space was far too small to ease her restlessness. 'Why this ship?'

'You needed a healer and we needed to hide.'

She swirled around. 'We're trapped here.'

He gave a curt nod. 'To evade my capture, you've been an intelligent adversary for months. Whoever plagues you won't expect you to make stupid decisions. They won't expect us here.'

'What of the owner of this ship? The men who operate it?'

'Extra protection, and even more so when we travel to France later today.' He pushed up on his knees. 'You reacted to that.'

Of course she did. Could she be that fortunate to go the very direction she was meant to?

His eyes narrowed. 'You want to go to France. You told me the truth when you said you were waiting for your family. You lost your father and now you're following him. He told you not to, didn't he?'

He did. But she couldn't follow that order. She was

a weapon, but she was a daughter first and a daughter would question why she had to remain behind.

'His missive told you to accept death, but if he's trying to kill you, why wouldn't you stay away?'

Because she had no one otherwise. She didn't need to tell Eldric anything; he was guessing the truth.

'It's the child, isn't it? You're after the child.'

She wasn't after the child. Without her father's love, without his missions and protection, she was nothing. Had nothing. But now, she was realising the child couldn't be incidental. Not since his message. Her father wanted her dead. He'd made her an enemy. It hurt. She had no one, but if she could save the child from the same fate as she...

If she was dead by her father's hands or by the King of England's, so be it. But until then she would escape, she would confront her father and she would rescue that child. Until then...

'If I tell you details, you'll take me to France?'

'Any details? What if I want to know about you, about your watching me? Is that why you scarred my arm and—'

'I started watching you when I was a child. Off and on for years.'

Eldric pinched the bridge of his nose.

'That concerns you?'

'I never saw you. I don't know *what* you saw.'

His whistling, his friendships. She'd learned from this man.

'Much.'

He exhaled and lowered his arm. 'With women? Did you see me with women?'

His was her first kiss; she knew what they shared wasn't his. Was it terrible, did he mean to mock her?

'Why is this important?'

'It's not.' He shook his head, waved his hand. 'Ignore it for now. No, wait. At what point were you to kill me?'

'That didn't come until later, when my father ordered—'

Eldric held up his hand. 'I won't understand this unless we start at the beginning. Tell me your tale of your childhood...before me.'

She'd regale him with all her observations of him over the years, but her revealing her childhood wouldn't be easy and she didn't know the purpose. 'So many questions, when your keeping me prisoner makes you my enemy as much as he is. And you haven't agreed to take me to France.'

He stilled. 'You'll get to France, but tell me this: I know who you are to me, but what would make your father your enemy?'

She was at the whim of men! She had thought her father was strict, but kind, and now he wanted her dead.

Eldric wanted vengeance for his friends. Even if she told him the truth, that she hadn't killed all three of them, but only one and accidentally, she didn't know if it would make a difference. For reasons she didn't understand, he wanted to take her to the Tower. All this time she'd thought, when he captured her, he'd simply kill her. Eldric, too, had his own schemes he wanted fulfilled.

She was merely an object for both men, but she wasn't the only one. That child, whom she thought only a rumour, was also at the whim of these men and it was up to her to rescue her.

But Eldric wouldn't let her go until he had his questions answered. Refuse him and they'd go around and around as they already had. Answer him everything and she would have given him too much of herself and he had his own agenda.

To tell him enough, to lull him into thinking she cooperated, could she keep her heart out of it? She wasn't sure. She had little experience with conversations and what did she know of this man?

Eldric wasn't her enemy, he couldn't be, but she'd been treating him like one. Oh, he believed he was and would, no doubt, want some retribution against her. He seemed determined to take her to the English King.

That was her fate and, given all her deeds, perhaps deserved, but her life wasn't the only one in the balance. Maybe if she trusted him with her past, he'd trust her or at least understand why she needed to save the child—her half-sister, she realised.

'What is it?' Eldric said.

'You asked if we were enemies,' she said. 'I want to answer, but I will have to start with my childhood.'

He gave a curt nod.

'You are not my enemy, Eldric, but I am yours. Even so, before I tell you all my past, I have two requests.'

'To which you want me to blindly answer?' He crossed his arms. 'Tell me.'

'When we are done, I want to find the child and return her to her family.'

'With my help.'

'My father is a demanding man, skilled, cunning.'

'And you want me to believe you need my help. No. You don't stop. You'll try to escape when we finally touch land. You won't, but what do you need from me since this is a condition?'

'Save her, if I cannot. Find her family and return her.'

'You can save her and I'll be at your side when you face your father.'

'If I survive, I want to talk with her.'

'You expect me to bring you to the Tower still.'

'What has changed?'

A muscle ticked in his jaw. 'Nothing.'

'Good, then, we are agreed,' she said.

'What is your second request?'

This…this there could be no compromise on.

His holding her, touching, his kindnesses—they were like tiny daggers filling her with such longing of needing more that she didn't think she could bear it.

'You kissed me.' At his curt nod, she continued, 'Don't do it again.'

## Chapter Ten

'My father raised me,' Cressida said. She'd do this her own way. He wanted answers to questions. She'd answer what he needed to know, which meant her childhood, her father, all that pain, would have to be laid out before this perfect man. Then she'd lose…no, she had never had Eldric in the first place.

'When I was very young, my father left me in one abbey or another. In between, he came to visit me, to give me lessons. When I was old enough, he kept me with him. He was always moving then and constantly changed camps and mercenaries. Though I was with him, he kept me separated from everyone, my hood always raised. Eventually, he sent me away on different tasks to complete for him.' This is where she deviated from the whole truth. Not quite ready to tell how she was abandoned, though she knew it was ridiculous. Eldric already knew her father wanted her dead. 'I was at Dover following my father. I didn't know I had a sister. But that mercenary made it all too clear I do.'

'Sister? But that's—impossible.'

'Half-sister. He wouldn't take a child who wasn't his. I think, I think my mother didn't die in childhood. I suspect that I was taken, too. That I was stolen and kept hidden until I was old enough to be who he wanted me to be. To be what you know. The mercenaries that come to train me—'

'Train you! That message said something else.'

He knew nothing and, if she had her way, he'd never know the pain she'd endured since last autumn. 'For months, my father sent his men to surprise me, to keep me ever ready. That time at the inn wasn't the only time. The messages before that were...different.'

He clenched his jaw. 'Orders to kill others.'

'Not kill. I haven't killed since—' She hadn't killed anyone since she accidentally killed Thomas. But she wouldn't tell him that. 'If you keep interrupting, you will know nothing.'

He gave a mutinous nod, so she continued. 'He wanted me to spy, but I suspect he was simply keeping me occupied while he attended to other matters. When the first mercenaries came, they told me my father had taken a child, one who was his, and I was no longer needed.'

Eldric lowered his eyes to the floor between his feet. His reaction didn't ease the pain inside her which just became tighter and tighter.

'You should be gloating, Eldric,' she pointed out. 'I'm sharing with you my greatest fear and agony.'

He put both his hands on his face and rubbed, but he didn't look up. 'You have to know, most of this tale makes little sense... I understand none of this.'

Words that she said to him when she felt at her most

exposed. She took the step back to sit in the chair opposite him. The stitches in her back pinched as she adjusted herself, as she stared at the man she'd admired first as a child and now as a woman. Despite his hatred of her, despite his treatment, she found she cared for him.

She couldn't hold back with him even if she tried. She might realise her father meant her ill will, but Eldric was her secret. For years, she'd watched the goodness within him.

She harboured no illusion he could ever care for her, let alone love her. Even if they shared no past, she wasn't beautiful. Her father, via his training and by his hand, had seen to that.

If Eldric was any other man, she wouldn't care about her looks. She'd be pleased that she could blend in with the crowd because it made her a better weapon. But the moment she'd first observed this man, she'd yearned to be someone else. Someone good and worthy of him.

That feeling became more acute as the years went by and she observed Eldric in one English camp, then another. Watched his very ease with laughter. Listened to the beauty of his whistling.

He was freedom to her. Like that moment when she released an arrow and it was out of her control. Anything could happen. The arrow could be anything it wanted to be.

Unlike her own controlled life. She was an arrow never released from the quiver. No, Eldric would never understand her life. Though she couldn't change it, she told him anyway.

'I was raised and he has made me this. That is all you need to know.'

'Yet you won't tell me who he is?'

'It's not safe for you. Your fate would be different if you let me go. By keeping me you've brought yourself only danger.'

'Even if he has abandoned you?'

She wanted to fight the truth, but the pain of the last message rang true. 'Especially because he's abandoned me.'

'You may have watched me, but you can't know everything.' At her shrug, he continued, 'Let me worry about me.'

Until she died, she'd always worry about him, even if he thought she'd failed in killing him. 'Dover port is where his trail ended when you—'

'Captured you in a tree.'

Eldric slowly exhaled his held breath. He felt as though he hadn't breathed properly since that moment he'd grasped this woman's ankle. That was so short a time ago, yet nothing was as it had been last night. Cressida was the enemy. He hadn't forgotten this. His vows wouldn't let him forget. Her father was to blame as well for every action she had done in his name, the man who had raised her, fathered her and now abandoned her.

Because that was what her pain was about, what she tried to hide at first. Her pain because she loved a man who hadn't any honour at all.

His life had been easy. His parents had cherished him as he did them. Even when he'd spied for the King, it had all gone without effort. But when his life crossed with this woman's, even before he knew who she was, he'd been on a perilous path. He just didn't know it.

He had several choices and only one made sense: to hide on the ship and, when it returned to Dover, take this enemy to the King. Any questions or concerns he'd chalk up to mere curiosity.

Except by turning a blind eye to it all, there was the potential to risk Robert's and Hugh's lives with their wives and families. He didn't fully understand the King's demand to have the Archer brought to him. And he still didn't have all the answers needed from Cressida.

What motivated a man to have such a daughter? He needed to know the identity and motivation of the man she called father, but to whom he could never apply the honour.

Then there was the other matter. The bone-deep certainty he was tied up with her somehow. But how? She had been raised by a madman who was bent on some vengeance Eldric couldn't guess.

Taking a child to replace a woman who was trained in deadly skills? Her father wasn't sane, yet she mourned him. It was clear in every tear she'd shed. Everything in him, absolutely everything, wanted her in his arms, to hold her, to not let go. To show her that the world wasn't her father.

He saw all of that now, yet the trajectory they were on could not change. Even if he abandoned the vow to his lost friends, there was an English king who would come and remind him. He needed to stay loyal to King Edward to protect his friends who still lived.

To do that, he needed to capture her father and per-haps rescue the child, Maisie. Because that was who the mercenary meant when he had said a half-Scottish bastard. Maisie of Clan Colquhoun. He had sent the message to Colquhoun land on a guess. But as time went on, as he discovered more, he was certain this girl was the missing child.

He needed to send a message to Hugh in Spain! Hugh, whom he hadn't seen since last autumn when they made a pact to exchange any information that could help Robert at Clan Colquhoun. Hugh's last mes-sage since then was to report what had befallen Robert and his wife, Gaira, that their youngest adopted child was stolen and they'd been searching for her ever since.

A child who couldn't possibly be Cressida's half-sister. The child was born from Gaira's murdered sister, Irvette, and her husband. Not from Cressida's father. Never him. Although…the timeline of their marriage… No, it was too unfathomable to be true.

Until he was certain, he wouldn't tell Cressida that he suspected he knew the family.

He stared at the woman, who stared back. Se-cluded in the dark room under the decks of a bus-tling ship, they'd already talked for hours, the morning gone. They'd be setting sail soon. It was a short trip to France, but he hadn't told Cressida that they must stay hidden until they were cleared by the Commander. He imagined that wouldn't go over well with his Archer, a woman who didn't seem to ever stop fighting him. Fighting everything.

To know this about her, to know anything about her, seemed impossible. So little time spent, but so much had changed since the tree. They'd fought, been injured, bloodstained their clothing. Hers were torn. Insignificant concerns compared to what was revealed today.

What she had revealed of herself. He had been beset with conflicting emotions as she told him of her childhood. So many questions he had, so much he didn't want, but needed, to know. Restraining himself from asking too much, because the little she did say revealed a wealth of pain and pride.

These months of pursuing the Archer, the vengeance that he seethed to exact upon his enemy, morphed to something darker, sinister. All aimed at a man she protected.

Mere hours in her presence and he had not only captured the Archer, he knew a bit of who she was, what she was. Why she cried. The pain in her voice. Her father…she loved him. Eldric could hear it, yet the man had abandoned her and now stolen a child to replace her.

But he'd been pursuing the Archer for months. He'd fought her. Between her beauty and her skills, there was no replacing her. And certainly not with a child. There was more to learn here.

'Why did you lose your father? Why is he trying to kill you?'

She paled, her brows drew in. 'I told you that, didn't I?'

'Not in so many words, but—'

'Because I betrayed him,' she interrupted. 'Surprised? Not more than myself. I was hidden in a village at a vantage point where I could protect him as well as complete a task he'd ordered.'

'Task? You mean to kill an enemy of his.'

'A woman and a man who travelled with her. My father stood in the middle of the village. The woman, she was distraught. Angry. They fought, he'd raised a dagger to kill her.' She stopped, took a quick breath. 'This is a woman who had something my father wanted very much. We'd been pursuing her for months. If nothing else occurred, I was in a position to kill her. One shot of my arrow and she would have been dead.

'But she talked. Before he raised his knife to her, she said things. One of my father's men had killed her brother. There was grief in her words and I… I don't know what happened. I released my arrow and it hit him. Stopped his arm from going any further and the man swept up the woman and escaped.'

'You won't tell me what the item was, or who the woman was, or whom she fled with?'

She shook her head as if she could dislodge the memories. 'No, it's not safe to tell you this much!'

Fear in her voice now. He wanted that bastard. Wanted him for creating every pain not only to his own life, but to Cressida's as well.

Feelings? Emotions? Too many now. He was no longer a spy and warrior bent on vengeance. On fixing rights from wrongs and proving his loyalty to the King, while he committed treason by not telling him that Robert lived among his enemy, the Scots, and Hugh hid in Spain trading English secrets.

Complicated. Entangled, and despite everything even if her father had ordered her to kill his friends, to mark his arm, *she* was the one who had released the arrow. She'd killed his friends. She'd never once said anything to the contrary.

He couldn't forget, yet he'd kissed her and, though she demanded he not do it again, he wanted to. Very much.

There was something that drew him to her. When she wasn't guarded, she looked at him, as if…as if he was more than someone she had run from and fought. Maybe if he could not think of his friends, and if they could resolve everything between them, he could understand their connection.

What was it about her eyes? The vulnerability, the fragility. She was raised in numerous abbeys, had been at her father's side ever since. There was an innocence when she spoke to him, but… He would be a coward not to acknowledge the look he saw in her eyes now.

If it was unfathomable that he desired her, it was equally confounding her wanting him. But she did.

The way her eyes darkened, the flush around her cheeks. When she had licked her lower lip and kissed him back. Wrapped her arms around his neck and gathered herself around him. She wanted him. How? Why?

'You were supposed to kill me, too, but you didn't,' he said. 'You haven't. Why are you protecting me from his order? I've been pursuing you to bring you to justice, and you've… You've watched me for years. Wasn't this another betrayal? Why didn't he know of it and why are you protecting me? Because I've seen your skill, Archer; if you meant to kill me, I'd be dead.'

Cressida felt the flush bloom from her heart and

cover her cheeks. She looked away even though Eldric could see it.

After all she'd told him today, this was one bit she was hoping to avoid. But, of course, he'd guessed. Or at least, was attuned enough to know something else was motivating her.

After that kiss, though, she was surprised he asked. Couldn't he guess she wanted him? No, now he wanted her to say it.

She could refuse. After all, she hadn't told him everything. Her father's identity, his schemes, those she hid from him…because it kept him safe. But her protecting him, watching him, truly had nothing to do with her father and everything to do with the warrior before her. Eldric was her secret. Did she dare to tell it now?

'When I was old enough, my father took me on trips from one camp to the next. For training, he'd have me go to neighbouring camps and hide. To bring back some snippet of information for a reward. I was a child when I first spied you from a tree.'

'Because he'd ordered you to kill me? When you were a child?'

His gaze was too direct, his body too close. She turned her gaze away from him and kept quiet; she'd said too much already.

'Do you need to rest?'

'Rest? I can feel the ship moving. We are no longer anchored. The trip to France isn't long.'

'Why be in such a hurry? What do you think to do when we reach France, Cressida—escape? We made an agreement to do this together and, if you must know, I made an agreement for protection on this ship.'

Had she foolishly trusted again? 'What do you mean? We're not sailing to France?'

'We are…but the Commander requested we stay below until the following day after we dock.'

'No! That puts us too far behind.'

'It puts us exactly on the time that we have. You are still now, but even you must feel the tug of your stitches. I feel the sting of your head butting mine. This ship was the best cover and so convenient it almost seems implausible. One more day of rest will not hinder you or me. You father will not be an easy man to thwart and you're not facing him alone.'

He then slapped his knees and stood. 'In any case, I'm hungry. Aren't you thirsty?'

Such a change of conversation, but now reminded she realised she was hungry, thirsty, tired. She was filthy. A day lost, but would it truly be so terrible?

Cressida hugged her arms around herself. Her injury was stitched, would heal enough to travel off the ship. When they docked, she would escape. She would make right the wrongs of her father. In the meantime… 'I need some clothing, something to wash with and mead, the kind infused with herbs or spices if they have it.'

'You prefer sweeter things. I am glad to know this.' His tone was almost playful as he opened the door.

'Eldric.' He turned. The cabin ceiling was low and Eldric could not stand at his full height. It should have made him look ridiculous, but it didn't. She suspected nothing could. He was a giant of a man, but everything in perfect proportion. The way his brown hair fell to his shoulders, the lashes that framed the blue of his eyes. Everything about him drew her.

It didn't matter, none of this could end well. If it was only her father's wrath she had to face, there could be a compromise, but her father was at the beck and call of the Warstone family. Even the King was respectful of their power. She'd go against her father and maybe she'd survive, but she wouldn't survive the Warstones.

'You confuse me,' she said.

'How?'

'I've told you… I told you how I was made. How I became what I did. You know what I've done, yet you're offering me food and rest. Time to heal. Why?'

'Does there need to be a reason?' he said.

She'd shared too much. She needed…she didn't know, some reassurance. She had told him enough so that her sister could get a chance should something happen to her and yet…she'd also told him so much more than she had intended.

She'd answered questions he'd been asking since he bound her to that bed. She'd refused him before, but him holding her while she cried had crumbled the few defences she had left.

His expression eased. 'Come, it will be easier after we clean and have some mead. There will be hours of rest before us.'

Her heart wouldn't survive the many hours with him.

'Ah, you're thinking again,' he said. 'If it has to do with avoiding the mead and talk and intentions to escape the moment we reach French soil, you need to stop. It won't happen.'

'You can't meet my father.'

He flashed a grin. 'You expect to protect me. I'll find out why. Maybe he'll just meet me instead.'

'I don't understand you.'

'I hardly understand myself right now, but it will all be over soon. When the Commander gives the all-clear we leave to find your father.'

'You keep saying we cannot go on as we had before, but you forget we do not have to proceed. I've told you too much. You think maybe this is all safe. That I'm not dangerous to be around.'

'You put scars on my arm, fought me and almost broke my nose. I know what you're capable of. And if that man raised you, I won't underestimate him. But you forget I am dangerous as well. And thirsty, too.'

She asked again, 'Why? Why the kindness?'

She didn't think he would answer her. His eyes stayed steady with hers, but his expression revealed nothing, whereas she felt as if she revealed everything to him.

'Because you deserve it,' he said, before closing the door behind him.

## Chapter Eleven

With a few moments for relief outside the room, to clean, to change clothes, they attacked the food and talked far through the day and into the night.

Maybe it was the mead, maybe it was Eldric. She didn't feel like herself. At least, not a version she was familiar with. She'd never been this free with anyone before. Never been allowed this much company, let alone a man's. And all the while, his words echoed in her head, that she deserved it.

They didn't approach any more dangerous topics. She was almost content as she told him about the times at the abbeys. The separation from the nuns, her father's visits. Their disapproval afterwards even though they took his coin.

When he asked why they disapproved, she told him about how her father had trained her in the abbey's courtyards. How he wasn't gentle, but he was free with his praise when she did well.

Despite knowing the truth now, the memory of her father's visits was still a happy memory for her, though the nuns' disapproval meant missed meals and extra kneeling.

And though Eldric almost smiled at her stories and especially when she regaled him with the time she threw a dagger backwards and stuck it in a tree, he'd quickly lose those almost-smiles. A certain faltering of his lips, a dullness to the blue of his eyes as if he'd remember her learning those skills had meant the death of his friends.

Still, he shared his own stories. Of being raised as the sole son of parents who were happily still alive. He'd told of being sent to Edward's court for training. How he'd wanted to cry, but he couldn't because he hadn't been able to hide like natural-sized children.

And that was the word he chose. She remembered all the times she'd watched him being careful around others and her heart broke a bit for him. She would have protested, but he caught himself. Asked if she already knew all this about him.

She lied because she loved hearing his voice tell the stories. She both revelled and despaired at it as the night wore on. Amazed she'd be able to have such a time with anyone, let alone this man.

It wasn't until it was time to sleep that she realised her dilemma. The room was small, the bed smaller. Cramped. She might not have access to her bow and arrows, Eldric had hid them somewhere on the ship, but if they were attacked, being in a cramped area was not wise.

She knew, logically, they were on a ship. If the mercenaries were to attack, it would have been done already, but she couldn't stop the years of training.

'You do not want the bed?' she asked.

'I could hardly fit my frame there.'

The bed was hardly a bed, but more a hammock. He'd managed to sit on it, but the length wouldn't support the rest of him.

As for her... 'Could I...also have the floor?'

He snapped a blanket in front of him. 'Worried that I'll tie you up?'

She didn't know how to answer that. 'With the low ceiling it is not as if I can spring from the bed.'

'No, but you could crawl out of it easily enough.'

Hours together and he jested with such an easy manner. She'd seen Eldric like this many times with his friends and, as he arranged pillows, he almost whistled under his breath. Not the long piercing one that first caught her attention, but a lilting tune. One that she wanted to follow.

She hardly knew how to respond to that as well. When she didn't answer, he turned to her, his brow lowering. 'You mean it. You truly want the floor.'

'If we're attacked or...' She nodded.

'We are on a ship. No one knows we're here. How can you expect an attack?' His eyes narrowed. 'You're used to sleeping in the open, aren't you, and I...pinned you to the bed. I'm—' He shook his head. 'I'm not letting you out of this room, so I suppose this will have to do.'

He laid down closest to the door, his weight dispersing the bedding outwards.

The floor appeared as though it offered plenty of

space until Eldric laid down and took up half the room. With raised brow, he grabbed two pillows and plopped them at his side.

She almost wanted to smile. Two pillows were hardly a barrier, but who was she to feign propriety? She had camped around men her entire life.

But this was different. Now she was alone with a man—this man—and it was entirely her actions that would dictate the course in front of her. The crux of the matter was she didn't know what course to take. She never did when it came to Eldric. He was her private wish and laid out before her, he was hardly a secret any more. Everything in her knew it, too.

Eldric made some sound and grabbed another pillow, adding it to the pile at his side. 'Is this enough?'

For a barrier, no. But she was lingering and there were no other choices. Gingerly, she stepped on the mattress and settled as much towards the edge as possible. It was more than comfortable, but she was all too aware of the man on the other side of the pillows.

'I could sleep on the deck,' she said, already knowing the answer, but suggesting it despite herself. They were on a ship, after all, there were hardly many places she could escape.

'Never.'

She flipped to her back. 'You sleep on the most ridiculous padding.'

'There's something beneath us?'

She turned her head towards him. The hill of pillows blocked a clear view of Eldric next to her. Still, with his size, there were glimpses of him. The spill of his dark hair over one of the pillows. The slant of his leg because his right foot was flat on the floor. Against his stomach rested a forearm. His posture was both alert and relaxed. Even in repose, he was formidable.

'Five pillows under your head and you feel nothing?' she said.

'You may think this is excessive, but if I had one less pillow, I'd never find sleep. When you're as large as me, your weight will go through any feathers and straw.'

She snorted. 'When I'm as large as you, I still would find this much padding frivolous.'

'A jest, Cressida?'

It was the almost teasing tone in his voice that froze her. No one laughed with her. Where did this ease come from? The mead or the conversation? It was too much, too soon. She was lying beside a man whom she had spied on and who had hunted her down. The day before they'd been enemies.

And she…made jokes, as though this was all some game? It wasn't amusing. It changed something within her and she could tell it changed something in Eldric for he was suddenly silent, a restlessness to his propped-up leg that hadn't been there before.

'No, it's more of those contradictions, isn't it?' he said. 'Hours of talking, but there's something still missing.'

'You haven't told me everything.' They had avoided talking about him bringing her to the Tower.

'True, but you haven't as well.'

What was she to say? She longed for something that could never be. To be raised as something other than a weapon. To have attended the Christmas dance in Swaffham as a true guest. To have danced the entire night with Eldric. To have accepted his kiss that night instead of waiting.

To truly understand deep inside her heart that she did deserve his kindness.

But those were all fanciful dreams. Oh, she wished she could trust him. He whistled, laughed. There was a bit of her that felt if she told him everything, he'd understand. He understood everything else. He wasn't her enemy, but she was his.

Between them should only be barriers, not comradery and conversations that lasted into the early hours of the next day. He shouldn't be almost whistling, and she never should attempt humour.

Death pursued her. Her father, the Warstones, the King of England and Eldric. At the same time, she was death. Raised as a weapon. Her arrow…piercing his friend, Thomas. That horrible moment when she saw the wretched grief in Eldric's expression.

No, she had one mission now, to save the child her father had stolen and then to beg death to be swift.

There was nothing humorous about her life. No lightness, no easiness. No *comfort*. She turned on her side and forced herself to sleep.

Someone pinned her down. Her father had never done this to her before. Always he threatened to bind her between two of his mercenaries. Always she behaved and freely knelt with her bared back presented to him, her hands folded in her lap.

But now, she fought against the clamp of his hold. She was trapped. Suffocating. Words were being said to her. She didn't want to hear them. She wanted to be free!

Wresting control, she released an arm, jammed her elbow back. A grunt, but the arm holding her remained gentle, large, strong. Careful.

Not danger… Not… She woke.

Eldric at her back, his hand on her shoulder, whispering words she didn't understand. Until she did.

'Shh, it's only me. No one's here. You're safe.'

She shuddered. 'I thought I was…' Held down. Her arm pinned, her hand splayed so he could slice each of her fingers. How many times did her father threaten an appendage? How many times did she dream—?

Panic. She couldn't catch her breath!

'Shh,' Eldric insisted, his words never stopping, the hand on her arm brushing. 'Be at ease. It was a nightmare. It's not truth.'

She stilled; he didn't know. Of course, he wouldn't. 'It was my truth.'

He pulled her closer and she let him. She wanted, needed that warmth. He couldn't know how much.

'You want to tell me your dream?'

She stared at her hand, splayed her fingers, counted each one.

'Cressida, what did you dream?'

'I told you things…good things. I thought they were good. I see now that they were merely ways he controlled me.'

She counted backwards. *Ten. Nine. Eight—*

'Don't.' He clasped her hand in his.

'I need to say this.' She turned into his arms. 'Where are the pillows?'

'Gone. You cried out and…'

He began to pull away and she gripped his tunic. She felt that uneasy thrill when she climbed too high. That moment when the branch under her feet swayed, but she saw further than anyone. 'I don't want that life any more. I don't.'

His arms were there, hovering above her back. Surrounding her, but she needed more than that.

'I know you don't,' he said. 'Don't you think I know that, after all these hours spent, all you shared?'

'I didn't share everything.'

She felt it then. His hand brushing down her hair, his fingers carefully unknotting each strand. 'Neither did I, but we'll remedy that. After this night, I can't go back to the way we were. You aren't just an enemy. But it's late and we can talk in the morning.'

She shook her head. Felt the press of time. She'd told Eldric too much, risked his life. That's what her nightmare truly meant. It wasn't only she who her father threatened. It was Eldric, too. He needed to know how much she risked everything. 'I don't want to wait. You don't understand.'

'Shh, in the morning. In the morning. We're tired,' Eldric whispered, the weight of his arms against her back now. Almost a true embrace. Heavy with the weight, but not trapped. She felt…secure. When had she been held like this? When had she been cared for? He was so large, it didn't take much to make him her entire world, to believe he could ward off true evil.

They stayed like this for a long while. Easing into each other's breaths. She grew quiet, letting the rhythm he rocked her with and his heartbeat shove the nightmare away, his hand at the back of her head soothing.

His breath, the murmurs, were everything to her and, for every bit that he tugged her closer, she pushed herself into this embrace and felt the tightening of his body. Until his rocking ceased and his heartbeat changed its rhythm. Until she felt a certain heaviness in her own breath.

He swallowed. 'Cressida, are you still awake?'

Ever since she'd been caught by him, she felt she was dreaming. 'I don't think I could sleep again.'

'Could you tell me one more truth?'

She felt his breath over the top of her head; even that she didn't want to end. If it would take her telling him more to hold her like this, she'd talk and talk and talk. 'Yes, I meant it. I meant it. If you need—'

'No, not.' Eldric hated the way he began his question, could feel Cressida becoming frantic again, which was everything he didn't want. Not when she had allowed him to hold her like this. When had any female welcomed all his touch? His frame, his weight. Most times he was so careful to keep it all away, but Cressida kept tugging him closer and he let her.

Everything about holding her was a wonder. But out of all they had discussed, there was one matter that he couldn't quite shake. One matter that he felt had to be truth, but he didn't know why.

'I need to know,' he said. 'I want to know… Why do you feel so natural in my arms? Why is it when we touch, when I can scent your hair, do you seem familiar?'

He felt the slight twitch of her shoulders, the hard swallow against her throat. 'Because you've... You've touched me before.'

Needing to see her expression for this conversation, Eldric cupped her jaw, gently pulling her face around. A tiny movement, but enough to partly turn her to him, to brush her shoulder against his chest, her arm across his stomach until it rested between them.

'Since I've captured you,' he said.

She shook her head and it released the fragrance of rain and forest that clung to her pale tresses. He inhaled deeply.

'Because I glimpsed you in that tree?' He brushed his thumb across her cheek, his calloused hand far too large for her ethereal beauty, but he couldn't stop brushing his thumb across again to continue to feel the softness. 'This—'

She laid her hand on his and stilled his caresses.

'What?' he said. 'What is it?'

'At Swaffham, in the winter, we—'

'We?' He released his hand, laid it on her shoulder and turned her completely. Pale hair, wide crystal eyes, lips a distinct shade... Slowly, Eldric laid a finger across her cheek just under her eyes. By no means was it a mask, but it was enough to cast a shadow, to darken that one eye. To change it to a darker blue.

'It was you.' He pushed up until she was beneath him, both his hands cradling her face to hold her still for his gaze. Days in her presence with him staring at her, hours that she slept where he couldn't take his eyes away from the improbability that was her. Nothing. Nothing gave away that he'd been this close to her before.

Except, from the beginning he'd felt this familiarity. He thought it was the shock of capturing her. Never in a thousand years could he have guessed that the woman he danced with at a Christmas celebration in Swaffham last winter was Cressida.

He'd been sent to Swaffham to spy on his friend Hugh of Shoebury, whom the King believed was a traitor. Hugh had, indeed, been sharing English secrets via a half-thistle seal, but only with their friend Robert of Dent who had married into the Scottish Colquhoun Clan.

All the time Eldric spent there trying to determine the truth, he'd eaten lavish meals, swum in icy waters, attended masked dances. There in the Great Fenton Hall, he'd spotted the dark-haired woman. She was no bigger than…than the Archer. But she stood in the shadowed corner, fidgeted with her gown and looked around her with a sense of wonder.

As he conversed with friends and drank far too much, he knew the woman in the corner also watched him with the same open expression.

Never would he have dared approach. She was far too tiny for one such as he and his size. Yet, when their gazes met, her delight turned to an almost fragile longing. It called to something inside him and he was halfway across the room before he knew what he did.

Most often when he approached women, they'd tremble, run or gloat as though he was some conquest to boast about later. When he was younger he didn't care, but over the years he'd found it difficult to be interested enough to pursue, persuade or negotiate.

Which was why, when the tiny maiden in the corner remained, when she raised her chin with a gaze neither shy nor bold, there was a part of him that exalted. For several heartbeats, they stood without words. He was transfixed and, despite propriety, despite etiquette, he held out his hand.

He didn't know what to expect then. Certainly not his reaction when she flouted the same rules as he, placed her hand in his and he brought them to the other dancers. By the time the music began he realised it was a piece that kept them apart far too much and, just as they were to meet again, just when she was at one side of the room and he the other, she disappeared.

He had searched for her after, but there was no trace. No trace, and now, now she was here. He couldn't truly believe his eyes, didn't dare trust her words as he tried to merge the details of that night to this woman under him.

'It was you I danced with,' he repeated. 'How?'

She nodded. 'I knew you were there. I thought to simply observe the way I always had and then——'

'Then I saw you and couldn't take my eyes off you.' She held still for him. Nothing but wonder and delight in her eyes. Years and years of derision regarding his sheer mass, only truly comfortable around his fellow warriors. Always feeling awkward around any maiden tall or not, for none was as wide as he. Knowing he could crush them and could do little about it.

But the maiden in the corner he could never forget. Not when she had stared directly into his eyes, like she was doing now. Unafraid…and wanting. She had no idea what that meant to him. How he had searched for her, couldn't forget her, and all this time… All this time she was…*this* woman.

Whom he touched, felt the softness of her skin, the warmth, saw the curves of her hips, her breasts.

Slammed with the utter awareness of her proximity, the fact the woman he had lusted over the last several months was beneath him, Eldric shuddered. He was surrounded with the way she felt, her scent, the stunning colour of her eyes and hair. All of her within reach for his pleasure. He hoisted himself up, poling his arms on either side of her body.

'You need to move from me, Archer.'

Cressida thought Eldric would be angry she had duped him last winter. That the shame would add to his revenge. He hated her, wanted her dead, then she had danced with him as if it was all a jest. *Flirted* as though she'd done it a thousand times before, their eyes clashing in a dance that went far beyond the steps they made in that hall.

But it wasn't anger that blazed through the warrior's eyes. Not wrath that shuddered his body because she physically experienced each of his breaths, observed the waves of prickles up his arms, the flush that spread upon his throat.

It was heat. Intent. Desire. And the more they stared at each other, the more it increased. All her life, she'd watched, observed until her prey was within her sights. All her life, she'd wanted Eldric. Could it be possible that he desired her, too? Never in her life did she think so.

Yet what did she do now? She had no experience with men, no experience even talking to others. Instead, she had watched. She had watched and watched and then, when it came to Eldric, she had dreamed. It was those dreams that kept her still in this moment.

'Cressida, this time, this place. *This* is why there's been a contradiction between us. I should hate you, but I can't. I shouldn't trust you, but I do. I shouldn't kiss you, but I did. This is what I was missing. You. I was missing you. And now you're here...'

The strain in his voice. One moment they argued; another moment she was asleep in his arms. She didn't have to wonder now why she fell asleep near him, why she allowed herself to be vulnerable to him.

This was Eldric and, from the moment she had heard him whistle, from the moment he had laughed, she was always vulnerable to him. Never more so than now, as she placed her hands upon his chest, felt the thump of his heart increase like her own and began to think back about the other times they had touched, the way he looked. She began to believe.

'What is this, Eldric?' If he truly wanted to be away from her he would have stood. Stormed out of the room. Instead, his arms on either side of her body shook.

'God's bones, woman, I'm begging you to move. I'm a man, do you understand? One who has wanted you for far too long.'

Cressida's heart didn't care if it survived or not. Eldric felt the same about her as she did him. This was like some promise of the ocean that didn't—hadn't—lied to her.

'And if I don't want to?' she said. 'You said I deserved kindness. What if I want more than even that?'

## Chapter Twelve

Another great shiver, his eyes blazing a warning she didn't heed. Then, on a hungry groan he lowered his head and took her lips. No hesitation this time, no waiting for this kiss. She knew what she challenged when she said those words. A roll of his hips until he was against her side, his arms lowering that bit more, so she felt the weight of him. Felt the answer to her question: he did want her.

Twining her hands behind his head, she pulled him towards her. His arms shook, his great strength affected by such a small touch. He kept that slight distance, trailing his kisses along her jaw towards her ear. Only his lips, only the heat and weight of his body to the side of hers. None of his touch.

'How did you hide from me in the hall?' he demanded. 'Your hair was dark.'

'I… I put oil and ash…' she caught her breath '…bound it up to prevent it brushing anything. I don't understand what's happening.'

'I searched for you that night.' He licked along the

rim of her ear, the warmth of his lips, the heat of his breath, making her shiver. 'The following day, again, I searched. So much pressure, so many demands and I wanted to find this one woman who left me wanting.'

Could she trust this? She wanted to. Threading her fingers through the length of his hair, she tugged and pulled, felt and saw the surprised curve to his lips, an almost disbelieving look in his eyes.

'Tell me more about that night,' he whispered in her other ear. 'How did you hide the colour of your eyes?'

More of him above her, more of him for her to reach—she arched her own neck, pressed her own lips under the line of his jaw at the tenderest of spots and mimicked what he was doing to her. The light kisses, the dart of her tongue to taste him.

Against his skin, she said, 'I shaped the mask to cast shadows.'

He groaned, raising his head. His thumb rubbing across her lips. Branding her as surely as his kisses. 'But this mouth, these lips.'

That night, she had meant only to observe, but he'd held out his hand and so she took it. Why did it feel as though it was happening all over again? She reminded herself she'd worn a mask, a gown. Now, with Eldric's dark blue gaze riveted to her lips, there were no shadows or mask to hide behind and she slid her bottom lip under her teeth.

'No, no, no,' he chanted. 'Release your lip, Cressida.' When she didn't, couldn't, he tapped the corner of her mouth until her mouth eased. Then he rubbed along the parted seam and she had an overwhelming need to taste the tip of his finger. To taste *him*.

A hum under his breath as if he knew that want. 'Across the room, I focused on what little I could see of you, what was not part of the costume, the headdress, the gown, just this jaw, this chin, these lips. This lip in particular, it looked so soft. It feels soft now.'

She couldn't stand it. She had to. Darting her tongue out quick, hoping in vain that he wouldn't notice. He did.

His breath hitched. Hers stopped completely.

'What is happening?'

'You know. Surely you know.'

Did she? She couldn't think! 'But why?'

'Because I wanted you at that dance. The duties I had to complete and there you were. I haven't stopped thinking of that woman at the dance.'

'But that woman...' she said. 'But I'm me.'

It was her. All this time, the Archer was Cressida. Cressida was the Archer. His enemy and the woman who haunted him.

Eldric only touched her hand at the dance, but she felt...right. When he spoke, bending to be heard over the roar in his ears in the din of the crowd, and caught the scent of her, he was snared. All through the simple dance, he kept his gaze on her. Then he'd turned, blinked and he only saw her back to him, the trail of her gown as she bolted down the shadowed hall.

Aware of his size and the distance, he waited one, maybe two more steps before politely disengaging and pursuing her, but she was gone.

Until he captured her. Even as he fought her, his body knew.

'I know who you are. All the more, I know, Archer, and something in me knew it, too.'

He noted the changes this intimacy had on her. The ones that were tightening everything in him, demanding him to claim this woman in all ways. The flush to her pale cheeks, the darkening of her eyes. He wanted her then and, now that he knew who she was, somehow, despite everything still between them, he wanted her all the more. But more words needed to be shared.

'Cressida, there are matters to talk about… I meant it when I said in the morning we'll talk. But now…with this truth between us, I can't deny the coincidences. I feel as if fortune or fate has brought us here. What are the odds that you would be you?'

Her brows drew in. 'I've always known it was me. I always knew I was there.'

What was she telling him? 'You were there…to watch.'

She nodded. 'I was there for you.'

He shook his head. 'All this time, I dreamed of you. Pursuing the Archer and dreaming of a woman who I shared only a few words with. Since last winter I argued that I had no time for any other woman, I needed no distractions. The truth was, I was only wanting you. Sit up.'

She did. He gathered the hem of her tunic, felt it tear as he whipped it over her head.

Her arm snapped across breasts he ached to taste. But it was her look of discomfiture that stopped him cold. A sharp reminder of who he was. Of what he had just done. Holding her tightly to him, ripping her clothes from her body. Like some…brute.

'What is it?' she said. 'Do you hear someone?'

He wished there was someone to have stopped him before… But he'd wanted to for so long. Eldric looked at his massive hands. One hand spanned her entire waist. He picked up her tunic, showed her the tear, readying for her to realise.

'Eldric?'

'This…this is what I'm like. In battle, it's… But here with you, I haven't been careful. You've told me the secrets of your life and I haven't been gentle. I haven't been—'

She swung up and slapped her hand against his mouth. The sound echoed in the room.

Very slowly she eased her hand away. He didn't like the uneasiness in her eyes.

'I need to explain,' he said.

'You've seen my back.'

He didn't want to think about those scars and the pain she'd endured.

'Cressida, if you only knew what was in my heart, the ache I have for you because you suffered any pain. I could hurt you. Like him. I could hurt you and—'

'I have other scars,' she said.

He waited. Something more important was happening here. 'More harm he did to you?' he said. This wasn't about him. If she needed him in some way, he'd be there. 'What are you trying to tell me?'

Her eyes widened. 'No, not…he never…or allowed others. These…injuries I caused myself.'

Only a bit of the wrath in his heart eased. Her father was to blame and he would get his due. For now, the woman before him captivated as she, still clutching her arm across her body, pointed to her opposite arm.

'This is when my arrow slipped. Over here, I was carving a bow and it splintered, puncturing a hole. I couldn't do anything for weeks.'

She bowed her head, a white-blonde curl slipping over her shoulder. 'You should know I've got callouses on my fingers and along my legs. I think I fell from more trees than—'

She was beautiful and the more she described herself, the more he wanted her. The more he knew he didn't deserve her. 'Cressida, we can—'

'Look at me, Eldric. I'm sturdy. My back doesn't hurt. You won't hurt me.'

'Sturdy.'

'I'm not some maiden who wears a yellow gown and—'

The description was too specific. It was a memory of his, one he hadn't shared. One she knew right down to the dress.

He pulled up, clenched his fists. 'You watched me, Cressida. You did see me with women. Then you know my brutish ways. My inability to—'

'No! I couldn't. I saw beforehand and I'd know... I always turned away. I could watch others. But never you.'

'Others? My God, the pictures you put in my mind.' He shook his head. 'Why, Cressida?'

'Because you're...you. I'm the one who watched you. I couldn't bear that, though. It hurt me to see you change in front of them. I don't want you to change for me. You're not brutish. Not to me, not ever. If we need to talk about causing injury, I've hurt you more than once. What makes you think you could truly harm me?'

He canted his head, the brown locks tumbled along his shoulder. 'You're proud of your body. You should be.'

She nodded. He did understand. Of course he did. She didn't want him to hold back. She was a warrior, too. She loved his size and strength. Wanted it.

Although that brought her to who she was. Her scars, the strength, the training, the fact she didn't own a dress.

'Not since I was training has it failed me,' she said. 'I am strong and can lift far more than my weight. I can climb trees and am small enough to reach branches others can't, but I can't wear dresses, not without feeling clumsy. I can't be—'

'You think because you're sturdy I wouldn't want you. Or because you are built like this, strong for a man like me, I wouldn't want you.'

He was right, but it wasn't all she meant. 'You make it sound contradictory.'

'Isn't it? Are we not just contradictions?'

'Can it...can we be both?'

'It could, but it's not. If you truly want me despite my size, then what makes you think I wouldn't want you despite your scars? Or maybe I want you because of them. Because they show your bravery. Your endurance.'

'Most men wouldn't like the fact I climb trees.'

A quirk to his lips, a dubious question to his eyes. 'You are a formidable foe, but I'm not kissing your lips,

I'm not aching to taste your breasts, begging to part your thighs, only because you climb trees.'

She shouldn't be shocked. She shouldn't. She'd seen men piss, defecate, throw snot out of their nose. She'd seen them shove their hands down their pants to fondle themselves in all sorts of matters. She had even seen sex.

But Eldric's words sent a hot spike right through her centre.

He knew it, too. His smile and the heat in his eyes increased, making the shot of need acute through her. 'It's because you're you.'

'Me?' She looked down.

'You.' The colour of her hair, the softness of her skin. The way she looked at him with that mixture of vulnerability and strength. Eldric tried to keep his control, lost it. 'I must kiss you again.'

So he did. He did. Ever careful she was under him, but losing that carefulness all the same. Noting the changes in her with each kiss he deepened.

Down the column of her neck, down between her breasts he had yet to touch, taste. So he did. Kisses, darting of his tongue.

She gasped. 'Eldric.'

He lifted his head. 'How did we get here? How? I want more of you.' He licked across her nipple, bright red and swollen.

She arched under him. So he did it on the other one and she clawed his shoulders.

'But for that time in Swaffham, I've never worn a dress. I know the best of wood for arrows, at what sharpness each arrowhead could be—'

'Cressida, my mouth has been along the curve of your shoulder, my tongue tracing the plumpness of your breasts.' She was beautiful like this. Flushed, her hair cascading outwards. Her lips swollen from their kisses.

He trailed his fingertips along her collarbone, down between her breasts, around her navel and back up. Revelled in the feel of her hands doing the same, her palm increasing with heat and every swipe along his stomach sending lust hard and fast through him. And still she talked!

'Are you doubting this?'

'I can't believe. I can't.' Her words like a pant broke him. Eldric grabbed her hand and pressed it between his legs.

Cressida was shocked out of her next words. Eldric had been so gentle with her. Every question asking her if she wanted him, every reassurance she gave him in return only emboldening her. His touch sending so much pleasure, bringing more want, but this…

'If you tell me any more of your accomplishments,' Eldric growled, 'how you carve your arrows, or climb your trees, I swear I'll spill in my braies. If you move one finger now, that's how close I am. All the scars on your body don't, could never—'

She curled all her fingers and he threw his head back. He kept her hand pressed hard against him and she felt the sear of one pulsing throb. She'd never felt anything more wonderous in all her days.

'Did you?' she whispered.

He sunk his chin to his chest, his eyes promising retribution. 'Think me finished yet?'

He felt harder than before. 'There's more?'

'Cressida, your curiosity, your beauty may be the death of me yet. Mine all the worse. For I want to ask and not ask. How much do you know? How much did you watch?'

Never him, but with the look in his eyes... 'I think... I think I should have watched more.'

'There are those images in my head again.' He gripped her wrists, clamped them together and brought them over her head. It stretched her body out as he eased her back to the makeshift bedding. His gaze swept to her bared breasts.

'You're beautiful. Perfect. I know some of this feels sudden. Some of it feels inevitable. And you want a man like me?'

'Yes, always.'

'Words we exchange while I ache, while I want to taste the tips of your breasts again, feel and see your response to my touch.'

'I don't know where they're coming from. I've never done anything of this before. It's not as if I trained—'

Growling, he lifted her bound wrists, pressed them back down again. 'I tied your hands like this. Did you know what that did to me?'

No, she didn't.

'Captured, made my prisoner, yet I couldn't stray from you. You compelled me. I was a prisoner of yours, did you not realise that?'

'You left the room.'

'And returned. Left and returned again. Always you felt familiar. This dance we've been playing, I've been aware of it since last winter. Wanting you for months and you want to train—it'd kill me!'

He sunk his head into her neck. 'How could I not know who you were?'

She felt his hot breath, the tenderness of his kisses. She arched her back to brush her breasts against the coarse hairs on his chest.

He hissed, pulled up. 'But you knew. You knew all this time who I was,' he said. 'You…you placed an arrow on my bed that night in Swaffham. Why?'

She curled her fingers around his own. He eased his grip until she could link her hands in his.

His kisses, his touch, his words. It was if all the turbulence between tumbled out at once. All of it true, all of it confusing—none of it would make sense until she told him the truth.

'It was my very best arrow, Eldric.'

The most perfect arrow she had ever created. She had made it years before and could never part with it. She did that night. She might not have been able to complete the dance…to…complete the promise he made with those dark blue eyes of his. But she had wanted him to remember her. Thought he wouldn't.

They held only fingertips, danced with others, she left when the music put her close enough to a darkened hallway. She turned one more time and disappeared—only to realise she couldn't exit down that hall. So instead, she'd raced to his room, the abundance of bedding pushed to the floor leaving the starkness of his pillows almost like a target, and it was with those errant thoughts that she'd placed that particular arrow on the pale linen.

His eyes widening, taking in everything all at once. Down to her hands, up to the arch of her brow as if he was looking for answers.

'It was not a threat?' he whispered.

'My best one, one I had spent more time carving than I did with any others, that I carried for more time than that,' she said. 'It was meant as a token. I wanted you to remember me. Remember that dance. To think of me as—'

Brows drawn in, he kissed her tenderly. Shared his breath. Hers. Kissed her again. 'I didn't know it was *you* who did that.'

'I know,' she said. 'But *I* knew and it was a memory for me, too. Something I stole for me, out of everything in my life. *You* were for me.'

*'Cressida.'*

Eldric released her hands. His touch could no longer be gentle. He needed to feel her everywhere, touch her in all ways at once. He wanted to kiss and taste and consume. The arrow on his bed. She did that for him. He didn't understand, his mind couldn't comprehend, but everything else in him felt it. Felt her.

He hoisted himself up, just enough to shove down his breeches, his braies. 'Tomorrow. We talk.'

She clenched her nails into his shoulders as he rolled the rest of her clothes off to throw them to the side. Until she was utterly, stunningly naked beneath him. Her skin could not be real. A bruise, another scar. Her pale breasts perfectly round to fit in his palm, the tips begging to be pinched. And then, the swoop of her waist before the flare of her hips, and then...between, where the palest of hair, like starlight, hid the treasure he knew was underneath.

'Eldric,' she said.

'Quiet, Archer, while I take in your beauty. While I try to remember why I need to go slow. That you've never lain with a man, that I out of all the men in all the lands you travelled am the one you chose. And I need…need my control.'

'Yes, but you're so messy.'

He clenched his eyes tight, looked to the right. 'Cressida, the images you give me. You'll undo me!'

'Tell me.'

He blew out a held breath. 'Not if you want this over before it's begun. I'm trying not to be messy. But my hands, my very body…you're shattering any control when I already warned you!'

'I meant… It's our clothes. They are…' her breath hitched as her eyes swept over his body in curiosity, in need '…everywhere. If someone attacked, we couldn't…'

Eldric swiped his large calloused hands down her legs. 'Cressida, your choice of words don't compare to how you appear to me. You're perfect. Exquisite. I can't think of anything. But before you say one more word of attacks or escaping, you should know I have no intention of you finding your clothes again.'

Startled wide pale blue crystal eyes darkened in the light of the room, in light of her desire. Utterly vulnerable, exposed to each other and still she gave him a look that drew him towards her. No fear. No hesitation. Another slip in his control.

He adored and exulted in her hands gliding along

his shoulders, around his sides and down his back. Hands that mimicked his own movements. Ones he wanted her to repeat.

'No more talking, especially about interruptions.'

Her Eldric. His hands, his kisses, his touch, gliding, caressing as if what he did couldn't be enough.

Days ago, this didn't exist. They didn't exist. She wasn't sure they did now; it didn't seem possible. Eldric knew about her, her family, her darkest secrets they had shared, and now she wanted only to stop watching, to stop hiding in dark corners, to *feel*.

To be with this man, who granted her everything. A press of his lips against her collarbone, a nip of his teeth and swipe of his tongue above her right breast. A soft sound was ripped past her lips, a sound that echoed how much more she wanted.

Eldric jerked, stopped his kisses, his caresses, his harsh exhale sweeping across her entire body, just like the shudder that rippled across his.

He yanked himself up, denying any of his touch, and the chill of the room washed across her overheated skin, against the dampness between her thighs.

Eldric's gaze drew down and his growl turned feral. With one hand, he reverently parted her folds.

'Oh,' she gasped.

'Yes,' he said. 'You like this. Do you know how many times I dreamed of you like this? How I wished we had this moment before? We only touched finger-tips, Cressida. But that brief touch. The feel of your skin. I knew, I wanted you to be like this.'

A widening of his fingers. Cressida looked down

her body, up to his, the feeling tightening inside her. She wanted more.

His gaze locked with hers as he slowly circled around and again. His touch tender, gentle despite the look in his eyes as he lowered his head, kissed along her collarbone, down the middle of her chest. His body lowering, she felt the hair of his legs against hers, the heavy weight of his hip against her upper thigh.

And that one hand, tenderly sliding fingers through swelling heat. His mouth now hovering above her breasts. Strumming his tongue across her nipples until she couldn't be still any more.

In great greedy handfuls, she rubbed her calloused palms across his form. Threaded her fingers through the sparse hair of his chest. Felt the fall of his brown locks against her shoulders, the side of her neck.

Her hips, her hips now arching to his touch. Begging. Needing more.

She laced her fingers through the length of his hair and pushed it back, all the more to see and not just feel what he was doing to her. A quick glance up, his mouth curving into a smile, his eyes gazing with a wickedness she had only dreamed of, but could never quite perfect. Not like now, the blue almost all gone, leaving only dark intent.

Another slip and he lowered that much more. A welcome heavy weight that anchored her as the circles at her core became tighter, the thrumming at her nipples became less soothing.

She no longer could caress him, instead her hands clenched into his shoulders. He only growled his approval.

'Eldric,' she warned.

He switched to her other breast. 'Cressida, let go. Let go. It'll be easier when I—'

'Oh!' she gasped. His touch firm, more intent than the dark in his eyes. So much more, until she shattered.

The pounding of her heart easing, her breath slowing until she only heard Eldric's thrumming heart, his harsh breaths against the side of her head.

He held himself aloft. The look in his eyes one of deep ache and his kiss utterly tender.

'What was that?' she whispered.

'There's more.'

She put her hand on his face. 'There couldn't be.'

He groaned. 'Please tell me you jest.'

'A bit.' She kissed him under his jaw and he shivered, swept her hands along the damp expanse of his arms and he groaned.

'Cressida.' Her name like a request. The tightening of his fist in her hair, the rolling of his hips, the plea.

There never was a question for her. When it came to him, she just wanted.

She pressed closer. Felt the hard, slick strength of his desire against her thighs. 'Please, Eldric. I'm sturdy.'

'That word!' On a half-chuckle, half-groan, he cupped her beneath him, his eyes fierce with some emotion she couldn't name.

She could only name her own. And as he waited, poised above her while she shook, while she needed, she told him. Each word of want between each kiss she peppered along every plane of skin she could reach. More words of trust in every swipe of her hands and fingertips.

And the more she did, the more his tension eased, the more his body shook, his head dragging lower into whatever it was that had got them here. Desire. Lust. Want.

'That's it,' she said, reaching between them, feeling along the hard planes of his stomach that rippled to the arrowing of his hips. When did she get so bold?

'I can't get enough,' he said. 'I can't.'

She both loved and loathed that he was being so careful with her.

He opened his eyes that had somehow closed. 'Cressida, you can't know. This isn't how it is between... This is different. We need...words said tomorrow.'

She didn't want to hear of others, she didn't want to talk. Somehow he made her want even more. 'Please.'

He gripped her thigh that bit tighter, pressed that much more weight of himself against her and everything between them fell. It was almost easy after that.

As if all the waiting, and need, all the longing and desire made the decision for them. As if they were, indeed, inevitable and fortune was finally satisfied.

'God's most private of body parts, Cressida.' Eldric nuzzled her throat, kissed along the tender parts of her shoulders and neck. 'That was...everything.'

She knew. She knew what he meant. She felt that difference.

Over the years, she'd accidentally stumbled on others. The most embarrassing was a couple using the very tree she'd hid in.

She'd once thought that she might love Eldric, thought what she felt was love. But this between them now. The sharing, the touching, the tenderness in his blue eyes. It was everything…

He pulled away. Flopped on his back, his arm thrown over his eyes. She felt the same languidness, the inability to have any sort of grace. If someone charged in to harm them, her reflexes would be slow and he was right. She didn't care where her clothes had gone.

But that fact wasn't what alarmed her. It was the fact that, despite the absolute ease with which Eldric moved his body, a certain tension was there in the way he breathed, too fast and laboured, in the jerky movement of his legs as he untangled them from hers.

She'd given everything to this man, everything. All her secrets, both of her body and her heart. True, he had them all along, but he hadn't *known* that until they came pouring out of her.

At his soothing touches and understanding words, her anguish and pain, need and longing had spilled out, more than she was aware of, and that still didn't deter him. He drew her closer, his touches turned to caresses, to kisses, to…

Her body, though so recently sated, wanted more. But Eldric did not talk, his laboured breath now turning uneven as though he couldn't breathe at all.

And there, under his arm that stayed across his eyes, slipped a single tear towards the bedding they shared.

'Eldric?'

'You're unhurt, aren't you? Please tell me I didn't harm you.'

There was a soreness that hadn't been, but the rest of her… 'No harm.'

He rubbed his arm against his eyes a few times, let

out a harsh breath and he sat part way up. One hand by her head, one arm holding up his entire torso as he turned to her.

He was beautiful. The various shades of brown in his hair slipping down over one shoulder towards her. Some so dark they were almost black, others so light they looked like streaks of sunlight. The dark stubble of the beard he'd grown since he captured her highlighted the brutal angle of his jawline, the softness of his lips. The blue of his eyes held every colour of the sky and all the promises of a new day.

Everything about him perfect, except for the look of doubt just behind everything else he showed in the depths of his gaze.

With his free hand he took one of her curls and wrapped it around his finger, the heat of his hand welcome after she felt the chill. She leaned her head in his palm, watching the quirk to his lips.

But that contact did not ease the troubled look in his eyes.

'I'm pleased, Eldric,' she said. 'Oh! Your shoulders.'

He looked to his right where her nails had dug in, a small smile to his lips before he turned to her again. 'Everything's changed now, Cressida. You know that, don't you?'

She could feel it, feel it, but instead of the elation she expected since she'd bound herself to this man, she only felt that troubled worry he held in his eyes.

She shook her head, not knowing or liking where the conversation was headed.

He threaded a few more of her strands through his fingers, not so much a caress now, but as if he was un-

knowingly pulling her to him. 'Your secrets. You...
your father...these missions he used to send you on.
This child he stole.'

Pulling away, she sat up, drew the bedding to cover
her when his eyes slipped down and the heat, newly
awakened, flared again.

'Is this your idea of later? I thought we were to talk
in the morning. I didn't expect it so soon.' Nor did she
want to go from such happiness to this uncertainty.

'I know,' he repeated. 'But my heart, what I feel, I
can't contain. My thoughts are overflowing.'

She knew how that felt. 'You have your own secrets.
Is that what you want to share first?'

He dropped his hovering hand. 'I can't help you if
you don't tell me everything.'

She truly didn't like where this conversation was
leading. 'I'm not asking for your help.'

'We go to France, we confront your father...' He
huffed. 'You don't expect to confront him, do you? You
want to simply steal the child from him?'

She wanted very much to confront her father, to
rage and rail at a man who could hurt her so much. She
also intended not to do it with the warrior in front of
her. She would, until the end of her life, protect him.

If it came down to simply sword skill, Eldric would
defeat her father, but with his alliances, his love of
games and surprises, no one stood a chance against
him, at least not for very long. For as long as she could,
she wanted Eldric to avoid him, though her now lover
seemed intent on not letting her free. But she had ways
of subduing even the most stubborn followers.

'You expect to go without me.' His expression

turned to forbidding. 'I won't allow it. You need me against him, if nothing else as a distraction so you can slip out with the child.'

'How do you know what my father would do? You're not even certain you can provide a distraction to him. I've told you nothing of his personality.' She was sure of that.

'I know you and, if he raised you, he'll fight with everything he is to achieve his aim. Just like you do with those arrows of yours.'

She felt the point of an arrow now. One he aimed at her whether he meant to or not. It was as if that weapon was merely lying between them at the ready for him to throw. There was truth to that, they hadn't resolved everything.

Her own emotions began to roil, as Eldric caressed along her hairline, his eyes roaming her face. They went from wondering, to wonder, from a tenderness to something troubled. And on that troubled look he asked, 'How?'

So much between them, but the past hurt and she wasn't quite prepared to talk of it now. Even like this, in the sanctuary that was his arms. In the firm knowledge that it was different between them. That Eldric was good and it was right to trust her secrets and her body with him. But still something inside her doubted, that something that kept talking while he touched her. Asking how it was possible they were together.

'How what?' she said.

'Out of everything. It's the one… I can't seem to rectify it with who you are, with what's between us. It's tearing me apart inside.'

The tear. She should have guessed what that meant. 'Your friends.'

He closed his eyes, took his hand away. She wished she could move out from the bedding without revealing her very naked scarred body. Instead, she lay there, waiting for the question she expected him to ask. After all, they did talk and had shared. He said he couldn't rectify that she'd killed them…now he'd ask who did.

Oh, it wouldn't make her perfect. There was still a part of her that felt she could prevent it, she could have in the past not released the other arrows her father requested, but in this…in this, Eldric would—

'How could you have aimed, knowing what would happen when you released the arrow? How could you, knowing it was their death?' he said.

That arrow between them wasn't merely pointed at her. Now, she felt the full prick of the iron. If he asked this question, after all she had told him, it meant there wasn't the trust she thought between them.

But that couldn't be. In this she must be mistaken. This was Eldric. Her Eldric. He would—should— understand even these darkest parts of her. She sat up and he did the same. She immediately felt the cold, but her feet still rested on his legs. In that there was still warmth between them. She took heart in that.

'I haven't been a good person, Eldric, but I've tried. To do that, along the way, I've made…difficult choices.'

He brushed his fingertips against her hand pressed to the floor. 'You've told me a bit of your father, how he controlled, demanded.'

This conversation hurt. Knowing now what role her

father had made in her life, hearing the truth was still too fresh.

She looked behind her, grabbed her flung tunic. Her breeches had been tossed the other way. Eldric's clothes were spilled even further than that. The entire room was in shambles. If they had to rush out now, there would be a strong trail.

He shoved his own tunic over his head. She was fascinated by the way his muscles shifted as he did so. When his head poked free, something in her expression must have given her away for he gave a slight knowing quirk to his lips, but the blue of his eyes still held the troubling look.

'I don't want to talk of my father, not now.'

'We must,' he said. 'We've docked in France, and we must plan for his protection, where he could be.'

'I'm thirsty,' she said. 'Do you want some mead?'

'Perhaps that would help.' He stood, then thumped across the floor to retrieve his strewn clothing. His back was to her, so she kept her back to him to prepare the drink. Eldric would understand in the end. The tiny vial of liquid she kept strapped in her boots wouldn't be enough to kill him. Not a man his size, but it would be enough for him to sleep. He'd still be angry, but she'd apologise for the rest of their lives if she had to.

Moreover, she wouldn't be gone for long, she already suspected where her father would go on this side of the water. It was where he usually went, to a house hidden between many others that had an attached building to house his men.

She spun around just as Eldric was at her back. She handed him the mead, watched as he took a drink.

'You have to know I'm not planning anything.' She took a drink of her own and swung the goblet around. 'I think you should stay here on the ship. It's not safe for you and—'

'It's not safe for you!'

She relished his words. He must care for her if he wanted to protect her. He cradled the goblet between his hands, his brow furrowed. Her heart flipped as he drank the remainder of his laced mead.

Then he looked at her. Just looked at her and she knew nothing would be the same again. Something. She felt it. Had she betrayed his trust? She shouldn't have given him the herbs!

'You're…strong, Cressida, so strong,' he said. 'I can't understand the hold this man has on you. How he forced you. Was it the pain of the whip? Did he threaten you another way?'

She had aimed and released those arrows to save him. She had laced his mead with a sleeping draught and she'd do it again. Eldric was good and must stay safe on the ship. She had to make him understand. When it came to Eldric, she always had a choice. Always. He was hers. Her secret, her longing. She had kept him safe for years, she would continue to do so.

'When it comes to you, my father has never had any control.'

He frowned. 'Explain.'

'He ordered me to kill you because he heard you agreed to spy for Edward. My father knows all of Edward's spies. There are few who survive. He doesn't like them.'

He gripped the empty goblet. 'This is treason. Something we must tell the King.'

'Must we?' she said, holding up her hand. 'I am not privy to all my father's secrets, but I'm not absolutely certain on the reasons he does things. He's...cunning.'

'Duplicitous. But your father was devoted to you.'

'For most of my life, until...' She purposefully trailed off. 'I don't want to talk of my father.'

'Your father must be committing treason and the King knows of it. He...ordered me to bring you to him.' He shook his head. Pressed his fingers to his brow. 'My head is hurting. I—'

The draught was working fast. She needed to talk because, when he woke, she wanted him to understand. 'Please, Eldric, listen to me. My father never had control over me with you. He ordered your death, I wouldn't comply. I pretended. I released my arrow to make it look as though I had tried. I marked your arm so that you'd feel the pain, so you'd veer away from it and out of my range. And you did. You always did. I protected you.'

'But you killed the others.'

She parted her lips, readied to argue how killing Thomas was an accident, how her father had killed the others, trying to reach Eldric.

But again there was that something that held her back. That doubt that would not end when it came to him. Maybe she felt this was a dream because it couldn't be true. And...she wanted him to love her even if she had killed men. Because Thomas might have been an accident, but it was still her arrow that felled him.

And there were others, when she was younger, when her father wanted her to practise. He'd point to men. Bad men, he'd called them, and she believed him as she notched her arrows.

When she was older, her father stopped asking her. No reason given, perhaps because he knew she'd question it. Or maybe he lost confidence because she 'missed' killing Eldric.

In the end, it didn't matter that she hadn't truly killed his friends, she wasn't a good person. She was trying to do better. Eldric knew her. He would understand.

But not for very long. His blinking was increasing as the draught took over. 'I killed them instead of you. To protect you. Maybe I'm selfish by doing so, but do my deeds make me a terrible person?'

He'd have to say no. Have to. He had to understand she was nothing but a weapon all her life, releasing her arrows with no thought just as her father wanted. Then she heard Eldric whistle and she knew there was beauty in life, something lighter.

Brows drawn in, certainty like flint in his eyes. 'Yes. Because you had a choice! You had a choice! What would your father do to you if you disobeyed an order? Chopped off your fingers? You could have made the choice to not end others' lives. What is the loss of a hand compared to another's life!'

She felt his anger, watched him shake his head to stay awake. She'd caused all of it, but suddenly she wasn't prepared to face it. She'd lose. She knew that now, unless she told him how difficult the decision was.

He'd kissed her so tenderly. Surely, he'd comprehend the choices she made.

'And you believe I didn't think that?' she said. 'A hand for a life? What would have happened then, hmm? My fingers would have been gone. My father would have assigned another mercenary to kill you. I had to stay alive, to be useful, to protect you.'

He blinked rapidly. Set the goblet on the table. It wobbled a bit and he frowned at it before returning to her. A steeling anger in his eyes. One of accusation. Judgement. 'You don't understand. They were my friends! I would have died for them! I should have died for them.'

Merely the thought of Eldric dying caused her more pain than losing her father. He couldn't die. He was what was good with the world. He was what she strove to be. Kind. Generous. He had not minded her scars, or her lack of dresses.

'What choice did I have?' she said.

He pointed at her. 'If I were you, if my father had asked me to kill others, those who were innocent, I would have killed myself first.'

His words struck like hot iron arrows through her heart. 'Then that makes you a coward.'

He stepped forward, unsteadily. Shook himself. 'A coward!'

'Yes, a coward. Because I stayed alive to make the difficult decisions, Eldric. Ending my own life wouldn't resolve anything, I would have done it if I thought it would make any difference. But it wouldn't have. I would be dead, your friends would have died and so would you!' She drew herself in, prepared for the rest of the damning argument.

He blinked. Staggered. 'What have you done?'

She had done it out of love for him. Because she'd do anything to protect him, she'd put the sleeping draught into the mead, knowing he'd drink, he'd sleep, and she would take the risks instead. Confront her father, steal the child. Keep everyone safe.

'I did what was necessary,' she said.

He shook his head, fell back into the chair, his great body sagging. 'You poisoned me.'

She had. Was doubly glad for it now. First to protect him, now to protect herself. She was wrong about him. Just as she was wrong about her father. There were no good people in the world. No one to make the great sacrifice for. Not her father, not Eldric.

He didn't love her. Didn't care for her, didn't trust her or know her. Didn't understand she had made the decisions she did even when her heart broke each time she did it. Her father ordering her to kill those men—men her father said were evil—but even then she'd had to find a sanctuary and cried afterwards.

When it came to Eldric, when it came to her accidentally killing Thomas, she'd shed torrents of tears she couldn't hide from anyone. The agony she caused Eldric, the agony she felt for killing a human being. Afterwards, for days, her father looked upon her with disgust and she had learned to hide her emotions more effectively ever since.

She had lost some of her father's respect and care that day. Now she was attempting to be someone she was not. Her father had made her one way, but she wanted to be Eldric's way. To hear music, laughter.

But Eldric wasn't what she had made him out to be in her childhood fanciful dreams. No matter how strong or mighty he appeared, how handsome, if he could judge her so easily, so callously, then…he wasn't who she thought he was.

He sunk further in his chair, fighting to keep his eyes open. One bright flare of pity at his condition had her hating him. He didn't deserve any kindness. She took a few steps closer to him and weighted her next words with all the meaning they could possibly contain. 'Yes, I poisoned you. And I'd do it again if I could.'

Without looking back, she carefully unhooked the latch bolting the small cabin door and left Eldric of Hawksmoor behind.

Eldric couldn't open his eyes. Couldn't move his legs or arms. Waves of sleep were overcoming him, but the rage inside him fought back and his mind, though not clear, stayed aware.

Enough to hear her feet up the steps, to know that if she wasn't stopped at the top, he would find her. Find the duplicitous Archer who had tricked him. Another wave. Darkness hovered along the edges. He slept, fought it. Lost time. Slowly, his mind became his own again.

The anger helped. The betrayal. He'd shared parts of his childhood with her, the times he was at Edward's court. Nothing he revealed compared to the agony of her life, but still she had asked him questions. Her eyes had lit like stars when he told her anything remotely humorous.

And she was...she was the woman he had danced with last winter. He tried to tell her the significance of that moment for him, knew he failed as his body reacted to her. As she responded. Each touch something new and, because it was her, startling in meaning. His heart...

The Archer had poisoned him! Killed his friends and... Some memory scraped across his fogged mind. He cursed the poison. Had he known she could do something so vile as to pour it into his mead, to give him...

Poured it into his mead. He had held the goblet when they argued, but he was given the drink before, when they were merely rising from the shared bed. When he wanted to talk of her father and make plans for his capture. She'd put the draught in his drink then.

Ah! A tingling in his right foot.

She hadn't done it out of anger. She'd poisoned him...to protect him.

As she told him she'd done before. He should have asked more questions. She had confessed to watching him since childhood, but her father hadn't ordered her to do so. How had she seen him? Why would he be of any concern to a child. His size? But she had never acted as if that was any significance to her. Which was significant to him.

When he saw her again, he'd beg to know more. Contradictions were everywhere and this sense of certainty with her did not cease despite knowing her past, her deeds. Who was she? How could he reconcile her acts with who he knew, what every instinct inside told him, she was?

He had held her while she cried, while she told of her childhood. Just the way she held her body, the way her voice changed when she told of the acts expected of her, he knew she hadn't liked them.

But she'd done them…and so he'd lashed out without thinking, his grief battling with the joy. The fact the foundation of both was the woman he held was too much.

Accused her of the most awful of things. Did he truly want her death? Never. And the most humiliating truth of it all was…what would he have done in her place?

Because she was right. Her death, any other action than the one she had taken would have only caused more death, more pain.

Instead, she had warned him away with her arrows across his arm. She had lied to her only protector by covering her actions. For months more, she'd endured more of his punishments and corrections. She'd harmed her body and damaged her soul.

A soul so bright, he now knew why her hair was the colour it was, why her eyes reflected light like the sun in a white sky.

Life had taught him that people were either good or bad. There were various degrees of both, but the essential core of them, the essence of the person, was always one or the other. He'd pursued the Archer with this premise: his friends were good and the Archer was evil. The cunning, the malicious personal targeting of his friends. The fact the arrows struck him as well.

He thought…he'd thought all this time that it was done…for amusement. A game. When he had captured her, he'd continued with this theory. The fact she was a woman hadn't changed his opinion, just confused it a bit. He understood there was more to her story, but it wouldn't change the result. He would still deliver her to King Edward, not only to keep his loyalties straight, but also to protect his friends in case King Edward doubted their demise.

But the more embroiled he became in all this, the more he realised there wasn't good versus evil. Life wasn't made that way. Robert and Hugh had already blurred the lines. They had committed treason…for a good cause. And Cressida…

Cressida was raised by someone who wanted her one way, all the while…

She had saved him by defying her father, saved him again by throwing that dagger at the mercenary.

Underneath her deeds, there was…goodness. Her heartbreaking cries from a daughter to her father. Her determination to save a child from her father's machinations.

And he felt that goodness when they touched, kissed, when they laid next to each other. When he cried.

And he…blindly erected barriers. Threw up walls that hurt her. For what? Assumptions. He'd never asked her about those days on the battlefield when she marred his arm. It never occurred to him…until now. The sequence of the arrows shot. But something of her told him that what he believed wasn't true.

She had told him of Thomas and her eyes filled

with tears. If she had killed him, it wasn't intentional. And for the others—had she admitted their deaths even once?

He needed to confess, to apologise to his friends that died. He didn't know if he could fulfil his vow to them. They'd probably laugh that he was embroiled in contradictions. His life had been so very easy before all this.

She was her father's daughter, yet when she could, she made decisions for herself and even those couldn't have been easy. She'd hadn't renounced everything of her life. When she talked of training, of her tries at accuracy, she had such pride. When the conversation turned to her father and his demands, her voice shook. Every arrow she was forced to release hurt her.

He *was* a coward.

He needed to face the fact that even if she'd killed a thousand men, she had reasons, she had had to make agonising decisions.

And who was he, a warrior who killed on the battlefield, to judge? Even if he was the holiest of men, even then he would not be worthy of her.

She had left to confront her father on her own. To save the child, whom she believed was her half-sister.

His hand twitched. Clever Archer. A sleeping draught and a good one. Valerian, possibly, nothing he could taste since she had ordered spiced mead. Regardless, a man his size needed so much more if she wanted him to truly sleep. A bit more time and his thoughts would be clearer, his body strong once again.

It was time for him to make difficult decisions. If

her father didn't kill him as Cressida thought he would, King Edward certainly would. His only goal now was to protect the Archer and the child she risked it all for.

## Chapter Thirteen

'Hello, my daughter.'

Cressida clenched the rafter in front of her and somersaulted to land in front of the man who had raised her.

It had been many seasons since she last saw Sir Richard Howe, also known as the Englishman. It was a name they used to repeat with amusement since few of his enemies knew his true identity. His hair was greyer and the lines around his eyes were deeper. Mostly, he looked tired. He had to have been to find him this easily.

The tall, narrow house was as she remembered it from before. Thick, brightly whitened walls and sturdy dark oak beams that matched the carved furniture covered in cream and green linen. The attached residence, she knew, was the same shape, but not so finely decorated. It was no more or less than quarters for his men.

But this residence, this space was where they used to rest when they travelled. It had made it all too easy to find him. 'You didn't travel far.'

He lifted one shoulder. 'I like this part of France.

With the docks and different people. The commerce keeps me amused.'

Many a time he had had her positioned at docks or inns. Anywhere people and information flowed. It wasn't exhaustion that kept him here, it was another of his schemes. 'What amuses you now?'

'You, coming for me. I thought you'd be here before now.'

If she had remained the daughter he raised, she would have been, but Eldric had found her, kept her, and she thought…she thought she could be something else. Until it was clear he could never forgive her, never enough to ask for the entire truth.

It was for the best. He was not who she thought he was and, even if she could change into someone she wanted to be, the scars on her body would always remind them both of who she really was. Who she always had been.

Nothing was going to change. Nothing, until she changed it. Her wishing and hoping for Eldric was over; she'd always have blood on her hands. There was only one choice for her now: to kill her father and to return a stolen child. When Eldric found her, as he surely would, she'd welcome his blade. She was death and all she deserved was death.

'Where is she?' she asked.

'Ah, you believe she exists now? My men told me you doubted.'

'Your message made it clear she is real.'

'Of course, your observing her this evening helped make that a certainty for you.' He laughed. 'What, you think I don't know you? You've been observing this building all night. It's almost day now. I'll be disappointed if you don't already know where she is.'

No matter how still she kept or how fiercely she fought any expression, her father always knew her thoughts. She had believed it was because he loved her. Now she realised it was part of his training, his madness, for she did know where her half-sister was kept. Right next door in the matching house, surrounded by five mercenaries. She'd only glanced in the window, hadn't dared linger in case she was discovered.

But she should have spared more than a glance to ensure her sister was safe and was all the more a fool to think she could surprise her father by hiding in the rafters of his home.

She knew everything he had taught her, but all was clear now, there were a few tricks he kept to himself.

He turned, making his back a perfect target, and strolled to the other side of the room. On a table there was a platter that held a few crumbs of food, an indication he'd been comfortably sating himself while waiting for her.

He waved to the flagon of wine and two goblets. 'Are you thirsty?'

She stayed even with her father. For every step he took, she took one as well. If others stormed in, he would be the first they protected and the first she threatened.

'I have questions.' Eldric had had some, too. That's all he had, until he ceased asking any more. He had finally finished with her, just when she wanted to answer him.

'Questions?' Her father turned. 'Do you want to

know why your sister isn't here? I would think you know the answer to that.'

She did, but now was different if rumour was right, if Eldric was right… Things were happening and the Warstone family was divided. Her father could take fewer risks. And he couldn't have had enough time to put her sister in the convent. If she knew anything of her father, he didn't move fast.

'Since you failed so miserably with training me, it would be foolish to proceed the same way with her.'

A quick grin. 'Ah, prick my pride to rile a response. This hasn't been your way before. What other skills have you learned since we've parted?'

Parted. As if that was what she wanted to do. She thought her heart had broken when her father banished her. She thought the bits still in her chest were destroyed when she received the message he wanted her dead. But nothing was like this moment before him. Without Eldric.

Because even before Eldric captured her, he was hers. To listen to, to watch, to yearn for. Now, he rejected everything about her, even the part that was trying to be good. She no longer had the hope of Eldric and all he had represented to her since she was a child.

But she might…she might have a sister. 'Who is she?'

He sighed. 'What are we doing here? Answering questions as if we are strangers? Don't you want to simply kill me and be done with it? I wrote you a message.'

To kill her father and not have answers. No. 'It's not like you to be blunt. You like to talk and explain. One would think you meant not to answer me.'

His eyes narrowed. 'Oh, you have learned skills.'

Days of conversing with someone had changed her, yes, but she wasn't about to admit that to him.

'Maybe I've chosen to follow in my father's footsteps.'

Frowning, he took a step back until his legs hit the chair behind him. 'She is mine, that is all you need to know.'

But not all she wanted. 'You intend to kill me. Wouldn't it amuse you to reveal secrets you've cleverly held from me first?'

A familiar gleam in his eye, one she only saw if he was particularly proud of her.

'Come sit. We'll converse until the end. I find I have some questions for you myself. Should we begin at the beginning? Would that help your curiosity?'

'I'd like to know why you always punished me when I asked about her.'

Slowly he arranged himself in the chair. 'Your mother meant nothing to me. She was simply another in a long line of women I borrowed for a time.'

She didn't need to know. Still she asked, 'Without their consent.'

'I did always choose those who would put up a fight. I wasn't sloppy about it. I didn't want a breed of bastards, but there were a couple. You, the girl. I don't think I left any others, but I do like to check. That's how I found you. I returned to the village a year later. Look at your hair, your eyes! There was no doubt you were mine. So…after removing your mother, I took you. Named you after her, or what her name should have been. I thought such a duplicitous name, Cressida, was appropriate for you. After all, you weren't supposed to exist.'

He splayed his fingers to the side. 'Sit.'

Cressida had guessed the truth of her mother's death, wished she didn't carry such a hateful name, but locked her knees against his words. 'I'd rather stand.'

He tsked. 'I did the same with that child next door. The woman I laid with was uninteresting except for a powerful family and glorious red hair. When I returned to the area, she had a husband, which surprised me. The man was beneath her family connections. He came from a more simple upbringing and they must have wedded quickly, perhaps because of her being pregnant.'

She didn't want to hear of marriages and husbands, of mothers being slaughtered. 'You're conjecturing. Why?'

'I can admit to you, my daughter, it surprised me because she seemed happy. Can you imagine?'

Her entire life, she'd given her father her undivided attention and being in his presence reminded her why. His charisma, the way he'd study the person he conversed with as if they were his entire world.

And he did that now. The soothing tone, his large eyes rapt on her. She felt the pull to keep her attention solely on him, partly from her lifetime of obedience, the other because of who he was. A predator.

But she knew what a dangerous game that was. Knew it and, this time, she ensured she kept abreast of her surroundings. A glance to the window by straightening her clothing. A perusal of the door's latch as she stretched her limb or neck.

Oddly, it remained only them. Having her father to herself was a rarity and one she meant to take advantage of.

'I'm not your daughter,' she said.

He appeared affronted. 'When would you ever doubt that?'

'When you sent your men to kill me—'

'Train you,' he emphasised. 'You understand how it has been. You betrayed me; you are being punished for your disobedience. When I deem that you are sufficiently chastened, we can begin again.'

She felt the pull. The need to believe him. After all, this was her father. The man who had raised her. He was all she had longed for for months. It was merely days ago she'd been in abject desolation because he'd shunned her. All she'd wished, all she wanted, was her father's love and approval once again. Except…

'You wrote me a message. Your parchment, your seal, your writing. I read it, over and over. There was no other interpretation.'

He crossed his legs. 'Don't you know my cruelty has to be all that much more when it comes to you? How can it be a punishment if you believed I cared for you still? Haven't I always been firmer with you than any of my men? Didn't I push you long past when I stopped their lessons?'

Repeatedly. Hours of throwing daggers from both hands. More times than that to run around the camp. And run around again. All while the men sat in the centre of the camp laughing, drinking, enjoying the warmth from the fire. And she…she had no fire. Even on the coldest of nights, her father allowed her no fire.

She had to remain in the darkest parts of the forest so she'd remain safe and unseen.

A strategic location to surprise anyone foolish enough to attack, for she always remained near her father's place of rest.

To be his own personal guard. To watch when the men failed to watch. She'd taken extra pride in those moments. Felt that pride as her father lavished praise on her for the extra sacrifices. Felt superior because those men enjoying the fire were weak. Her father knew they were weak and only trusted her to be truly vigilant.

Yes, he had trained her the severest of them all. It was logical his cruelty would be just as harsh.

'Hmm,' he murmured and Cressida snapped out of her reverie. She cricked her neck and searched the room for any differences. The shutters remained in the same position, the latch on the door stayed still. All the while she was disturbed she had let her thoughts drift enough that she'd lost track of her surroundings and the man who watched her all too closely.

'I hope that you felt the loss of my careful guiding hand,' her father continued. 'My protection. My coin. You've been wandering all over England on these useless tasks, all the while wondering where your home was any more. I have to admit, it was one of my more brilliant schemes.'

If it truly was one of his schemes, it had worked. She'd felt every pebble under her foot, every bitter cold rain that fell upon her unsheltered head.

Mostly, always, she felt the lack of this man who had been a constant for as long as she had memory. This man who she could not trust or believe.

'One of your mercenaries confessed to the note, told me more about your hatred of me, about the child you stole,' she said.

A slight tightening in his brow was the only indication of her father's displeasure. 'You killed him, I hope.'

Eldric had killed him and now she wondered why. The man had been spitting each hateful word, words that had felt like cuts against her soul, and Eldric had thrown that dagger. There was no reason for it. Still…

'He's dead,' she said.

A gleam of victory in his pale eyes. 'Good, I will not have my first daughter lied to.'

Her father's expression seemed to have eased, but the tenseness in his shoulders remained. Because of what the mercenary had told her, or because he truly did care for her?

If she hadn't conversed with Eldric, if she hadn't received the message, there would be none of this doubt. She would know, with absolute certainty, that he was angry someone had lied to her.

She'd seen the punishment of any man who had looked at her. And the one mercenary who had dared nod his head in acknowledgement when she approached the camp for food? He was never seen again.

She'd revelled in her father's protection of her. Now, now she hated that it was all in doubt. She should be certain, shouldn't she? But she'd been certain about Eldric and look what that got her.

'I am pleased you finished him,' he said. 'It reveals that you are embracing your proper way of life again. Perhaps it is time for you to travel with us once more.'

Her first reaction was to reject him, only because

there was still doubt she could trust him. The note had been too cruel, the mercenary's words too cutting. Even if it was all a lesson, she still felt the slash of the whip. Her father's rejection was a cut and she didn't know if it would ever heal.

And if she did reject him, where did that leave her? With no coin, no shelter. No skills to get her through the rest of her existence. No one would hire a woman who could throw a dagger. She couldn't clean, sew, cook. She knew nothing of men. She didn't own a gown with skirts to toss for anyone. Moreover, with her scars, what price could she charge?

And in the darkest of her days, when starvation or cold got the best of her, she'd have no dreams of a warrior who whistled. No man who was good because even that was gone. Eldric was a lie.

Eldric, who would recover from the poison, who would pursue her once again, his vengeance fiercer because she had escaped. She'd ensure it would be that much more difficult to catch her again. She wouldn't be lulled next time because there was a part of her that believed she had wanted him to catch her in the tree. But not now. Not ever again.

To survive she'd need the protection of her father's force once again. Could she join now knowing that he might reject her once again?

She liked to pretend she was wiser now. No, she was wiser. She could take his protection, but she wouldn't do it blindly. There was more here than just herself now and that posed a problem. She had come to rescue her sister, to escape Eldric. Yet…her father compelled her as he always did. He was her father. Her family. He might have rejected her, but she now knew she hadn't truly rejected him. The child complicated everything, but perhaps…perhaps she didn't need to be alone.

'I did feel the sting of your lesson, Father,' she said. 'Very much.'

His lips curved. 'And?'

'It is a lesson I do not want again,' she answered. The conviction of her voice did not waver. And it wouldn't as long as she kept to the truth.

He rested his elbows on the chair's arms and steepled his fingers against his lips, but it did not hide his quick smile. 'That pleases me very much.'

'It pleases me to please you,' she said. Again the truth.

'Of course, you know I cannot completely trust you now.' He waved his fingers. 'Did you think it would be that easy? You'd find me, you'd offer a few words telling of your inconvenience? You haven't even apologised.'

Inconvenience. The months had been sheer torture for her, but the word was a testament to the difficulty of pleasing this man.

She sank to the floor, clasped her hands behind her back and bowed her head. If he wanted to whip her again, he could. She'd let him. 'I am sorry, dear Father. I was sorry the day that I displeased you. But in the weeks, months since then, there is no word in all the lands to represent my sorrow for your displeasure. So, I offer all that I have left: me. My service, my skills, my body from now until my death. And if you so wish, I will haunt all your enemies for all eternity.'

He uncrossed his legs, but she did not look up. Not

even when he stood and circled her. How easy he could take a dagger to her. How easy he could end her life, but she kept her hands clasped. If he attacked, she couldn't defend herself in time.

He would know this. Perhaps that was why he took a dagger to her neck, held the point there until he pricked her skin. Until she bled, the hot trickle sliding down along her collar and dripping to the floor.

Still, she held steady and did not defend herself. Still, she remembered Eldric holding the blade to her neck, but not damaging her even when his anger was at its height.

That memory hurt worse than the sting of her father's blade. Eldric might have never permanently harmed her body, but he had destroyed her far worse.

The release of the blade stopped the sting, but not the trickle of blood that took several more moments.

'Very well, first daughter.' She waited until he sat again before raising her head.

She expected his expression to hold a mocking victory, or a fatherly gleam of pride. Instead, he looked paler than before, his wide eyes swirling emotions that were partly controlled, partly wild. As if something she'd done scared him. She had done what she had always done with him: submit. Why would he be looking at her this way now?

'Have I suffered enough, Father? From the cold, from the lack of food. With no protection. Without your firm hand to guide me. Has the blood I spilled here pleased you?'

'Perhaps.' Again he steepled his fingers to his mouth.

She wasn't deterred by the word, not with the slight tremble in his right hand. 'If it pleases you, may I travel with you once again? May I climb the dark trees and protect my father's camp?'

His expression stayed the same. She didn't need to know his emotions, she just needed to know his actions. Needed to control her own. Just because she was within her father's care once again didn't mean she'd forget these last months.

'You may protect your father's camp. You may not protect me. You are not trustworthy as yet, first daughter. That right must be earned.'

If she was to protect the camp, but not him... 'Will my father not be attending camp?'

'That is no concern of yours. Just know, with reservations, you are now in the fold once again. You should be pleased.'

Standing, she laced her fingers behind her back. A reminder of what he liked when he whipped her.

His eyes lowered to her chest. Stayed there. 'Yes, very pleased, and your *protection* will please my camp.'

His voice, his eyes—nothing about either of them had changed from before. This was her father. Or at least, the father she'd had. The one she knew the best. But Cressida had been in another's company and now she could compare her father to Eldric. Neither good, but...her father's gaze was not natural. His words were innocuous, the meaning of them depraved.

And Cressida realised everything. Her posture was not reminding him of her submission to him, but that she was a woman. The outline of her breasts stark against her tunic and he watched her. Watched her as he had been doing these last few years.

Her hands, clasped behind her, shook.

# Chapter Fourteen

To think for one brief moment being before him she'd almost, almost, truly returned to his care. His voice, his attention. He'd almost turned her again. This man wasn't good. No matter how much she longed for it, no matter how much she wished otherwise. He meant to give her to the camp and, now she realised with the darkening of his eyes as they rested along her body, he might have kept her to himself not for her safety, but for him…as a man.

The roil of her stomach wasn't anger, it was sickness. She breathed through her mouth, calmed the shaking of her body.

Her sister was now in his care. Her sister was to be raised as she had been, to be loved, to be… Never!

How long had she heard the rumour and denied it existed? How many months had the child been exposed to the abomination before her? Was it too late?

Her sister…maybe…she hoped upon hope because she was so young that the child was untainted by her father. Didn't he say she came from a happy home?

Whatever it took, by whatever means, she'd protect her sister. Protect her and get her far, far away.

'If it pleases you, I will protect your camp even in your absence.' Slowly she disengaged her arms and brought them to her sides. 'And of your other daughter. Will I also be providing protection for her?'

He frowned. 'No one looked after you.'

Save for the nuns in the abbeys, whom she realised must have given her more protection than she'd ever realised. And all this time, she and her father had greatly mocked them.

'But you stated she is from a happy home. That would make her weaker than me, who has had the benefit of your training,' she said, playing into his ego.

'True.' He turned contemplative. 'They shouldn't have been happy. I sired a babe and the woman married and built a home.'

'That angered you,' she said. He'd want the woman he raped to be unhappy, alone, scared. Was that how her mother had been when he found her and killed her?

He wagged a finger at her. 'You know me so well, Daughter, but their happiness was merely an annoyance. What angered me was the environment she lived in. A hut in a valley? A mix of clans, a tiny village. No strength, no wealth. I didn't breed with a commoner. I never would. But she'd married one. I could never tolerate such an existence for my offspring!'

'But you did not take her then. I would have helped you!' She made her voice as conciliatory as possible.

'Unfortunately, she was too well protected and I couldn't rid myself of the mother and husband without some distraction. Thus, I involved more mercenaries than I'd have liked.'

Cressida's stomach flipped. 'When was this?'

'It was Doonhill. Don't you remember? The King was already in a rage over Scotland and sanctioned that massacre in Berwick. So I thought I'd have one myself.' Her father shook his head. 'No, that's right, you weren't with me.'

If she had been, would she have betrayed her father and saved her sister's new family?

He exhaled. 'Because I had to involve my men, it became complicated. I didn't want her killed, she was mine and therefore worthy of life. But it wasn't necessary to keep the child since I had you. All these decisions to make when my lookouts warned me of riders approaching, so I left her.'

He grabbed the nearest goblet and sniffed the contents inside. 'I'll confess I thought it a weakness that I didn't kill her, but now realise, with your betrayal, it was fortuitous.'

Her father was a madman. She had been raised by a monster. Why hadn't she seen it before? Maybe she had. Maybe she was fascinated by Eldric's strength and loyalty because her father had none. She must save her sister, but to do so, she'd have to lead him where she wanted him to go.

'Now that I am with you, we could leave her again.'

His eyes narrowed. 'Jealous, Cressida?'

The widening of her eyes wasn't false—he never said her name—but she used it to keep her appearance innocent. 'Your daughter is my sister and family. What is her name?'

He took a deep sip and wiped his mouth with the side of his hand. 'Can't remember girls' names. Why couldn't I have bred men? It doesn't matter. I'll change her name, just as I changed yours.'

She went cold. Cressida. She'd change her name if she lived through this. She almost laughed. She wasn't going to live. Her only hope was to free the child before the end so she wouldn't be raised by this monster.

'You took me, named me. Weren't you disappointed I was a girl? She's a girl and too young yet to train. She seems…burdensome now.'

He tapped the goblet against his palm. 'You are jealous! I like that. I like that very much. No, we will not leave her behind. And… I'm…yes, I want you to take care of her. Any harm to her and it'll be your life. But it is too soon, isn't it? I may need—'

He stood suddenly, held up his hand. 'Did you hear that?'

Irritated at herself for obeying him, she listened. When she heard nothing, she wanted to fight his authority, but she was playing a game she intended to win. 'Do you want my protection now, Father? I can go outside and investigate.'

He gave her an enigmatic look and strode towards the door.

She didn't care what was happening outside, she needed more time to convince him. 'I can give you protection the way I always have before.'

He looked to the door, but no sounds broke through. He cupped the goblet once again. 'My men are next door; they'll provide me enough. And you…betrayed me. I've got a scar because of you. I don't even know if you're worthy of being in the fold.'

She'd followed her father blindly until that day. But seeing Mairead Buchanan brandish her weapon, hear her grief over her brother as she accused Cressida's father of his death…she hadn't been able to release her arrow. For one, it was true. Her father's man had killed the brother who had somehow got hold of the dagger hiding the Jewel of Kings within its handle. And for another, at her distance and hidden away, Cressida could only hear every other word exchanged. But it was the way Mairead said it. With fire and vehemence, with desperation. Cressida had felt Mairead's agony, her wrath. She…had felt. Thus, when her father raised his blade to Mairead, Cressida released her arrow and struck her father. Just a graze, but enough to stop him and let the woman and the man she was with escape.

Something inside Cressida woke up at Mairead's voice that day. She didn't fully understand it then; she did now. As she faced her father, as she truly understood all that he was, a roiling of emotions flooded her as well. Now, she felt all too much.

She wished, with everything in her, she could brandish a dagger. Instead, she needed to think of her sister, to hold back and have him believe she was his once again. And, when the time was safe for her sister, to release an arrow into her father's black heart.

Her arrow.

'I did not mean to scar you, Father. I released that arrow to remind you.'

'A reminder?'

'You controlled that village. You didn't need that

woman or the man trying to protect her. She didn't know what she was saying, she was grieving for her brother. Her death would have been a complication.'

'That woman was Mairead Buchanan, as you well know, and she held the secret to the Jewel of Kings. Her brother stole the dagger holding that gem.'

'That gem is just a legend. Who believes in legends any more?'

He scoffed. 'The King of England does. He believes in Excalibur and wants that gem so he can rule Scotland. Doesn't matter what we believe. And you knew how important it was.'

'You weren't going to give it to the King, you were giving it to the Warstones.'

His wide eyes gazed rabidly around them. 'Quiet!' Her father brandished the goblet over his head as if to strike her. 'Spies everywhere and you say their name.'

She had said it because she knew it would rile him. 'If they come, I will protect you, not that child.'

'Hmm,' he said. 'Almost believable.' He lowered the goblet and stepped back. His eyes still looked around him, searching for their enemies, no doubt.

Despite herself, she listened just as hard as he, but heard nothing.

'You forget, however, that I know you too well,' he said. 'My men said there was a man who accompanied you. Were you captured or was this person an ally?'

Person. Her father would have gleefully commented if he'd known the identity of her captive. The fact he didn't know about Eldric was a traitorous relief. She didn't owe any loyalty to Eldric now and she'd prove that.

'Captured by a man who thought to ransom me.'

He glanced at her clothing. Her reasoning was sound. Everything explaining Eldric wouldn't be. Her father had sent her to kill him. If her father knew she yearned for him, he'd never take her back and she could never save her sister.

'You've never been captured before. A man who knew you?'

'A man who believed me an enemy and to him I am. It was Eldric of Hawksmoor.'

Her father let out an almost gleeful chortle. 'That took time.'

'Time, but now it's done and I sought you out immediately.'

'A true penance.' He cocked his head. 'There's that sound again.'

'Your men are next door. The walls were always thin. If there is trouble, one of them would have come here.'

'True. They are good men. Not the best. You were trained better. Which always made me wonder why you didn't immediately kill that spy.'

'I shot my arrow three times at that man.'

'Yes, but three times you grazed him. That first time, you merely killed his friend. Hardly a satisfying end.'

His words were a stab to her chest. If Thomas hadn't moved at that moment, she could erase Eldric's grief! Eldric, who didn't deserve her guilt. How long must she remind herself of that?

'Isn't one English warrior as good as another?' she said.

'But something wasn't right about that either. I saw your arm, you weren't aiming for his friend. I think it was an accident. And as for the other two times…to miss your target twice more? I couldn't suffer it! I had to let loose my own weapons to kill the others.'

'Why didn't you kill Eldric?'

'Everything I do is to train you so you can become a better warrior than any we face. I ordered it and therefore you were required to kill him. The others felled by my own hand were simply to ease my annoyance.' He smiled. 'But now my annoyance has ended since you are here after he captured you. How did you finally kill Edward's spy?'

'He hid my weapons and, when I could, I gave him a tincture.'

'Poison. Well done.' He eyed the dried blood on her neck. 'I've created you well. Yet…why did you harm me that day I faced the Buchanan and Colquhoun? Me, the one who loved you most. We were close to finishing our mission. I would have laid the world at your feet.'

Always back to that day. Her father wouldn't understand if she told him she was brimming with Mairead's grief and frustration. There was nothing she could say. She'd already bled for him this day. The sting in her neck from his dagger wasn't enough, her poisoning of Eldric barely registered. What else ever satisfied Sir Richard when his anger was at its peak?

Ah.

'Take out your dagger, Father.' Turning to her side, keeping her gaze on him, Cressida knelt. Felt the unforgiving cold of the floorboards seep into her knees. This wasn't like before when she apologised. Now she knew she had to do more.

Sweat pricked her back as unwanted memories lashed her heart. All these years and the feel of this posture was familiar. She swore she felt the cuts against her back all over again. She'd suffer them as many times as she had to, to rescue a child from the fate she'd been met.

'What do you play at?' he said.

She lifted her tunic to show him her back. 'Many a winter I was left in the trees by your camp, but for the first time in my life, I felt the cold. You won't trust me, so I will do what I must to secure that trust once again.'

He dropped his empty goblet, she heard the whisper of a released dagger. 'Yes,' he said. 'Yes, this pleases me very much.'

His voice was steady...but his eyes held that maniacal gleam of victory and that look she understood now. Lust.

She shivered again. Braced herself for whatever he'd do to her. Now that she fully understood this man, whatever he decided, whatever action committed, would scar her back...and her soul.

But she'd do anything to save her sister, for the chance to return her to a happy home. One that could never be Cressida's.

When she felt the prick this time, she knew, absolutely knew, he would slice along the scars he'd already made. She slowed her heart. Exhaled and prepared for the worst.

An explosion of splintered wood!

Her father spun, sliced her back. 'What have you brought to my—?'

The door slammed open and Eldric stormed into

the room. Dark clothing, even darker expression. His hair unbound, his blue eyes blazing.

A vengeful angel and one who was not welcome.

## Chapter Fifteen

Eldric almost collapsed the moment he took in the room. Cressida kneeling, a man with a dagger, the bright stream of blood trickling down the pale curve of her spine. The angry welt of the freshly stitched wound a glaring reminder of what she already suffered.

'No!' Leaping over the space, ramming his elbow into her captor's weapon arm, shoving him to the floor.

Why he didn't kill him immediately he didn't know. Instinct? Cressida's warning gasp?

A gasp he knew with utter certainty wasn't for his well-being, as he raised his gaze to her. Her pale hair was ruthlessly plaited back, her expression absolutely devoid of any emotion. Gone was the elusive vulnerability that had once captivated him. This wasn't the woman he'd held, touched, kissed. Everything in her was as still and silent as death.

This woman was one he'd never truly met. She was as he always imagined her being: the Archer. His enemy, a nemesis, a killer, her demeanour as iron-clad and cutting as the weaponry she wielded.

Except…except her tunic was still hitched around her hips where she had pulled it up to present her back to the man he had captured beneath his body.

He ruthlessly dug his knee into her father's shoulders. The man's grunt was merely a low chuckle. He hitched his arms further back and revelled in the hiss.

'Release him, warrior, or I would think you mean ill will to us both and will act accordingly.'

Her voice. When had she ever spoken to him in such a cultured monotone? Even when she pretended to be a healer, there was a softness to her. When she became Cressida she swayed him with the emotion in every syllable that fell from her lips.

When he said the words he should never have said, her words wobbled, then shouted her disappointment. Now she was only empty glare and empty words.

How long had he been incapacitated by her potion, delayed by the search and the mercenaries he fought to gain entry? What had she endured in the time he couldn't get to her?

His eyes locked on hers. 'You poisoned me. Left the ship. This is your father, isn't it? I have him beneath my knee. Tell me what to do.'

Her eyes widened. 'What to do? I thought it was clear, when I fed you that tincture, what I desired from you. I poisoned you just as you expected I would.'

She'd poisoned him to keep him on the ship to protect him from this insignificant man, from the mercenaries whom he'd already dispatched. There was no danger. They simply needed to retrieve the child and return to the ship. There he could apologise to her. Explain what a fool he'd been.

He'd heard the exchange between father and daughter. The secrets revealed! He needed to tell her his secrets. Tell her everything.

But what to do when she acted so at odds with who she truly was? He was here—couldn't she see that the danger was over? He scanned the room; listened for any outside disruption. Nothing. Yet her expression never changed. Did she know something he did not? He would proceed with caution.

'I never expected poison,' he said. 'Nor was it something I wanted.'

A slight curve to her lips that did not soften her eyes. 'I poisoned you as *I* always wanted. As you deserved.'

Her eyes. There was what he was looking for and hoping never to see.

He was a fool. An utter fool. This woman before him wasn't cold and distant because she was hiding some scheme, because she played some game. It was because he had hurt her. His words he never should have said, that he could never take back, had done this to her.

The man attempted to rise. Cressida's attention went to him.

'Release my father, warrior, or else you'll wish the poison had done it's foul deed.'

Her father, who had held a dagger to her back, who had injured her already. A trail of dried blood curved like a macabre necklace along the pale column of her neck.

Release this man after all she had shared, after what he'd done, what Eldric knew he would do again? This man who'd kidnapped a child and meant to do them all harm.

He wanted, needed, to deny her. But he'd only deny the Cressida from before. This woman was not she. Until he apologised for the rest of their lives, he needed to grant her what she desired. Her father. A man who, no matter how foully, had raised her.

With a curse, Eldric released him and stood in front of the exit. Cressida grabbed a table linen and went to her father, felt along the arm he'd pummelled and twisted.

'It's not broken,' she said, wrapping the linen around it.

The man remained on the floor, cradling his limb, a sweat on his brow.

There was some resemblance between them. Their height, the pale hair, though his was much darker than his daughter's and his eyes much paler. Unlike his daughter, however, everything about him was withered. An odd glint to his eyes, though he was in pain.

Eldric had just fought five men far more trained than he'd ever encountered before. If he hadn't had the element of surprise, he wouldn't have succeeded. But he hadn't felt fear at all, not once, until now. This diminished man with colouring similar to Cressida, but with none of her elegance, none of the warmth in her gaze, but a fanatical sheen, chilled him to the bone.

'She was supposed to kill you,' the man gasped. 'Help me up.'

'Forgive me, Father.' Cressida supported her father until he stood.

Eldric glanced to the woman who seemed infuriated by his arrival. He didn't know what to expect when he pursued her, certainly not her rushing into his arms because he'd rescued her, though a part of him wished for nothing else. But this wasn't anything he could fathom. Siding with the man who had harmed her, asking for his forgiveness! He needed to step carefully. To hold back.

But the battle roared in his veins. His sword hand twitched. He wanted nothing more than to rage and fight. To finish this. He must, he must hold!

'The amounts of poison it takes to harm me varies, but the quantity is not for the weak-hearted. Most would get it wrong.' He addressed her father, said what needed to be clarified in case…in case this miniscule man intended harm. Cressida might side with her father, but he would continue to protect her.

'Pity. Healing is such an inaccurate occupation and it would have made it simpler if you were dead already.' His gaze swung to the door. 'How did you get in here?'

'He's felled our men, Father,' Cressida said.

The man's eyes turned calculating. One man. One trivial man and no other enemies to surprise him, but somehow Eldric didn't like his odds of surviving this encounter. Not with Cressida acting as she was.

She had been…she had been kneeling before this man, presenting her scarred back to her father's dagger. Now, she stood beside him as if to protect him. And all this time she'd known Eldric had killed the other mercenaries. Eldric clutched his sword. Willed his arm to remain still.

Cressida's father was evil incarnate. There could be no good in him. None. He'd harmed her! Even now her tunic was plastered to her back from the cut he had given her. This man would be dead but for the woman who stood beside him.

Again, he had to re-evaluate everything and came to only one conclusion. She knew everything and there was nothing to hide. He'd apologise, but only in private, when he could confess. Declare all of himself. Dedicate his life to her. God's heart, he wanted that now!

'Tell me what to do with him,' he demanded of her. 'What is his fate?'

'Do what with whom, Eldric of Hawksmoor?' The man smirked. 'Hmm, hardly polite, my not introducing myself. I am Sir Richard Howe, at the English King's demand.'

Cressida gasped.

'Don't worry, dear, he won't live long enough to tell the tale,' Howe said.

'Your men are dead,' Eldric said. 'How do you think to rid yourself of me when I intend to live long enough to kill you?'

'Now I know those were the sounds I heard earlier. The ones you dismissed, my daughter.'

'I gave him the tincture held in my boot. The one you perfected. I thought it stronger than that. I don't know how he found me. Nor is he welcome.'

'Where are our manners? Of course he is welcome. I had always wanted to meet one of Edward's privileged men.' Howe wagged his finger. 'You understand, though I attempted to prevent it, it was only a matter of time before we met. I know friends of yours and have heard many tales.'

Eldric feared to ask whom he knew. Were they

merely other of Edward's spies, or the friends he protected, Robert and Hugh?

Everything about this meeting seemed fated. There were too many coincidences, too many ties between them. Years of entanglements until they were all snared. Trapped. Is that why Cressida acted the way she did—was she trapped? Where was his training? As a spy, he knew to observe, to wait, but the longer he stood, the more the warrior side of him emerged.

'They were clever like you,' Howe continued. 'How did you find us?'

He shrugged. 'Fortune.'

No matter how much training he had, Eldric wasn't prepared for the outcome before him. When he had woken, he knew Cressida had fled the ship.

After a few choice words with the Commander, who pointed the way, he came to the cluster of houses. All the while he searched, he worried she could be somewhere else beyond, where he couldn't find her.

The desperation, the words he had stupidly accused her with pounded in his head, his heart. One look. One look from her as she accused him of being a coward was all it took for him to remember who she was and who he needed to be for her. Not some naive warrior, but a man prepared to make the difficult decisions for her...with her.

He searched and searched until he heard her voice, heard words that he couldn't quite comprehend. So he stepped closer to listen, which was a mistake. Five men with swords rushed out of the attached house. Mercenaries who had to be killed.

But no matter how brutal the fight, no matter how

much he was knocked back, none of it affected him as significantly as this seemingly simple conversation. None of them affected him like the truth.

He'd heard almost all the conversation between Cressida and her father. Heard about the Jewel of Kings, about Warstones and Buchanans and Colquhouns.

Heard that Cressida hadn't killed his friends. Thomas! It had been but an accident!

And even with all these certainties, he could tell her none of it. Not with her father watching them both, not without understanding what he'd landed himself in.

The father must be attended to before he could have Cressida again. He knew what mistakes he had made, but he didn't know what had transpired while he recovered. He didn't know what her decision would be when it came to him, her father or the sister they'd agreed needed rescuing.

But his patience, his training, was fraying when faced with the ultimate truth: he didn't know whether he'd get a chance to love her.

Cressida felt the dull prick in the back of her neck. The sharp wetness of her tunic sticking to the fresh wound in her back. Everything else about her was numb.

Eldric was here. Eldric who rushed in, took down her father, killed his mercenaries, all as if he cared. His eyes, blue, clear, looking on her with determined devotion. Then the confusion as she stared blankly at him, determined not to reveal any of the treacherous emotions overwhelming her when it came to him.

Now, now he looked as if he valued her. As if she

was some prize he could never win. Cressida refused to believe any of it. Yet she hated he was here confusing her. He thought her soul beyond repair, that she could never be good. Never…right.

Eldric had told her that, so why was he here?

Worse, she wanted to poison him again, but not to kill him as she told her father. She wanted to save him. Foolish man! She'd done it to protect him. To keep him on that ship, to never become entangled with her father, his spies, the Warstones. His insurmountable alliances. Even if her father died, there would be others and more after that.

When Eldric took her to the Tower, he might as well be right along beside her.

All the while, for her sister's sake, she stood beside her father. Because her father was cunning, because Eldric had killed some men, but she wasn't certain he'd dispatched them all. Because she needed more answers from her father.

But her intentions wavered under the useless hope Eldric's presence created. She couldn't help but think they had a chance. He'd killed the mercenaries. Her father's arm was harmed and he was no match against Eldric. Better still, the child should still be safely ensconced in the attached house.

What chance? Eldric had said those words to her. He'd made clear he didn't want her.

She couldn't trust either of them. She only had herself and her sister only had her. She would not fail the child.

'Fortune brought you here!' Her father laughed. 'We'll see how fortuitous it is for you soon enough, shall we? In the meantime, would you care for wine? I'm afraid I don't have any food left.'

'Father, what would you have me do?' Cressida said, pleased her voice remained devoid of her thoughts.

Eldric's gaze went to her. His stance ready to fight, his eyes... Was he pleading? 'I won't dine here. I'm... done with this. What's going on? Tell me.'

'You can leave, Eldric, and never return,' she said, 'or, since you dispatched my father's men, I can fight you.'

'Cressida. I'm here—'

'To rescue her?' Howe laughed. 'She's my daughter, though I have toyed with the idea of not keeping the responsibility.'

'No,' Eldric said. 'God's bones, this is an untellable situation. You know those men are gone. What more do you need to end whatever this is? Is it the child?'

'The child!' Howe's voice cracked. 'What do you know of the child? First Daughter, what have you done?'

Curse Eldric, he'd made it worse. 'Eldric was there when the mercenaries came and I read your message.'

'He knows too much,' Howe said. 'This man, out of all men, cannot walk around knowing—'

'Why not?' Eldric interrupted. 'Is it because my identity has something to do with hers?'

'I won't let you take her back,' Howe said.

'That's all I intend to do. Where is she?'

'Stop!' Cressida said. This was unbearable. Her heart couldn't take it. 'You'll leave us alone. You'll leave all of us alone. You must go. What are you even doing here? There is no reason for you to be here. Do you know what—?'

'I'm done. Blood splatters my clothes and I would spill more, but I refuse to simply stand here. You never stop. We can't go back, or spin around each other as we have. Is he holding you to ransom? Whatever was said, it can be undone. I'm here now. The men are dead. There's only us.'

'How are the scars on your back, First Daughter? Finish him.'

'Leave,' she begged. She was believing, hoping that Eldric cared. It…sounded as though he did and it hurt, it *hurt*.

'Kill him, Daughter, as I require you. As I have always required from you.'

Sick rose in her throat. She'd do anything for her sister. Was this what it came down to? To kill the man she now knew she loved, the man who had hurt her, for a child she'd never met, but who was her family?

# *Chapter Sixteen*

Howe clapped.

Cressida jumped and he started laughing.

'You're protecting him! Why didn't I see it before? Three times failing to pierce him with your arrows. I was fooled. Fooled because you marked him. You didn't even kill the men flanking him. I had to.'

He looked wildly around, a harsh laugh escaping him. 'Oh, this is almost divine in its familiarity.'

Her father's pleasure was exactly what she feared. When he was like this, people died.

'This isn't familiar, Father. I'm not protecting him.'

'You are. You are. You are. How did I get here? Hmm.' He pointed. 'You! Always you. You've put me here again. All my mercenaries dead and before me is a woman protecting a man. You might as well be brandishing a blade at me like that Buchanan woman had. Even your voice has that tinge of desperation as if I had killed someone, but who do you grieve for? Ah! You worry over the child!'

Her hesitation caused this. Eldric caused this! Her

father wouldn't ever accept an apology. Spilling her blood, carving more scars wouldn't ever satisfy him now.

She couldn't simply bide her time until it was safer to take her sister. To protect her became infinitely harder. Impossible! She pulled the dagger at her side.

'Cressida,' Eldric said. She heard the warning in his voice. Hated it. His pleading eyes were a lie, all of it false. He had no rights to warn her. No rights at all. She'd lain with him. Loved him, and he…believed she was evil just like her father. That she could never be good. She knew better now.

He was the coward. Spouting words he shouldn't have that made everything worse. Storming in here as if a simple rescue was all that was needed. It was up to her to make the difficult decisions. Again. Alone. For her sister, she must.

'Look at your arm trembling,' Howe said. 'What has become of you? How far have you fallen?'

'Fallen, Father? Fallen? I'll show you who will fall.'

'No!' Eldric cried out.

Ice. Cold. Dread. Eldric realised his impatience, his need to hold and protect this woman had tipped some balance he didn't understand. He warned himself to hold on, to learn from her, and instead…twice a fool!

Howe cackled. 'I should have drowned you when I could. Ended you. You worthless, ungrateful child. You foul, low-born, unwanted—'

Eldric charged, slamming his fist against her father's head. The force spun him over and he crumpled to the ground.

Cressida shrieked, jumped around Eldric, her dagger aiming for her father's heart.

'No!' He grabbed her shoulders, gripped her wrist and forced the dagger away from them. 'Drop it, Cressida, it's over.'

Steel in her eyes and death in her skill. She could physically do it. When he met her, he would have said she could do it without a backward glance. He knew better now. It would kill her to harm her father.

She wrenched her arm; he didn't let go. 'He won't stop until we stop him. You don't know him. I do.'

'I may not know him, but I know you. Though he breathes, he's down, Cressida. His head bleeds from my fist. That is all that will happen to him. Let…let the King decide his fate.'

'I'm his daughter. I will decide whether he lives or dies.'

'Truly. Defenceless like this? I won't have it. You are too good for this; it would harm you and—'

'Harm me! Nothing can be done to me that wasn't already done. Protecting myself when there's nothing to protect will solve nothing. You're a fool, Eldric. Naive! This isn't some simple battle. Some right and wrong. The enemy isn't felled; all is not solved because he's transported to the Tower. I can only do what must be done. I must—' She stopped. Her eyes, darting to the wall attached to the men.

'The men are felled,' he said. 'No one is coming.'

'But the child.'

'Do you know where she is?'

'My sister was in that room where the men were.'

She paled. 'You didn't see her? Are you certain you got them all?'

She yanked; he didn't let go. 'You bastard. Release me. If she's gone, and now I can't ask my father questions, I'll have your head!'

'Your father deserved my fist and then some. I will never tolerate cruelty towards you.'

He'd killed that mercenary in the inn, too. And the way Eldric said it, she could almost believe him. Almost, but never again. 'Let me go! You shouldn't be here. You have no right to be here!'

'Well, I am and there's someone else here who needs us, so control yourself, Archer. I won't let you go so you can kill him. And if there is the child next door, we're risking her life with your inability to give up.'

He felt her stiffen, braced himself for the blow. Instead, she relaxed. 'Take me, then.'

He took her dagger, tucked it into his belt. Watched her stare at her father for one, two heartbeats, her entire body ridged, her fists clenched.

'Let's go,' he repeated, easing his grip, ready to defend her again if he must.

Cursing, she rushed past him and out the front door, then stopped. 'You left all the bodies just lying around! A trail for anyone to see! To know we were here!'

'I was trying to save you.'

'Save me!' She slammed into the house. Left enough space for him to follow, but she didn't step any further inside.

Everything was quiet. Too quiet. Terror froze Cressida's feet.

Curse her father. Could he have sent a signal that

she missed? Was it possible her sister wasn't in this house any more? Before she hid in the rafters, she'd only had a chance to glance in. Saw the five men, the small child sitting on the floor between them.

Seemingly well fed, dressed appropriately. Clothed. Content. But no one was playing with her, acknowledging her, and she was so very, very quiet, Cressida's heart had broken for her. She remembered those forced silences. Remembered how she was protected, but allowed to talk to no one.

'Take care of the bodies,' she bit out as silently as she could.

'We need to get your sister.'

Her sister might already be gone. An unknown mercenary taking her far, far away, some place she didn't know. It'd been luck her father stayed here. Most likely his arrogance, thinking he'd controlled her still. She wouldn't get that chance again.

'Drag the bodies inside and hide them in that room. The light comes. People will wake.'

'Cressida, let me—'

She glared at Eldric. If her sister was gone, she'd never forgive him. Never. 'Now.'

His nostrils flared, but his eyes… He pivoted and left the house.

Cressida released her held breath. The house was too silent. Tears pricked. Was it all for nothing? Slowly, forcing her feet to shuffle forward, dread weighing down her heart, she entered the adjacent room. And there, right in the centre, right where she was once surrounded by five deadly mercenaries, sat a little girl. Abandoned.

She must have made some noise and given away her position because the child's head whipped around and, for the first time, Cressida saw into her eyes— extremely pale eyes, though their shade was different— and knew with certainty she was her sister. A cascade of white hair like a cloud around her head. Exactly like hers had once been.

Cressida went to her knees and sat very still while the little girl turned towards her, a look of extreme wariness on her small face.

Everything in her trembled. The relief, the fear. This was a child. A child she needed to protect. Her father alive, but an enemy for evermore. With all his alliances, he could and would send the worst of mankind after them. She'd never know who was an enemy or whom to trust. And it was just her, just her to protect this young—

'Cressida,' Eldric called a warning from the other room.

Cressida wouldn't speak. Didn't want to raise her voice and scare the child any more than she already was. And she was scared, her entire body was trembling.

Then Eldric was there, at her back, standing in the doorway, and the little girl swayed, her chubby fist going to the ground.

Cressida wanted to straighten her up again. To use the hand that held a dagger to help this child. She couldn't. She just watched as the child found her balance.

'Cressida.'

'Eldric,' she said. 'Stop.' She was trying to make a

connection. She refused to snatch the child and run out of there, though every instinct told her to return to her father, to finish what was started.

'Try Maisie,' he said.

The child's head whipped up and wide pale green eyes stared at Eldric as if wishing he'd talk again.

'What?' she whispered, keeping her eyes on her sister.

'I believe that's her name, Cress. Use it.'

'What did you call me?' She shook her head. 'Never mind. How do you know her name is Maisie?'

At that, at that name, the little girl's face crumpled and, before Cressida could reach for her, before she could provide another word, the child stood on wobbly legs and barrelled straight into her arms.

Warmth straight through all her defences, her body, her heart. Warmth after a lifetime of being cold. Was this what being raised in a happy household felt like? She'd never let her go.

'Cress,' Eldric said.

'Why do you keep calling me that?'

'Look at me.'

Over the shoulder of her sister she did.

'Your father's disappeared,' he said.

## *Chapter Seventeen*

The pull of the oars against the choppy waters didn't ease the raging force inside Eldric. Wrath, possession. Shame.

If Cressida wanted to kill her father, he wanted to do it a thousand times more. But clashing like waves against all that shame and need for the woman who rushed into death's den was the absolute certainty that nothing of her father flowed in her veins.

Cressida might share Howe's traits, but her heart, her soul was nothing like that man. Not even a full-drawn breath in that room and he knew that man was evil. The insidious kind that no matter how much you shove it away, like some oily entity it creeps back in another form.

And she had faced him alone! Why?

Because he had sent her there. Rejected her. Said—

He needed to beg for her forgiveness. To grovel. Spout words that wouldn't be adequate no matter how many times he repeated them.

Over it all was this unending possessiveness a thousand times stronger now that she clutched her sister against her chest. Defending them. Dying for them. Waving his sword and roaring to all the entities in all the world didn't come close to describing what he felt beating in his chest.

Cressida must have sensed how close he was to the edge for when he grabbed her and Maisie, then ran out of the camp, she hadn't said a word. Was quiet now as he shouted up into the night for the ladder to be thrown down.

Cressida, with Maisie strapped to her, wrapped the rope around her until someone on deck pulled them both up and over the ledge to safety.

Moments passed. Too many of them while he waited for them to throw down the rope. When it finally happened, he noticed the lack of customary loops and knots for such a climb and cursed the wily pirate who meant to detain him. With a leap, he hoisted himself to the top.

Terric was there. When he stayed still and quiet, chin raised, Eldric clenched the oar in his fists before he hurled it into the Commander's gut. To his credit, Terric let the oar hit him before he clasped it.

'Why?' he demanded. Terric knew not to let Cressida off the ship. Knew there was danger. She could have died long before he got to her.

The Commander eased the oar off his stomach and coughed. 'I pointed you to where she went.'

'You shouldn't have let her off the ship and you know it.'

'I am new at this loyalty thing, my friend. Maybe

you can explain what to do when it is shared equally between two?'

Eldric still itched to harm him. 'Some day, you will feel my fist.'

Terric grinned. 'Not today. The child was taken by the healer to get fed and clothed. However, it appears your captive is trying to lower a boat on the other side and I promised to give her a head start.'

Eldric cursed; he couldn't fault his loyalty. 'Eldric. My name is Eldric of Hawksmoor and when this is done, we will have words, Commander!'

'Terric!' he called out, but Eldric was already sprinting across the boat.

'I won't ask if you ever give up, because I know the answer to it,' Eldric said, enclosing her from behind and oddly, gently, extracting her fingers so they didn't burn on the ropes. 'But some day, Archer, you will tell me why.'

His gentleness irritated her. Cressida wrenched her arm out of his and punched him in the heart with the heel of her palm. 'We won't have some day! You let him live. You left him capable of making decisions that will ensure our death. My sister's, too.'

'I didn't let him live,' he said, attempting to grab her free hand. She wouldn't let him. 'You saw his head wound. He bled.'

'Worse! Someone came and extracted him.'

'When would they have done that? We were right next door. I was dragging bodies inside.'

'We were both inside. They could have sneaked past us, or worse, they could have been already in the house and listening to everything my father said. Do you know the information extracted? What that could do?'

'No one was in that room or house. We were both there—when I came in wouldn't they have declared themselves to fight me?'

She poked him. 'You don't know the lengths he goes to train us. I waited in the rafters of his home for hours before he decided to acknowledge my presence.'

He didn't want to think of her training, or what that madman had put her through. They were done with his schemes. Whatever she'd suffered from before was over.

'Let him come. I know what the bastard looks like now. I know exactly who he is.'

She laughed. 'No, you don't. Only I realise who he is, what he is capable of, what he will do.'

'And so you'll kill him?'

He caught her hand, clasped it tightly in his. 'You kill him and another will kill you. I won't have you die.'

She wrenched her fingers free, but he tightened his grip on her palm. 'You don't care for my death!'

'That's not true. We need to talk.'

'No, we don't. I need to find my father and end this.'

'You would leave your sister behind on this ship?'

Her sister. Terrible, horrible decisions left to her. She'd make them. She'd always make them. 'You said her name, and she recognised it. You know who she belongs to. You can take her back to…to her happy home.'

'You believe I'll return her.' She felt his exhale along her cheek. 'You trust me with her.'

'No!'

'Which is it? Either you trust me with your sister, or you don't.'

She didn't know. She knew what she needed to do, what action to take. But for feelings? She wanted to lean and fight against the warm support Eldric provided.

'Cress, there are things I—'

That name. It, too, was contradiction inside her. She loved and hated it. Wrenching free, she jabbed her knuckles just under his ribs. 'My name is Cressida. Greek, meaning treachery. That's what he called me, then made me...made me a treacherous killer! Don't you dare shorten it. Don't you dare make it out that we have endearments. What am I to call you, then?'

Another jab under his ribs had him sidestepping away from her. She immediately felt the cold.

'You can insult me with names many times, I'd welcome them,' he said, 'but we'll talk first!'

'I don't want to talk to you. I want to be away from you! You should have just left me in the tree. Should have just let me bleed out from the back wound instead of stitching me. Should have let me face him on my own as I should have done a long time ago.'

Snarling, she swung and elbowed him in the stomach, then rapped her knuckles where she'd jabbed before. That time, air rushed satisfactorily out of him. 'Felt a bit of that, did you! Good! Maybe you'll feel this as well.'

She locked her ankle around him, grabbed his arm. A simple move would have him flipped to the ground where she could pummel him. Pummel him so he'd stay still, so he wouldn't put her sister, himself, in danger.

She twisted and jerked back.

Eldric hummed in satisfaction. 'Not going any-where, Archer.'

She wrenched again. Nothing. He held fast and now she was locked with him. A manoeuvre she'd executed a thousand times didn't work because Eldric was a thousand times larger.

Gritting her teeth, she screamed in frustration. He whipped around until her back was to his front again. And she was bound! But not her feet. She kicked, and kicked, feeling every strike of her heel against his shins.

'Enough!' he growled against her ear which sent shivers down her spine. 'You think you want to fight me. But that's not what you want. There's something else we—'

'He'll kill her. He'll kill you and all the years I spent saving you will be for nought. The one good deed I ever did will be undone. And she'll never get to her family. To be happy again.'

She folded her legs into herself, to land one telling kick that was sure to fell any man. Mountain or not.

'I don't think so, Archer,' he bit out, clasping her left leg and pinning her lower half to his.

Defeated. 'No, let me go.' She squirmed. 'You have to let me go.'

He hissed. Spanned his fingers against her thigh to secure her and stopped them both. The rock-hard heat of his frame, the thick band of his right arm leashed across her chest, his hand secured on her opposite shoulder.

His left arm dropped firm along her body and

locked on the juncture of her left thigh. And higher. Her squirming, his fingers, the grip slipping. His palm cupping now at the juncture and not moving.

'I won't let you go. Neither one of us wants that. It's not a fight you want from me, Cressida. I was a fool, but even I know that now. I know what I want: it's you. It's you.'

Words when she felt the thickness, the insistent heat of his fingers. Could feel the slight tremor there that vibrated through her core.

She couldn't breathe as something akin to shock, then blinding need, flamed through her. Her body acted as it always did. On instinct. She flung her head back against his collarbone, dropped her legs and let Eldric take her weight.

At her capitulation, he groaned, seemed to collapse against her, his cheek rubbing against the top of her head.

'There you go, but not yet, Archer. Not yet, there are words that must be said between us. Words I want to say to you.'

Words! Soft words. Endearing words! 'No!' she cried, jammed her feet into his thighs and kicked off, until she landed on her feet, her hands balanced on the wooden planks. Her eyes darted to her left and right, looking for a way to escape.

The only exit was behind him. She straightened. Readying to dash. She'd fling herself over the side!

If possible, Eldric seemed larger, almost feral. 'The ending of this will be the same, Archer. It was always going to be the same. With you and me. You made me yours when you marked me.'

'To make you go the other direction. Why didn't you go another direction?'

'No more. There are no enemies on board. The babe is safe; you are secured. We begin tonight.'

He lunged, she darted. Not fast enough. His grip like iron around her waist, he strode to the entrance to the below deck. When he got to the doorway, he clasped the ledge above and swung them down into the tween deck.

Another few steps and he got them into their room, the door closed, the latch lowered. Locked. Then he set her down, slowly, steadily, as if he was reluctant to let her go.

It was that, that difference. The tenderness, the just-under-the-surface edge that changed everything for her.

Everything.

'You bastard.' Cressida seethed with hate, with want, and all it was aimed at the infuriating warrior who locked the door and stood in front of it. Trapped again. Why did he keep trapping her?

And worse, all of it worse because he held her as if he wanted her. For a moment, she forgot, she forgot. Never again. 'Let me out of here.'

'You know I won't do that.'

Wishing she had a dagger, she slashed out with her hand. 'What are you doing? I was gone from you. Isn't that what you wanted? A killer like me away from your precious life?'

She threw words instead of arrows, but it didn't feel like enough. The fact he flinched was no relief. She needed more. Spinning, she spotted a candlestick, threw it at him. He dodged and it thunked against the thick wooden wall.

She grabbed the other.

He held up his hands. 'I was wrong!'

'You were wrong finding me and bringing me back here.' She hurled another candlestick.

He darted, but she anticipated it, and the spin got him across his temple.

'My words were… I was wrong.'

He widened his stance, his hands still up. A trickle of blood at his temple. She'd caused that. She'd caused that and was all the madder for being concerned about it. She turned again—the room wasn't full enough with weapons. She didn't care, the act of throwing things helped. So she reached for the wooden basin and chucked it over her head.

He caught it and threw it behind him.

She threw the pillows, the quilt. The chair padding. All of it he caught and set beside him.

Until everything was behind him and she had nothing left, and he carried on watching her. Then slowly, keeping an eye on her, he lifted his foot to his knee and began to unlace his boots.

'What are you doing?'

Eldric's entire focus was the woman in front of him. It would take every bit of thought and reason to get her to stay.

But he had none. Once he knew she was safely on this ship, that her sister was taken care of, his usual ease with the world stripped away, leaving him nothing but a man before a woman. Full of need to hold her, to make sure she suffered no further injuries. The possessiveness inside barely contained. But first, first he needed to tell her, show her, how utterly wrong he had been.

'I am done being a coward.'

'Put your clothes back on.'

## Chapter Eighteen

He loved the imperious way she spoke. So different than when they first met. He knew that fire was in her while she hid it under her lies. Then the trip here, the unsure silences as if she wasn't used to talking. Now he was beginning to know why.

'They're just my boots, Archer.' He tossed the one to the corner of the room. 'Getting nervous?'

'You said—'

He threw his other boot to the wall with a resounding thud. 'And now I'll say just the opposite of all those asinine words that had you rushing out into the night.'

'So you can take me to the Tower.'

'You know I'm not doing that now.'

'I haven't changed.'

'It's me who has. I don't want you to change. Not one freckle off your nose or scar on your body erased. Because you're perfect. Perfect.'

Another mutinous look around him. No doubt calculating how to gain access to the candlesticks behind him. 'That's rather sudden,' she said. 'No time has passed since you thought me a murderer and most of that time you were—'

'Wearing off the draught you gave me, yes.'

She stilled. 'You heard. That's what it was. You heard my father and I.'

He nodded. 'This is what I wanted to tell you. I heard everything. Everything. I understand now and—'

'That's why you're holding me. That's why we're here again and you're taking off your clothes.'

'Only boots, yet.' He reached behind him and yanked off his tunic, felt the curve of his lips as her eyes widened. She wasn't thinking about throwing things at him now.

'Put that back on.'

'No. You're not getting away this time. I heard everything, but that wasn't what made me rush to you. Think, Archer.' He backed up, unfasted the belt around his breeches and pushed them down.

'I was already there. If you hadn't poisoned me and run off, you would know. I understood what you told me before I heard your father's confession. Before I knew for certain you didn't release the arrows that ended Michael's and Peter's lives.' He stepped out of his breeches, until he stood before her only in his braies.

She wasn't saying a word. Not one. He wasn't sure she was breathing except the odd hitches that happened with every bit of clothing he removed.

'Eldric,' she said.

'There you are.' He took a step closer, relief easing his movements when she didn't run away, when she didn't throw things or rail at him. Cressida before him. The Archer. She was fierce, but right now there was that bit of vulnerability in her. That uncommon fragility that made him want to wrap her in the finest of blankets and protect her with everything he was.

'What are you doing?'

'What I should have done when I had you in my arms the first time.' He knelt before her, his head bowed, showing her what he didn't say adequately before. That he was hers, that she could do what she wanted with him. Even walk away.

'No!' she cried and took the remaining step to him, her two hands on the sides of his cheeks. 'Please get up.'

'Not until you forgive me.'

Her hands trembled. 'Eldric, please.'

He liked her saying his name. He raised his head. 'Please what, Archer? You still demanding to leave? I can't stop you.'

'You just did!'

He stayed on his knees, she stayed touching him. 'I can't now. If you run out of here, how could I dress quickly enough, reach you in time? I'm baring myself to you, for you. I want you to stay because *you* want to stay. When I have said everything, if you still want to go. I won't stop you then.'

'And if I leave with Maisie?' she said.

'She's your sister. I'd even tell you where her family is. I just…want a chance to tell you everything.'

'You'd really let me leave?'

He wanted to say no, but this woman knew her own strengths, believed in herself. Was a far better human than he was. Who was he to tell her anything?

'If you…needed to go, I'd let you go.'

Her eyes narrowed. 'You wouldn't want me to.'

'I love you…so, no.'

Her expression went from some crumpled confusion to a frustration that lit everything in her. He wanted to pull her down into his lap and just hold her for the rest of time.

'*These* are the words you say to me,' she said. 'Out of all the words you could choose.'

'These are words you could say as well.'

He said that too easily, as if he already knew the answer. '*If* they were true. You can't love me. You're angry at me.'

As if that would stop him. 'Furious. So many ways I'm furious at you, my hair will be grey by the time I'm finished listing them all. But now, now, you're on this ship, you're safe and I'm dying to hold you in my arms again.'

'You pursued me. You hate me.'

'I hated you before I knew you. Once I caught you, I wanted to keep you.'

Her eyes narrowed. 'You didn't like me then either.'

'Cressida, you're breathtakingly beautiful.' Didn't she know? He wanted to laugh at her mutinous expression. 'But there also was that familiarity which drew me to you. I didn't want to want you, but I did. Very much.'

'That's lust. Doesn't mean—'

'You have to know, after what we shared here, that what we have goes beyond lust. You threw that dagger into the mercenary's chest to protect me.'

'That shows what my feelings were before, not yours.'

Her phrasing hurt, but he deserved it. Her love, her care was so sweetly given. Everything between them new. He'd do anything to earn her trust, her love again, but he knew the Archer and she wouldn't make it easy for him.

'You poisoned me and I came after you before I knew any facts,' he said.

'All these emotions, all this *love*, and you'd still let me go after your confessions.'

'I wouldn't want you to go, but, yes, I would if it's what you want. Contrary to reason, yes. But I am your enemy you protect. We have numerous contradictions when it comes to us, Cressida, but not how we feel.'

'How we feel? How dare you presume I feel anything for you other than anger.'

Cressida took a step back, wobbled. Her legs wouldn't hold her, but all this room had was the small bed, a chair behind Eldric and the strewn bedding on the floor, none of which would do her any good right now.

The bedding especially since Eldric had told her he loved her. So…easily. As if it was a foregone fact and not one she had whispered and prayed for in all her childhood prayers at night.

He loved her and she wasn't sure if what she felt was love any more. What she felt inside her wasn't what she grew up with. That had been some beacon inside her. A lodestone to keep her focused.

But he'd taken that away. Made her doubt and question to the point that her father, for just a moment, had almost convinced her to return to his fold.

She couldn't be trusted with feelings of love, not when Eldric knelt on the bedding where he'd whispered such fervent words. Not when he was almost naked and far too close to her. He knelt, but with his size, he wasn't that much smaller than her. It would be so easy to feel the roughness of his beard, the softness of his lips. To claim a kiss of her own.

She stepped back. His eyes took in her weakness and the slight curve to his lips distracted her.

Everything about him distracted her. It hadn't been that long since she had touched him, kissed him. It hadn't been that long since she had bared her own body to her father for forgiveness. Eldric knew this.

'Put some clothes on. You can apologise, but do it clothed.'

His eyes swept over her, a muscle ticking in his jaw. 'You know what I meant.'

'I'm taking it that way. Just—' She grabbed his tunic, handed it to him. 'Wear this. Say your words. Then I'll see if I can accept your apology.'

He pulled the tunic over his head. 'I have one more request.'

'I didn't know those who begged forgiveness could make demands.'

He held out his hands.

'You're shaking.'

'I'm trembling because my body hasn't caught up with the fact that you're safe. You're safe and alive, and I never want to see a dagger at your back again.'

'Why are you showing me this?'

'I'm kneeling and baring myself. I'm showing my fear because my words, or maybe my lack of words, caused this. I hope my body could tell you more of how I truly feel.'

'Eldric, stand.'

He shook his head.

'I need you to—'

He grabbed her hands and pulled her down to the bedding on the floor. 'Better.'

He said the word as though it wasn't a question. She was uncertain it was better. Eldric seemed larger than he usually was and sitting on the bedding only made her think more about the kisses they had shared, a blush beginning across her chest.

He was a calculating warrior, no doubt he'd use her weakness for him to his advantage.

'You can't sway me this way,' she said. 'I can't trust you again. It's not safe for me.'

He closed his eyes. Swallowed hard. 'Very well. But would you stay long enough to hear me?'

She crossed her legs, her arms. If she had to sit on the bedding, had to look at him, she would do it with the least amount of contact. She couldn't trust herself around him.

'Talk,' she said. Eldric inhaled, but then stopped. 'You won't now?'

'I don't know where to start. My words weren't good before. Do I tell you my feelings or the facts? What do you want to know?'

Eldric was always at ease with the world. His laughter, his friendships. To see him like this…she rather liked it. He deserved any bit of uncomfortableness. As for the feelings…

'Why are you giving me these choices?'

'I never gave you choices before. Tying you to that bed, locking you in this room. Not consulting you about staying at the French port a day longer. So when you poisoned me, I know it was because I gave you no choice but to do that rash act. I hadn't shared everything that motivated me to capture you and I certainly never told you how I felt.'

Her father hadn't given her choices before either. Her father who had betrayed her far worse. Who had made her believe he loved her when, in fact, she had always been a weapon. And that look he gave her, that one that she could only now interpret. How long had he looked at her that way? Cloistered, she had no references to know if people were good any more.

'How can I trust you again?' she said.

'I will tell you everything and then you can decide my fate.'

He shifted, but didn't move away. A part of her knew it wasn't his fault. The room was far too small for two, especially since Eldric was so formidable. She wished there could be more space between them as Eldric's expression turned grave.

'I went after the enemy who killed my friends,' he said. 'I was in pursuit of you when the King sent me to Swaffham to find an English traitor who traded secrets to the Scots. Imagine my surprise when I discovered the traitor was my childhood friend, Hugh of Shoebury.

'Now I wouldn't be very helpful to the King if I didn't garner facts for myself. And I knew that Hugh was also a spy. I also knew that Edward had asked one more person in Swaffham to also find this traitor. That was Alice, whose family had the dance at Fenton Hall.'

'Three spies in one small village?'

'Yes, and Hugh and Alice? They had loved each other since childhood, though it wasn't a love without some obstacles or separation.'

'There's a story there.'

'Oh, yes, and some day I want to tell you how amusing it was watching those two realise their love.'

'I was there.'

'You were and we danced.'

Eldric was looking at her too warmly. Too happily. 'We don't have a story yet.'

'Yet,' he repeated. 'I like that word.'

Too much! 'Tell me more facts.'

He shrugged. The tunic did nothing to cover the breadth of his shoulders.

'How to say this?' he said. 'Hugh was the spy I was sent to capture. Obviously because of our friendship and their past, I and Alice were compromised to ever report him.'

'But you did anyway? After all, he was a traitor.'

'No, because he had a good reason for trading secrets: he was protecting someone.' He nodded. 'I thought that might interest you.'

'Who?'

'A mutual friend, Robert of Dent, who fell in love with a Scottish lass of Clan Colquhoun.'

'There seems to be a—'

'Pattern? Perhaps. I like to think it's fortune smiling down on my friends.'

No, this went beyond a mere pattern.

'I also believe in contradictions and coincidences. You shouldn't know these facts, yet you do. I, too, heard everything between you and your father. I think our understanding the rest will tell you whether to leave me behind or not.'

'I am leaving you behind,' she said.

'And yet, you're still here,' he answered. 'Now where were we…? Robert of Dent, who was nearby, travelled with Gaira of Clan Colquhoun and four adopted children to return them to the safety of her Clan's lands. They're a family now, but to be so he had to fake his death. To keep his family safe, in case Edward attacked Colquhoun land, he and Hugh of Shoebury exchanged messages sealed with a half-thistle. And you know Robert and Gaia took in that family, adopted them, loved them?' he said.

She didn't want to answer this question. She didn't need to answer it because Eldric already knew the truth. Yet it was clear he wanted to say so much more, and she wanted to hear it.

'Because my father massacred the entire village of Doonhill,' she said. 'He killed everyone except his one bastard child named Maisie, whom he was deciding the fate for before she was rescued.'

'Her name is Margaret, actually. Her family calls her Maisie.'

She uncrossed her arms. 'You told me to call her Maisie!'

'Of course I did. After seeing your father, there is no doubt in my mind he sired her. It will cause more heartbreak when the truth is revealed as it must be to Robert and Gaira.'

To know Gaia's sister had been forced and Maisie's father was a madman and very much alive. Eldric even sounded concerned for them. Cressida couldn't believe everything he said and yet… 'And this half-thistle seal?'

He nodded. 'I have one of my own. One I used when I sent a message to Clan Colquhoun. When that mercenary at the inn said there was a half-Scottish child, I had to take the chance and tell them. I paid Terric's men to carry the message out before we sailed for France. It's well on its way to Scotland by now.'

Cressida's mind reeled with all the entanglements. And yet… 'My father stopped trusting me when I shot him in the arm, but until that point, I was privy to information that also involved the Colquhouns.'

'And thus you prove you're a worthier human than I. You'd help them.'

'They're my sister's family—why would my…hatred of you cause me to ignore them?'

'When you want to tell me, I'll use the seal.' Eldric rested his hands on his knees. 'So…these secrets would harm your father.'

'More than you could know.'

'Was it about his pursuit of the Jewel of Kings and that he intends to give it to the Warstones, though King Edward would very much like to have the legendary jewel that would give him true sovereignty over Scotland?'

'How did you know?'

'I killed those mercenaries quickly. Left them strewn about to get to you. I heard everything.'

'All the more reason for him to kill you. If you'd have let me finish him, most of this would be over.'

'I gave you a chance to return to him, to kill him, or capture, or whatever you want to do with him, and yet you're here with me. You want to stay with me, want to listen to my apology, want to believe I love you. And I want you to, too.'

She did. Her defences were weak when it came to him. 'Delusions only. I'm here because too much time has passed, he could be anywhere!'

'Cressida.'

'This is foolish and stop moving closer to me.'

He grabbed her hand. 'I want you in my arms!'

She yanked her hand free. He let her. He hadn't done that before and suddenly she had a mad desire to seize his hand again. Instead, she clutched her own in her lap.

'He has powerful allies. They're everywhere and could be anyone.'

'So do we.'

'We?' she whispered.

'We, Cressida. Despite your words to the contrary. I know your hand feels as empty as mine. And it's not foolish to stop pursuing him. I won't have you releasing arrows unless you must to protect your life.'

'He will try to kill everyone around me.'

'You're not unprotected. For all his power, he still preys upon the weak. Do you think they'd let Maisie have any freedom for the next twenty years? I almost feel sorry for your sister.'

'I don't want him haunting her.' She raised her chin. 'What if, as a test of your love for me, I asked you to kill him?'

## Chapter Nineteen

'Then I'd argue with you why we shouldn't,' he said.

'I'd love you again if you did it.'

'You love me now; I don't need to kill your father to prove it. You just don't know when to stop.'

It unnerved her that he knew her so well. She'd had years of observing him to understand the man he was. She'd only been talking to him for a few days.

'You can't know my feelings!'

'I only had to take your hands and pull you down to sit with me and listen to know you loved me. In truth, I didn't think it would take this long. Don't get up.'

She already stood. 'Will you stop me?'

'I told you I wouldn't. You choose this time.'

His words, the way he said them. Tears pricked her eyes and she blinked them away. 'I wish for his death.'

'You wish it was over. So do I. But to simply go after him? There's too much between you two. You feel too much right now and I won't put that burden on you.'

'You're angry with him. But you're not burdened with being his child.'

'Oh, yes. Always and for ever I will burn with hatred for that man, but...he brought me you. Because of all his deeds, he forced me to be with you. To see you.'

'And I don't know what benefit that's been to me.'

'I'm so, so very sorry for my words. I wish a thousand times to take them away or at least to explain.'

His voice. His eyes. She was believing and this time was different, more real, so she gave him a truth right back. 'I haven't exactly been a benefit to you.'

'You're my heart!' he declared, standing up. 'Don't you see? It will always be we. I regret not knowing of you sooner. Of not recognising you for what you'd be to me. I regret letting you go that night we danced in Swaffham. I had you in my arms.'

'We barely touched.'

'My fingertips never forgot you.'

'That's a ridiculous thing to say.'

'But truth.'

He almost smiled.

She almost gave in.

'I can't believe you let him go.' She turned to pace. The room hadn't got any bigger. 'He killed your friends.'

He stepped back. 'I won't kill him, Cressida. Because of his deeds, he brought me you. What other miracles in the world would I be stopping if I killed him? What other wonders?'

'You're saying you're grateful he asked me to kill you.'

'I can see, touch—know you. Grateful is the least of what I am feeling. He is also Maisie's father. She may have questions some day. How do you want to answer them?'

She stopped, stilled, bowed her head. 'She is young. I cannot think of that man as her father.'

'I won't—'

'She's my sister, Eldric. I'm related to her and I can't suppress my feeling of joy, though for her it will only be horror.'

He took the step towards her, placed his hand gently on her arms. 'No! Never think that. She will be proud she is related to you. Proud.'

'You know what I am. What I have done.'

'And I know what you are trying...what you have become.'

'But you said that didn't matter. You implied that I am what I am and will carry their blood on my hands for ever.'

'I'm a fool for saying anything close to that. I was absolutely wholeheartedly wrong. Your father isn't good, Cressida, but you...you shine. You're good and all this time you've been fighting what he was trying to make you.'

'I still did his deeds.'

'Forget his deeds. Let the past be gone...no. No. Not even that. The past simply is, good, bad, up, down, it doesn't have to be anything other than what it has been. We can't change it and I don't know whether I would want to.'

She stepped away. 'You lie.'

'No, there was pain, but there was joy, too. You watched over me for years though I didn't know it. Why would I want to take that away?'

'Because it hurt me? You were there and I could do nothing about it.'

His heart broke all over again and a large part of him wished he could thrust a sword into Howe's entrails and gut him. But it wouldn't be enough to end the need to harm him. Eldric wished he could take him in to King Edward and demand justice, but that would risk Cressida's life.

'I'm sorry if I hurt you back then.'

She shook her head, wiped at her eyes. 'You didn't know. I just had my father and you.'

Maybe, just maybe he would want to change that part of the past. 'What would have happened if we'd met earlier?'

'I would have trained you.'

'What?'

'You crook your head to the left a bit when you run.'

His mouth gaped and he was quick to close it. This woman was a terror at observation. 'I do what?'

'When you run and you're full out, your head tilts a bit to the left. It changes your even stride and puts more weight on your left foot. That's why when you attack someone you're always a little off-centre from them.'

He felt off-centre now, with her. Their words exchanged were lighter. He felt she was believing him now. It wasn't enough, he knew, and he still had secrets to tell her, but it was good to talk to her of this. Almost fun.

'I want to be off-centre, it gives me greater arch with my sword.'

She pointed at him. 'It also tells your enemy what direction you're going.'

'Then you'll fix me.'

She snorted.

'It's too ingrained. Maybe when you were being trained, a quality knight could have helped you, but doing anything with you now would be too arduous to comprehend.'

She made him sound like the very worst of warriors. He'd survived several battles—did she give him no credit?

'I was trained at Edward's court by the very best men. By Edward himself!'

'That was your weakness. You needed a woman to train you.'

He wanted to laugh, especially when he saw her lips twitch. He feared he'd never see a true smile again. Still, it irked him and gave him a twisted sense of pride that she had noticed.

'So I'm flawed.'

She looked at him, her eyes gleaming with something he didn't think he'd see again. Amusement. 'With certainty.'

'Well then, for our future, after we return Maisie, you'll train me.'

It wasn't the correct thing to say, again. He could see it because the light in her eyes went out, because she turned her back to him again. Because he'd reminded her that a sister she thought she'd never have wasn't hers. Cressida couldn't keep her.

'Cressida, look at me.' When she didn't, he continued. 'You haven't forgiven me yet.'

She shook her head. He knew that was the answer.

He could feel it. If she'd forgiven him, he'd be kissing her.

But…she hadn't left the room yet either. She was still willing to listen to his apology.

'I'm glad you haven't forgiven me because I have more to confess. I made a vow to the King about you. I took a hunting horn as promise. I carry his seal as insurance and clout.'

She did turn then. 'When?'

'After Swaffham.'

'So…' She waved around the room. 'So what's the point of any of this? You want to make these confessions. Tell me you love me, then take me to the King anyway. You can't avoid him. Why are you looking at me that way?'

'You look as though you're about to notch an arrow into your bow and go to war for me. I think that shows you care for me still.'

'Stop looking so smug and tell me what you mean to do. I'll have more facts before we ever talk of feelings.'

'I have a feeling our facts are too enmeshed in our story. But at least you know there are stories of love as layered as ours. Look at Hugh and Robert, they, too, had obstacles, and now are secretly living happily—'

'Eldric.' Cressida didn't want to hear about happy married couples any more. She wanted to be one and, with everything Eldric said, she was starting to believe she might be able to until he told her King Edward would be after them both if she didn't go to the Tower.

Why couldn't, for once, just once, some happiness come her way?

'Whether you acknowledge it or not, we have our own story,' Eldric said.

'And it ended when you said those things to me!'

'Not hardly, you're sturdy. I simply need to tell you more.'

'You've told me enough. More than enough to interest the English King. Maybe he'll hang you instead of me.'

'Yes, if you wanted to send me to the Tower now, you could.'

He looked so pained, there was a part of her that wanted to tell him it was all fine now. He'd swayed her, but though so much of her doubt was gone now, it was still there. But what more could he say to make it go away? Ah, yes, he needed to tell her there wouldn't be proclamations by the King of England for the death.

'What do you intend to do with the King?'

'I haven't unravelled that conundrum yet.'

'You were told to bring the Archer to the King himself. That person is me.'

'I suspect the King knows who you are, your gender and who your father was. I think he found it convenient that I, too, was after the Archer and planned to use me. Since he wasn't exactly truthful with me, I am not under any obligation to be truthful to him.'

'You can't do that. That won't be safe.'

'Are you protecting me again?'

He said he loved her. She believed him. The way he had kissed her, all of that was true. It was also true she loved him still and a thousand times before now she could have told him.

Now, however, it seemed harder to say the words,

probably because this dream could never become true. It wasn't only the King of England that would separate them. It was her past.

'Storming into an enemy's camp,' he said. 'Bringing a swift death to everyone you faced and you can't answer a simple question. Or are you scared to?'

'I loved you before you knew I existed, Eldric. You hurt me, but I know why; I killed Thomas. It may have been an accident, but my arrow still—'

'Stop,' he said. 'Don't even carry any more burden on it. Thomas would never want you to. And as for the other two—they would have given me a terrible time about my fumbling with you. They would have loved you.'

He breathed deeply. 'I do miss them. They were good men. I did not say it lightly when I said I would have died for them. But after everything, I wonder if you would have notched your arrow if you had known them. Known that Philip made crude jests and Thomas separated his food in his trencher. Would it have made a difference?'

She would answer him honestly. 'It would have made the decision harder, but not changed the decision I made. I chose you.'

He clenched his eyes. 'I feel as though I killed them…' His voice broke. He waited, took a breath and looked at her again. 'Do you understand? Not because they were protecting my back as I first believed long before meeting you, but because I existed. Because you chose me.

'I think that was why I was so angry. I hated myself.

Who am I to even question your decisions? I am a coward and I was a fool to say those hateful words to you.'

'No, you're not. We've only known each other for days. Though our lives have connected many times over. You were justified in your anger. It makes no difference whether I killed your friends or not. The fact is I killed.'

He stepped closer to her, she didn't step away. She spoke the truth. One that he had known since before he met her. She was her father's weapon. This was something they needed to face.

'I've killed, too,' he said. 'You know I have and yet you don't judge me. I, too, have killed far too many to count. I think, in this war, we all have.'

Eldric saw it then. Saw something in her ease and he knew they'd have a life together. Just a bit more and he could hold her.

'I have been death for many years,' she said. 'I'm trying to be life. I was nothing for so long. And then there was you. The woman that I was then is not the same one I am now, but you have to know, if you truly want this between us, I would still choose you no matter what the cost.'

His heart! 'I don't want you to make any costs. As for the rest, it's what I was trying to say when I kissed you, when I clumsily told you what that dance in Swaffham meant to me. I had already chosen you.'

She stilled. 'Will you then forgive me for Thomas?'

He understood now the difficult choices, understood it fully. He now only hoped for forgiveness. This time, he took the chance, pulling her into his arms, and when she didn't move away, when she seemed to pull him just as close, he wanted more. So much more. He sat on the bed, pulling her with him.

'There's nothing to forgive and nothing will hold me back from you. I went after you to save you from your father. Forgive you? I beg you to forgive me! How many mistakes have I made? It's a miracle you could have any feelings for me before, that you shared any of them now. And I swear, I'll spend a lifetime apologising for not recognising and trusting you.'

'I accept,' she said, adjusting her body so it was mostly on top of him. The bed wasn't meant for two, or even just for him, but to feel her against him was heaven.

For her to tell him she accepted his apology, he was beyond joy. 'You accept my apology?'

She nodded and, when he smiled, she smiled right back.

'So now you can kiss me and declare more love words,' she said.

He chuckled, playing with one of her pale tresses. 'Not yet. I have one more question. Just one and it's very pertinent.'

'Ask it,' she said.

He loved the way she was with him. Not afraid, she saw him just as he always wanted to be seen. Not for his size, but as a man. And he wondered if it all had to do with when she was a child in the trees. 'You said you loved me from before. I don't know how that's possible.'

He watched the blush grow up her neck until she was bathed in its pink glow. Her hands went to her cheeks. 'No!'

'Well, now I have to know.'

'It's silly. I was a child then.'

'What was it?'

'It was because you whistled, Eldric. I was at the English camp to spy on trivial matters to practise my father's training. You whistled some tune I'd never be able to name because I'd never heard it before and I noticed you.'

'Of all the things you could have said to me, that isn't one I expected.' He gathered more of her tresses, threaded his fingers through them. She rested her chin on his chest. Except for the fact his feet and most of his legs were dangling uncomfortably over the side, he'd stay there happily. 'Why the whistling?'

'It was beautiful. I'd never heard music until then. The nuns kept me away from them. Sometimes, I thought I heard voices, but I was never sure.'

'I am confused now. How could my whistling have caused you to watch me?'

'You whistle constantly. So year after year, I easily found you. It's not a very safe hobby. It makes you such an easy target.'

'A target. And how many men did you continually watch over the years?'

'Only you.'

'Others must have whistled, sung.'

She lifted her chin. 'None were as good as you.'

'There were other men who were large with hair like mine, eyes like mine.'

'But not all together.'

Her blush increased that bit more for that answer and he liked that very much.

'And you didn't watch them awkwardly try to kiss a woman in a yellow dress.'

'Don't mention that woman in a yellow dress,' she said. 'I hate the colour yellow.'

He couldn't hold back the smile then. 'How many other warriors noticed you, Cressida, over the years as you travelled from camp to camp, all the hours hiding in trees, waiting for your target? How many looked up and saw you, ran after you?'

'None.'

'Except for me.'

'Except you,' she acknowledged.

'Did you never think, then, never wonder, not once, if I was meant to find you, too?'

'You're making me believe in this all over again.'

'Good, because you accepted my apology and I do want you to accept my love. Although I don't know how you can doubt any of it. Every action we've taken for years and years have brought us here together. In fact, I think I love these coincidences between us as much as I love you.'

'Now you're being contrary,' she said.

'If by contrary you mean I'm still waiting for an answer from you, yes, I am. I'm still wanting to know if you'll spend a lifetime with me. If you'll be my wife, and we'll just…sort the rest of it out later.'

'My father won't wait to go after us and I'm surprised the King of England has not already stormed this ship in pursuit of traitors.'

'Those are facts. I thought we were on to the feelings part of this discussion.'

Cressida laughed.

'Tell me, Cress, what you want to do.'

'We've already docked in Dover, haven't we, and we don't have to wait for Terric's illicit affairs to be completed this time before we disembark.'

'Even if we did, I have a mind to ignore his wishes for a bit. I'm still not pleased he let you off the ship.'

'Well, then, I know what I want to do. First, I think you should kiss me, then I want to spend time with Maisie.'

'You've got family now, Cress.'

'I love you,' she blurted. A full grin from Eldric, one with a devilish look in his eyes. A warrior who had conquered all and expected to enjoy the spoils of war. 'And now I have you.'

'No, I think I had you first. Now, can we get up? This bed is entirely too small for me.'

# Chapter Twenty

'You look like a man who could use help.' Terric bounded over the deck as if he had been merely waiting for him to emerge from the room down below. Once they had got Maisie from the healer, they'd returned to the room. To chat, to play, to exchange glances and promises for later. So little time together, yet Eldric felt as though he'd always known Cressida.

As for Maisie, to see them playing together—it was as if they'd always been sisters. As for the rest, Cressida was correct, he did need to plan.

The fact that Terric could see it plainly on his face was no comfort.

'Where I go, what must be done, I wouldn't even risk the life of a pirate.'

The Commander chuffed. 'It's been a while since I've conversed with an honourable man. It's refreshing. I wouldn't mind keeping such a novelty around a bit longer.'

Eldric gave a curt nod. 'And I wouldn't mind a pirate such as you on the seas.'

'Of course not, look at me! Who wouldn't?'

Eldric's laugh sobered. 'You can't. If you're at all true, I have to decline your offer of help.'

'You're not a fool. You can't do this task alone.'

Eldric wouldn't ask how the Commander knew what needed to be done.

Terric's eyes stayed steady on his before he whistled low. 'You have friends. You're *not* doing it alone.'

Eldric shook his head.

'I hoped...' Terric shrugged one shoulder. 'I was hoping for a friend.'

'And because I have some, we can't be?'

'No, we can't. Conflict of interest and all that. I already have difficulty with loyalty. Moreover, I may know you, but your friends, not so much.'

'What if they are like me?'

Terric laughed. 'And a sense of humour as well. It looks as though your lady love is ready to depart.'

Eldric looked behind him. Cressida, carrying Maisie, appeared to be in a very animated conversation.

'Are you prepared?' Eldric asked her when she finally reached them.

She jiggled the girl on her hip. 'As much as I can be. We'll need supplies before we journey with her.'

'You won't have to travel far,' Terric said.

'Are you referencing the message we sent? It couldn't have reached them yet,' Eldric said.

'Have you looked over the railing?' Terric said. 'There's a very large red-haired man and a woman holding his hand who have been demanding, constantly, to come aboard. I didn't want to disturb you and made them wait.'

'Red-haired?' Eldric said, looking to Cressida. 'Colquhouns,' they said together.

Terric crossed his arms. 'He says he is Bram of Clan Colquhoun, former Laird, and she is of Clan Ferguson, but, honestly, I don't understand what the Clans are about.'

Eldric walked to the railing and looked down to the Dover docks. 'They're here!'

Cressida looked to Terric, who watched them both with curiosity. 'What is it?'

'I don't know, but I find myself wanting to know, which I don't know if I'm entirely comfortable with.'

She hadn't talked with the almost noble Commander as much as Eldric, but she sensed something in him that was all too familiar and wanted to tell him something she wished someone had told her when she gazed over the ocean. 'You'll find what you're searching for. If you keep looking.'

He arched a brow. 'I have coin and adventure, there isn't anything else a man could desire. I've never needed more, yet…why is it when I watched you that I suddenly do?'

'The need part is easy.' She adjusted Maisie on her hip. The child was almost as big as she, but she was loath to let her down. 'It's the want that keeps you longing. But if I, of all the people in the world, found what I most yearned for, you will, too.'

The Commander gave a quick bow. 'It's probably best if you get off my ship; these conversations aren't appropriate for a man such as me. I have…affairs and people that desire me to keep doing them that occupy my time.'

'Fair journey,' she said.

'Isn't that what I should wish to you?'

'No.' She gave him a smile. 'Because I have a feeling you're about to go on one as well.'

Cressida joined Eldric at the rail. 'Do you see them?'

'I think that's them.' Eldric pointed. 'Right—'

Maisie squealed.

Bram's eyes snapped up. The gaze of the dark-haired woman by his side did as well. They both shouted with joy.

Then Maisie tried to launch herself overboard.

Cressida knew she would be devasted when she eventually returned Maisie to her home, but she thought she'd have more time to enjoy this feeling of not being alone. Maisie was just so full of laughter and light. She didn't want to go back to how her life was before, but this new life seemed to be literally ripping her from her arms.

'Steady,' Eldric said, taking the squirming Maisie. Cressida, whose arms felt all too weak, as did her legs, handed her over. Her heart panged, as he adjusted the child in his arms.

'They're here already,' she said. 'I thought there would be more time. Foolish, I know, since if it were my child missing, the very devil couldn't be faster than me. But…'

'I, too, am surprised. None of the Colquhouns should be here and I don't know who that woman is.'

'It's his wife. He hasn't let go of her hand.'

'My soon-to-be wife thinks all the world is love.'

'Wife?' She shoved his arm, Maisie laughed and they descended to the docks.

\* \* \*

The woman at Bram's side immediately flew forward, Maisie's arms were extended and Eldric handed her over. The child's words were clear as could be as she addressed the crying woman who squeezed her.

'I am Lioslath,' she said, turning to Eldric, 'of Clan Ferguson and I am married to that man who—'

'Who wants to hold his niece as well,' Bram laughed. 'I am Bram of Clan Colquhoun, former Laird,' he said, for Cressida's benefit. 'I live in Ayrshire now with the Fergusons. Though you wouldn't know it. Family of her own and she's still greedy for mine.'

'It's not my fault.' Lioslath wiped her face on Maisie's shoulder. 'I didn't always want them; you've just rubbed off on me.'

Lioslath's tears wouldn't stop and Eldric found he didn't know what to do with the abundance of family; he was an only child. He looked to Cressida.

'You weren't expecting us,' Bram said.

'No.' Eldric looked around. This wasn't the location to discuss any of this.

Cressida handed the other woman a linen. 'Here.'

Lioslath took it. 'Thank you.'

'I'm Cressida, daughter of Sir Richard Howe.'

Bram stopped babbling to his niece and stepped back. 'What is the meaning of this, Hawksmoor?'

Obtaining and earning Cressida's love was not an easy task, showing the world the woman she truly was wouldn't be either. But as long as she was by his side, he'd face any and all storms that came their way. Family. It appeared he had one as well now.

'She is who she says she is,' Eldric said. 'She is his daughter, but she isn't him.'

'Your missive said nothing of her presence or of his. Is he here, too?'

'No,' Cressida said. 'We left him in France.'

'Dead?' Bram said.

Cressida flinched.

'Careful, Colquhoun.'

Bram's expression turned cold. 'That man stole my sister's child. We've been searching for months for Maisie. Our hearts haven't healed. There's been rifts in the clans. The damage he has done, not to mention what Caird had to go through.'

'You mean Mairead,' Cressida said.

Bram's eyes went from Eldric to Cressida and back again. He handed Maisie back to Lioslath, who rocked her back and forth. Maisie whacked the same rhythm on Lioslath's head.

'How do you know my sister?' Bram said.

Bram's eyes had narrowed on Cressida and Eldric didn't like it. 'She's his daughter, Bram. She's also the Archer. And she will soon be my wife.'

Lioslath gasped.

'Do you take issue with that?' Eldric said.

Cressida laid her hand on Eldric's arm.

'Now, it's your turn to be careful, Hawksmoor,' Bram said.

Eldric had had enough.

'I think we should talk somewhere else,' Lioslath said.

Cressida squeezed his arm.

'I agree, let's return to the deck of the ship,' she said.

\* \* \*

Once Terric saw them return, he ushered his men somewhere else and Eldric turned to Bram. Cressida didn't know what to expect. She hadn't meant to blurt out her identity, but just giving away her sister was already stabbing at her heart. The fact that her father was this family's enemy made the situation all the more uncertain.

She wanted, at least this part, to be ripped away. As though the decision was made and she merely needed to release the arrow.

Except after she said what she had, Eldric had come to her defence, announcing he wished to marry her. And Bram and Lioslath hadn't acted as she had expected.

'You are the ones who received our missive,' Eldric said. 'Though it wasn't addressed to you.'

'Your wife?' Bram said.

Cressida wanted to interrupt. This wasn't something they'd talked of, it wasn't something she thought was for her. Their love they'd announced. But as for the rest of it... Marriage meant family and happiness. It was too much.

Eldric looked at her as if he knew she was doubting. 'If she'll agree, Colquhoun. This journey we've been on has not exactly been a way to woo a female. But I have faced her father, as your brother did, and she is, and will always have, my trust.'

Bram chuckled. 'Is there a right way to woo? Lioslath and I were enemies.'

'Then you know,' Eldric answered.

'Perhaps,' Bram said. 'I have a feeling there are

differences. But even so. If your trust runs the way it does, then I will tell my side of this tale.'

Cressida didn't understand. 'She is yours, isn't she? Your family. You could simply go.'

'If you were my enemy,' Bram said, 'we would already be gone, but Eldric sent the missive. And you... I saw you holding her. You care.'

'There are four of us siblings still living,' Bram said. 'I am the eldest, then Caird, Gaira and Malcolm. The youngest, Irvette, was killed at Doonhill, along with her husband. Maisie was one of the few survivors. My sister Gaira rescued her and a few other children who fled.'

'Eldric has explained, and I also... I also know of the Jewel of Kings, of Robert...of Hugh. I know some matters.'

Bram's face darkened.

'Not all, Colquhoun,' Eldric said.

Cressida laid her hand on his arm again. 'It is fine. I understand. Up until the last few days, I knew only pieces.'

Bram and Lioslath looked at her expectantly, but not with any malice.

'You're not angry with me,' Cressida said.

'I've got to put Maisie down,' Lioslath said, slowly lowering the child, who took off in the opposite direction immediately. 'And there she goes. Bram, explain to her, will you, while I run off?'

Cressida watched Maisie run, but felt Bram's eyes studying her. Knew that Eldric studied them both.

'Cressida, we won't ever condemn you based on the deeds of your father. It's not within us to do so. Especially not I or Lioslath. If she even caught a hint that I held you responsible, she'd find a way to keep me out of the keep…again.'

'But it goes further than that,' Bram continued. 'You are the Archer. Am I right in thinking it was you who let loose the arrow that saved Mairead, my brother Caird's wife?'

So they were married now. 'I did.'

'You fought your own father.'

Cressida didn't want to answer. That question hurt somewhere that she couldn't rightly explain. Everything was still so new.

'Bram,' Eldric said.

'Forgive me,' Bram said. 'When he attacked Caird and Mairead, we were already sending missives and people to track him. Then Maisie was stolen.' Bram looked to Eldric. 'Maisie belongs with Gaira and Robert; they love her. But Gaira was pregnant when Maisie was stolen. They couldn't travel far, so Lioslath and I, we've been gone from our home a long time, searching all the south.'

'How did you get the missive?'

'By fortune.'

'Oh.' Cressida looked up at Eldric.

'Nothing by chance, Archer,' Eldric told her.

'After a day where the rains would not stop, we arrived in an inn and overheard two men talk about a message they had to deliver,' said Bram. 'They weren't loud, we were just huddled and silent.'

'It was open?' Eldric said. 'They knew the contents?'

'When I received it, it was sealed, they merely

talked of the delivering. It took me the better part of the evening to convince them I was exactly who they wanted to give it to. My clan, my hair, helped.'

'You didn't just take it,' Cressida said.

'Two men and I had Lioslath. Why resort to violence when just sharing family tales would do?'

'Don't concern yourself, Cressida, I would have stolen it, too!' Lioslath called out as she passed the group once more.

'That's how we received it, read it and came here. If you paid those men coin, Hawksmoor, they were worth it. It wasn't easy. They were a fair choice for messengers. But as to the rest...'

Bram turned to Cressida and she braced herself. Once she boarded the ship with Eldric and Maisie, once she truly didn't return to France to pursue her father, this would be the course she chose.

It would be a great hardship for all of them. Her father knew her well, could guess at any moment what choices she would make to avoid them. But she put her life, her trust, her love in Eldric and in Eldric's circle. With Maisie, who stumbled and laughed along the deck of a ship.

'Your father has schemes that involve obtaining the Jewel of Kings and you know why.'

'I know some. He trusted no one and, since I harmed him last autumn with the arrow, I've been in the dark.'

'Can you tell us anything—?'

'Not now, Bram,' Eldric interrupted. 'I've got to woo her first.'

'I'll tell him,' she said.

Eldric's gaze held hers and she fell into all that he

did not say as she always did, despite Bram's sudden laughter.

'I understand this all too well.' Bram slapped Eldric's shoulder. 'Will you be travelling with us now?'

Eldric shook his head. 'We're staying for a few days and then Cress will want to visit with her sister.'

Bram's eyes went to Lioslath slowly chasing Maisie on the deck. 'Sister.'

'That is why Maisie survived Doonhill, why he kidnapped her.'

Cressida watched Bram give a hard swallow. 'We always wondered. Their marriage was hasty, but they were so happy. I could deny her nothing. And Margaret—Maisie—doesn't have Irvette's hair and didn't look like either one of them.' Bram looked to her. 'She looks like you.'

'My father—'

'I think Eldric's correct,' Bram said, his voice devoid of emotion. 'We'll talk about these matters later. A few days, perhaps?'

'We'll be a sennight behind,' Eldric said.

Bram gave a curt nod. When Maisie toddled close enough again he scooped her up in his arms.

Eldric and Cressida watched the three disembark the ship.

'They're your family now,' he said, trying to ease the pensive look on her face. Years of her watching him, months of him pursuing her. Then in a matter of days both of their lives completely different, and yet... In all the dreams and wishes she had made as she hid in trees and travelled from camp to camp, this, right now, standing next to this man, was a dream that far surpassed any other.

'I have only just accepted that Maisie is true,' she said. 'Anything else, I can't quite believe it.'

'How about us—are we true?'

She laid her hand on his arm over the marks she had given him. 'All the years of wishing, of wanting. You should be still just a wish, but you, us, may be the truest thing of all in my life. I know that. I can feel that.'

'If there's any part of you that still doubts, Archer, I mean to prove it to you.'

Oh, yes. 'And just where were you intending to spend a sennight with me?'

'I know of an inn nearby,' he said.

She took her hand off his arm. 'You want to stay at an inn that my father's mercenaries know of, when he is but a day away?'

'We've been on that ship, he could be in England even now,' Eldric said.

Cressida turned her back to him. Eldric scanned the deck. There was no sign of Terric or his men.

'Cressida.'

'Don't tease about it. It's too soon. If they are my family, I risk their lives simply by continuing to exist. We stand on a deck of a ship, when right there on the street, one of his men could release an arrow and kill you. I can't bear it.'

Fair enough. He wrapped one arm around her shoulders, the other around her waist, and pulled her tight to him. She came to him willingly. He hoped he'd always earn the trust and love she gave him. It did come at a price. Even now, her comment was that an arrow could harm him, but not her. Did she not realise that he would protect her just as fiercely?

'Then we talk about some of that future now,' he said. 'We need to hide, like Robert and Hugh. I owe Edward a hunting horn and an Archer. I don't mind returning the horn to him. It was his first wife's.'

'He gave it to you on the day you negotiated? Why?'

'Because he sent me on a quest. I don't truly know. It's not the first time he's loaned it. It has some significance for him that we may never know. Oddly, I do wish for it to be his again.'

'Then we'll ensure it is returned to his keeping.'

Which was a risk. By returning the horn, the King would know he was still alive and disobeying the King's command. They'd have Howe's men and the King's men after them. Eldric wouldn't fool himself that they could evade both for ever. Still, if it was possible, he'd do it for her. For the family they'd have. He'd risk everything.

He squeezed her against him. 'He can have the horn, but not you. Now, where to go and hide. To Ayrshire? That would hurt Bram. To Ffords? That would harm Robert. We couldn't even go to Spain for there live Hugh and Alice. I fear travelling to any location close to the others will jeopardise their families. I won't live in France, not after our last trip.'

Cressida loved this man for even talking as though they had options. Pretending they could have a life on a plot of land and a little family of their own. To live in peace. It would be theirs some day. She vowed it. But he didn't know just how precious to her it was that his arms were around her. That she could feel the reverberations of his deep voice against her back.

This moment was her peace.

'We could go north,' she continued to pretend. 'Far north where the winds never die and the rocks are barren and the sea consumes all except the most hearty.'

'Where is this magical place?'

'To the Isle of Skye in the north of Scotland.'

'You'd take us to the ends of civilisation.'

'We don't need it, you and I,' she said. 'You can whistle and I'll hunt since I'll be better at it until I train you up.'

He chuckled. 'It's a good life we'll make there, then. Along the way, we could visit your family.'

'Certainly,' she agreed. And as they watched the birds swoop in the sky, she envisaged the entire sweet dream.

He rested his head on the top of hers. 'We're not going anywhere, are we?' he said.

'I do want to see my family if at all possible.'

'I can see why Terric does this,' Eldric said. 'Staring out at the waters—the roll of it all is calming. We could even stay on this ship and never touch land again or sail far into the deepest of oceans.'

To the end where the oceans are. Cressida turned in his arms and gazed at the man she loved. Loved enough to keep the life they needed to lead. To help themselves and others.

'Because that's where promises are kept,' she said.

He looked down. Confusion in his eyes. 'Promises?'

'We could sail on ships into every horizon. We could

go north, to the end of civilisation. Journey. Adventures. Because far ahead is where promises are kept.'

She laid her hand against his heart. 'Except I don't need far away or horizons. All the promises I ever needed or wanted are right here.'

He placed his hand over hers. 'What are you saying?'

'You must return the horn to Edward. Yourself. Robert, Hugh and you all disappearing? It'll never hold. We'll put them at risk.'

'But you?'

'You'll tell him of me, of my father, you will report it all except that which still protects your friends. That secret will have to remain.'

'And when he decides to execute me because I didn't bring him you?'

'That's why you don't take me. Because I'll be the one rescuing you.'

'Cressida.'

Eldric's voice saying her name, warning her, and she knew what he wanted. No more circumstances where she made choices that risked her life or her soul. 'I'll come to him, if he still desires it. But my father has alliances and they'll be there in the palace as well. They can't see me, or none of this will work. That should sway him.'

'You believe he'd want us in his service.'

'You already are, remember?' she said. 'Perhaps that's why he bargained with you to bring me to him. Not to execute, but to bring me to his side. He knows he has traitors in his midst. Perhaps he knows more about me or my father than we know.'

'If he knew about your father, wouldn't he have already done something?'

'The King can't go after the Warstones directly. They haven't gone after him and I don't know whether he'd survive that warfare. He's spread too thinly. The Crusades harmed his coffers and his obsession with Scotland may be the death of him.'

'I don't want you working for the King,' he said. 'Your entire life has been dedicated to others. Don't you understand I want to protect you? You were always there in the shadows. No longer should you make the difficult decisions. It's my turn now.'

No words could have been sweeter. 'You're already protecting me, saving me. But whatever the King wants, there are ways to appease him. If we simply disappear, we cannot help your friends, their families, my sister. For her, for you, I'll do anything to stop my father's ambitions. He cannot gain access to the gem. I may have let him go, but I won't stop or give up. I won't let him win.'

Eldric gave her the gentlest of kisses. 'We'll win,' he whispered against her lips. 'We already have.'

Another kiss.

It was the true and right decision. No children, no lands or responsibilities between them. His parents were well. Already, he'd been conversing with Hugh and Alice. If they could combine the clans and families, if they aligned with one effort, together they could make the world right again.

He ran his hands down Cressida's back, cupped her to press her close, parting her thighs just a bit, just enough for what was to be between them.

The world was already right. He ducked his head under her chin and kissed the tender skin there, felt the fluttering of her pulse.

'Where,' she shivered, 'where was this inn again?'

'Just a few steps away.' He nudged her ear with his nose.

'It's good it's so close.'

'On that we agree.' He pulled back, cupped her face in his hands, tucked a pale tress behind an ear and absorbed all that he saw in her stunning eyes. 'I love you.'

'I loved you first,' she reminded him, a gleam of challenge in her eyes.

It was a challenge he accepted and one he was eager to begin. Swooping down, he scooped her up in his arms.

'I'll love you the best,' he promised.

\* \* \* \* \*

*If you enjoyed this book, why not check out*
*this other great read by Nicole Locke*

Her Dark Knight's Redemption

*And be sure to read her*
*Lovers and Legends miniseries*

In Debt to the Enemy Lord
The Knight's Scarred Maiden
Her Christmas Knight
Reclaimed by the Knight